Operation: Endeavor

When the Mission Ends Book #2

by Christi Snow

Christi Snow

This book is a work of fiction. Any names, characters, events, or incidences come from the author's imagination and are not meant to portray real persons or events.

Texas Tech University and Lubbock, TX are real places, but again they are used only as settings in this very fictional world. Any similarities are purely coincidental.

Published by Christi Snow

Edited by Sarah Negovetich

Cover Design by AM Design Studios

Copyright © 2013 Christina Snow

All rights reserved.

ISBN: 1481035614
ISBN-13: 978-1481035613

DEDICATION

This book is for my siblings:
Daniel & David
(yes, they're twins who just happen
to be four years younger than me)

I love you guys.
I know you'll always have my back…
And then give me a hard time about it later.

BOOKS IN THIS SERIES

When the Mission Ends Trilogy

Book #1: Operation: Endgame
September 2012

Book #2: Operation: Endeavor
January 2013

Book #3: Operation: Endurance
April 2013

Book #.5: Before the Mission Begins
Valentine's 2013

ACKNOWLEDGMENTS

A huge thank you to my family: Ben, Jacob, and Kat. You guys have been my biggest cheerleaders and support and you rarely complain when we have frozen dinners…again. I love you three more than anything!

Mom, this is my official apology for not calling as much as I should and for the scattered conversations when I do. You've been wonderful to let me ramble on about Colton and Penelope and simply the ups and downs of doing what I do now. Thank you for always being there, for always listening, and for always doing a last-minute read when I need another opinion. I couldn't do this without you!

My betas…. Girls, I love you for the support you offer and the advice you give. This book has changed so much since you originally read it. I hope you still like it. Thank you to: Amber, Amy, Anso, Jennifer, Kara, Kim, Aunt Marcia, Michele, and Mom. Sabrina = proofreader extraordinaire!

And to my real life version of the Abilene Authors…I love all you guys from SAW (San Angelo Writers). We may not have a Tony, but we sure do have a LOT of fun! Nikki and Ben, your feedback on this book was INVALUABLE. Thank you for the time and effort you put into your feedback.

I'm a lucky girl. I had two wonderful editors work with me on this book: Sarah Negovetich and Mia Downing. Because of you two, this book is so much better and I owe you so much for that! Love you two and that you always kept me giggling, even while looking at the never-ending edits.
Sarah's favorite phrase: "What does that look like?"
Mia's favorite: "Show more, go deeper."

Finally, thanks to you, my readers!!
I was completely overwhelmed by your support on *Operation: Endgame*. I hope that you love *Operation: Endeavor* just as much!

Prologue

22 Years ago
The Chapel- Fort Hood, Texas

Ten year old Colton stumbled down the hall of the chapel and worked to keep a tight rein over his emotions. Tears battered at his insides, trying to get out. He wouldn't cry. If he started, he wasn't sure he'd ever be able to stop. Don't think about it, he berated himself. Don't think about his parents lying dead in the next room.

He needed to focus on the twins. Chris and Cassie were only six years old, too young to understand why mom and dad weren't coming home. Not that he really did either, but that didn't matter. Not now. Now, he needed to be there for them. But first he had to find them. They were always wandering off. The twins lived in their own little imaginary world where only the two of them were invited.

He started to turn the corner of the hall, but two female voices stopped him.

"It's just so sad. Those poor kids. What's going to happen to them?"

"I heard their grandfather, Lora's dad, is coming to get them, but as far as I know, he doesn't even know the children. He and Lora were estranged. He never approved of her marriage to Major Robertson." The women murmured their disapproval. "There's nowhere else for them to go. There aren't any other relatives willing to take in all three of them. You have to wonder about a man his age living by himself. How is he going to handle three young children?"

That ball in the pit of Colton's stomach started spinning. Estranged? Colton had no idea what that word meant, but it couldn't mean anything good. A grandfather? He didn't think they had any grandparents still alive. Who was he and why hadn't he ever met him? And now they were supposed to go live with him?

The women continued talking as they wandered down the hall, but their voices were too quiet now for him to hear any more. He peered around the corner toward their retreating backs. He still had no idea where the twins were and needed to find them before they all got into trouble. They were his responsibility now and losing track of them wasn't acceptable.

He gritted his teeth and looked in the doorways, searching. Finally, at the third door, he heard whispering in the back corner.

Creeping in, he approached the voices, just in case they didn't belong to the twins. But as he got closer, he realized it was Cassie he heard. She was crying and Chris comforted her. Colton swallowed the lump in his throat as he crouched down beside them. He hated how helpless he felt when she cried.

Chris looked up at him with anguished eyes. Colton reached for him, but Chris shook his head vehemently. "Leave us alone. We'll be there in just a minute."

Colton stumbled back to the door to wait for them, trying not to let the rebuff hurt. He wrapped his hands around his stomach to control the shaking of his body. He'd give anything right now for a hug from his mother. But she would never hug him again. He gritted his teeth again. *Not gonna cry. Not now.*

The twins always turned to each other before they turned to him. He knew that. He shouldn't let it bother him. But in this case, they were all in this miserable circumstance together. They needed to let him help. The twins walked up behind him and Colton clenched his jaw to get his anger, fear, and hurt under control. They were scared enough already.

He turned to them and asked gruffly, "Are you guys okay?" He watched them. They were still young enough that they looked identical despite being the opposite sex. The only difference between the two of them was their hair. Cassie's was flame-red and Chris's was blond. Right now both of them also shared identical red-rimmed, sapphire blue eyes.

"We need to get back before someone starts looking for us." He looked down the hall and Colton's stomach sank at the sight of his father's commander coming toward them. At first glance, the commander didn't look happy, but when he spotted them, his face softened.

As he walked up, the tall man looked at them kindly even as he quietly admonished Colton, "We've been looking for you three. We need to get started and I need to introduce you to someone."

Colton looked beyond the Colonel to where an old man stood observing the three of them. Colton immediately stood up straighter and reached for Chris and Cassie. As they approached the man, Colton watched him. He looked at them unsmiling, but his blue eyes were kind.

"I'm sorry we weren't there, sir," Colton said to the Colonel, but then he nodded his head at the man. "Is that our grandfather?"

The Colonel looked at Colton in surprise, but nodded. "Yes."

Colton stretched out his right hand toward the man. "I'm Colton." He drew his siblings up beside him. "This is Chris and Cassie. This is hard for them."

The man cleared his throat as he said, "This is hard for all of us. I'm your grandfather. Your mom was my daughter and I hope you three will come live with me. I'm sorry this is the first time we've had a chance to get to know each other."

As one, the twins grabbed hold of each of Colton's hands. He squeezed them in reassurance and swallowed his own fear and uncertainty. He had to be strong for them. "Do you live here?"

The man shook his head. "No, I live in a town further north of here called Lubbock. Have you ever heard of it?"

Colton nodded. "Yes, we went to a Texas Tech football game there last year." Hurt flashed in the old man's eyes, but Colton didn't know what he'd said wrong.

The man cleared his throat. "Well, from here on out, it'll be your home… with me, if that's okay with you three." He looked at the three of them questioningly.

The twins began to cry. He couldn't blame them as he wanted to do the same thing, but they didn't have any other choice. Their parents were dead and no matter how much they wanted it to, that circumstance wasn't going to change. Going with this man was the only way they'd be able to stay together. They didn't know their grandfather, but he had nice eyes. That would have to be enough.

"Yes, sir. We appreciate you taking us in." Colton looked down at the twins and tried to give them a brave smile. They would make the best of it, the three of them together. He was the oldest. He'd be strong. The twins needed that from him.

Chapter 1

Present Day
Lubbock, TX

"Dammit, Colton. Leave me the fuck alone." Chris leaned on his crutches glaring at Colton. The effort it cost him to simply stand there showed in the paleness of his features and the sweat on his forehead, despite the cool March day.

Colton ground his teeth together and mentally counted backwards. He was not going to lose his temper with Chris. Not this time. It had only been three months since Chris was rescued. A rescue from a madman who'd tortured and starved him for over six months. All things considered, he was doing pretty well. But pretty well wasn't good enough. Finally, after weeks of infection and possibility of amputation, his doctors were able to fix his knee with a host of surgeries. Everyone was relieved, but all that pain and effort wasn't going to do any good if Chris didn't start putting an effort into his rehabilitation.

Even without the rehabilitation, Chris was young and his body was beginning to recover, but his mind wasn't. That worried Colton. They had to break through this lousy attitude of his. Colton understood Chris had been through a lot, but he couldn't deal with this belligerent and defeatist attitude.

"Chris, if you don't work at your physical therapy, you aren't ever going to fully recover. You're lucky you even have your leg. Why can't you be grateful for that and use it? You've got to start doing the exercises. I'll do them with you. If you want, we could even head over to the gym…"

Chris interrupted, "Fuck! Don't you get it? I don't want your help. I don't want your pity. I want you to leave me the fuck alone!"

Chris turned quickly to try to get away from the conversation, but he moved too fast and lost his balance. Colton reached to help him, but Chris righted himself and glared at Colton. "I've got it. I'm not a complete cripple."

Running a hand through his hair in frustration, Colton sighed. "No, you're not a cripple, but if you don't start working your leg, you will be. You know what the doctors said. If you want full use of your leg back, you need to build the strength back up. Now, before it's too late. It's going to take time and it's going to take work. That's why I got out of the Air Force… so I could be here to support and help you."

Chris stared down at the floor and spoke low. "No one asked you to do that." He looked back up at Colton with hard, angry eyes. "You shouldn't have done that. I don't want you here. You shouldn't have given up your career."

"Well, that's too damn bad. That's what family does for each other. I'm here now and you're going to have to deal with me. Now, you have two choices. We can work out here or at the gym." Colton eyed Chris warily. He knew he was pushing him, but someone had to. The problem was Chris's fuse was getting shorter and shorter.

Chris clenched his jaw and Colton couldn't help but notice how gaunt he still looked. He'd lost so much weight and bulk. Three months ago, he'd been a virtual skeleton. He was better now, but still had so far to go to get back to where he'd been before his captivity. His eyes were haunted and the circles under them showed he wasn't sleeping well. Colton was worried. Chris needed to see a counselor. He'd mentioned it once before and Cassie shot him down because they needed to focus on the more pressing physical concerns, but he thought it was time again.

Officially, Chris medically retired from the Air Force after they discovered he wasn't dead. The Air Force provided counseling for him, but with all the vets returning back from the war zone traumatized, the therapists were overworked and he'd fallen through the cracks. Now with his retired status, no one could force him into the counseling sessions. It was like talking to a wall to try to get him to spend some time with a therapist.

"I'm not going anywhere," Colton told him. Why couldn't Chris get that through his head?

They were at a stalemate. Chris wasn't going to give in. Colton could tell by the aggressive stance he'd taken and the anger flashing in his eyes, but he gave it one last try.

"Fine, then we'll do your exercises here." Colton said softly, and that was all it took for the explosion to occur.

Chris's muscles bunched up in anger and he launched himself at Colton. They tumbled to the floor. Colton was 6'3" of pure muscle after spending many hours at the gym pounding weights. Chris's 6'0" lanky frame, still recuperating from physical abuse, was no match. Right now, though, Chris had anger on his side. Colton was trying hard to subdue him without hurting him. They rolled into an end table, sending the lamp on top of it shattering to the ground.

It was in that moment, Cassie walked in. "What the hell is going on here?"

Colton looked up. Chris took advantage of his distraction and punched him right across the side of his face. Colton growled and rolled Chris so that he was astride Chris's torso. "Goddammit, Chris. Hold still." He grabbed hold of him so he wouldn't hurt himself. They were both breathing hard, but Chris was sweating and pale.

Cassie rushed up behind Colton and shoved him. "Get off him. What the hell are you thinking?"

Colton slowly moved off Chris to make sure that he wasn't going to over-react again. Chris, for his part, didn't say anything. He just scowled at Colton as Cassie helped him to the couch.

Colton stood watching Cassie as she coddled Chris. Chris's chest was heaving with the effort their tussle had taken.

"He lost his temper again," Colton explained. "I was just trying to get him to do his exercises."

Cassie's eyes lit up with anger. She rounded on Colton, her temper matching her flowing, fiery red hair. "So you thought it would help to start a fist fight?"

"Physically fighting with him was never my intention, but yes, he needs someone to push him. Cassie, he's not going to get better as long as you let him get away with excuses. He needs to work out. He needs to see a counselor. He needs to move forward rather than languishing in this house every day."

"*He's* sitting right here," Chris interjected and Colton could see him clenching his jaw in anger, but that was okay. Anger was better than apathy any day. "I can also make my own damn decisions about my own damn life."

"Chris," Colton began, trying not to show his frustration, but Cassie cut him off.

"Colt, that's enough for today." She eyed Chris's pale complexion worriedly. "Why don't you take off for a little while and let things calm down around here?"

Cassie began to clean up the lamp. He knew she wanted to protect Chris, but couldn't she see she just enabled his bad behavior?

"I don't think—"

She cut him off again. "Not right now. Just go. Give us some time to cool things off around here." She eyed Chris worriedly.

"Fine." Colton shrugged on his jacket and stormed out of the house.

Chapter 2

The muscles in Colton's arms screamed, but he hardly noticed. He focused on the pounding beat of heavy metal pulsing through his ear buds as he counted off the reps. He channeled all his frustration into pushing the weights slowly off his chest. Fourteen, fifteen…

He'd been home two weeks, and already his siblings were kicking him out of the house. He ignored the sweat dripping off his body as he thought about the scene he'd just left at Cassie's house. It was time for him to find his own place to live. Maybe if he gave Chris a little bit of space to find himself again, then he would begin to heal faster.

He also needed to figure out what he was going to do for the rest of his life. He'd planned to make a career out of the Air Force, but when they'd found Chris six months after he'd 'died', Colton knew that Chris was going to need his help with his recovery. Luckily, he'd served his time so he had the option of separating. The situation with Chris allowed the process to go easier than normal. He'd been a good officer so he was widely respected, which helped clear the way for his separation paperwork to move faster through the system. So he'd separated from the Air Force and left a career which had been shaping up to be a successful one. Luckily, he'd been too busy in his career to do much besides work, so he had some money saved and had a little bit of time to figure it all out.

He moved to the leg press machine and ratcheted up the weight. It was different working out at the Fitness

Center on campus. He glanced around at all the young coeds. When had he gotten old? The sad thing was most of these students had a better idea than he did about what they were going to do for a career.

In the Air Force, he'd flown Hercules C-130's for Special Operations forces. He could fly low-altitude, high-risk missions with people shooting at him, but that didn't translate well into life in West Texas. Last time he checked there wasn't a whole lot of combat flying out here. Regardless, he wasn't ready to give up flying, so he needed to go check out the local airport soon.

He moved to add more weight to the machine and was surprised to find himself staring straight into gorgeous jade green eyes filled with concern. He quickly pulled out his ear buds. He hadn't even known she was standing there. So much for his combat-readiness. He looked at her warily with his heart pounding much faster than it had been just moments before.

Penelope Pruitt was one of Cassie's friends since her college days. Colton didn't know her very well except that she was blond, beautiful, and flighty as a butterfly. From what he'd seen, she was the modern age equivalent to a flower-child. A flower child who looked damn good in her low-riding yoga pants. She had a natural beauty that showed through even when glistening through the sweat from her own workout. He tried to ignore the alluring bead of sweat that dripped down the side of her neck. He needed a distraction, but she wasn't the kind that he needed right now.

***

Penelope had watched Colton through the workout room windows while she finished teaching her yoga class. He'd easily been pounding weights for over an hour and from what she could tell, he didn't have any intention of stopping anytime soon. No wonder the guy was so cut.

After her class filed out, Penelope walked over to Colton, who was dressed in jeans and a plain black t-shirt that hugged every hard plane of his very impressive muscles. He wasn't dressed for a workout, but he lifted like he planned to stay the rest of the day. She'd lay good odds he had another fight with Chris, especially given the bruise forming on his cheek. From everything Cassie told her, things were really tense between the two brothers. All she knew was this guy needed to relax and his current method wasn't doing it for him.

As she mused and watched him from behind the weight stack, he became aware she stood there. He pulled his ear buds out and stood abruptly. Jeebers, this guy was huge. It wasn't just the fact he was built of solid muscle. At 5'9", she wasn't exactly short, but he towered above her. She craned her neck up to look at him.

Surprise and wariness flared through his eyes. "Hi, Penelope. I didn't see you."

"Hey, Colton. You've been working out pretty hard." She leaned her head toward the weight bench as he nodded. She stepped back and looked him up and down. After lifting for so long, his muscles were literally bulging at the seams of his tee. His sweat made the shirt cling in all the other areas where it wasn't straining. He made for a very impressive picture for men's fitness, if you could ignore the lines of fatigue around his eyes and face, the tenseness of his shoulders, and the general tautness of his neck.

"What are you doing?" He looked at her with a raised eyebrow.

She ignored his question and grabbed hold of his arm. "Lifting weights isn't helping you. Come with me."

She dragged him into one of the workout rooms and pulled two rolled-up mats from a bin in the corner.

When she spread them out on the floor, he held up his hands in protest. "Wait, what are y—"

"Listen, I can tell by watching you that your stress levels are maxed out. You're trying to work off your frustration, but at this point, all you're doing is giving yourself muscle fatigue. Give me fifteen minutes and I promise you more stress relief than you'd get from lifting weights all day."

Colton looked from the mats to her suspiciously. "What are you going to do?"

"*We*'re going to do some yoga."

Colton shook his head and eyed the door to make a retreat.

"Don't tell me you're one of those guys who's too much of a manly man to do yoga." She crossed her arms over her chest and raised her eyebrows.

"No, of course not. I just don't think—"

"Good. The point is not to think."

He muttered under his breath, "Something you're very good at."

Penelope stuck her tongue out and glared at him. She had to remember he was stressed out. It was her job, albeit self-appointed right now, to help him release some of that stress. On a normal day, Colton was uptight. As tightly wound as he was right now, he was in danger of a mental and physical breakdown.

"Colton, fifteen minutes is all I'm asking for. Give me that and if you hate it I'll never bother you again. I promise." She leaned toward him, trying not to get lost within his wary, navy blue eyes.

Colton gave a short nod. "Okay, you have fifteen minutes to do what you want."

She gave him a flirtatious smile and a long, lingering look up and down his hard body. "Hmm, what I want? Now that has possibilities, but unfortunately not what I had in mind when I dragged you in here. That's a relaxation technique of a different sort. Besides, I don't think fifteen minutes would be long enough." She shook her head to dispel the notion, but already the ideas tumbling through her head sent tingles throughout her body.

His eyes had darkened as she rambled and now he looked at her like she was going to be his next meal. Okay, so no flirting with the dark, moody guy especially when he was in this kind of mood. Normally, she would be all over that with a guy who looked like this, but she knew enough about Colton to know that wasn't a good idea. Dark and moody were not her idea of a good time. She needed to refocus. Penelope turned on the sound system to slow methodical instrumental music before joining him on the mats.

"First, we need to regulate your breathing. Breathing methodically is just as important as the physical movements. As you breathe in and out, center yourself. Use the movements and the air moving in and out to calm your soul and your body." He gave a short nod, watching her closely.

They faced one another on their mats. "All yoga starts at what is called the Mountain Pose. Stand with your legs and feet together, shoulders back, abs tight, head facing straight forward. The goal here is to get your spine in complete alignment and concentrate on your breathing."

As Colton stood, Penelope stepped closer to him. "Good," she said and adjusted his body slightly with a gentle nudge against his ass, and at the same time she pushed his abs. A spark of electricity arced up her fingertips through her arm. His muscles contracted under her fingertips like he'd felt the same jolt. She glanced up sharply at his face. His eyes were dark and intense and his breathing had grown more erratic. She ignored her own pounding pulse and continued to instruct him.

"You need to concentrate on your breathing." She concentrated on his lips which were firm and enticing. They were parted slightly as he breathed. She'd love nothing more than to take a little bite from them before she worked her way around his neck, lapping at the sweat that beckoned there. The spice of Colton wafted toward her, a scent that drew her in. She wanted more. "Breathe in slowly through your nose. Good. Now release just as slowly through your mouth. Good." As she focused in on those gorgeous lips, Penelope fell down a dark hole of desire. "That's good. Just continue doing that for a count of five breaths." Penelope realized that her own breathing was out of synch at the same time she also realized her palm still rested on his hard abs, where she could feel his muscles bunching and clenching. Penelope snatched her hand away and fled back to the safety of her own mat.

She gave herself a mental shake as the vibrations of desire worked their way through her body. What was she thinking? Oh my God, this was Colton, Cassie's uptight older brother. A man who was about as far away from her type as you could get.

It was time to find her own center. She concentrated on breathing through the yoga pose with him, closing her eyes as she did so. Three breaths later she was more in control.

"Good. Now we're going to move through some of the other poses. I'll do them for you first and then I'll help you as you get your form correct." He gave another quick nod, all his focus on her and what she told him.

"First, place your palms together at your chest, breathe in and circle your arms out until they are stretched out above you. Reach over and touch your toes, keeping your back as flat as possible, exhaling as you go down. Hold this pose for the count of five and then walk your hands out until you are in Downward Facing Dog position.

Hold and breathe, feeling the pull through the backs of your thighs and buttocks."

As Colton watched her move through the slow poses, he groaned internally. He was definitely feeling something pull, but he it wasn't his thigh muscles. For the first time since he'd gotten to the gym, he was glad that he was wearing jeans because the thick denim helped hide his growing erection. With her bent over like that, her toned ass up in the air, he could think of several things he'd like to do with these yoga poses.

Maybe yoga wasn't so bad after all.

"Now lower down into plank position, being sure to keep your body as straight as possible as you hover. Hold the position and then lower into Chaturanga, as you transition into Cobra. Remember to breathe slowly the entire time as you move through the poses. Move back into Plank, back into Downward Facing Dog. Walk your hands back and end with a Sun Salutation."

She stopped moving and looked over at him, completely oblivious to the way he'd been ogling her body as she sensuously moved through the poses. "Now let's have you try it."

"Okay." Colton's voice sounded gruff as he worked to follow the positions she'd just showed him. As he moved, she gently corrected him with a nudge here and a touch there. The feathery guiding touches were driving him insane as lust pounded through his system. As he moved to fold down to touch his toes, his jeans were suddenly even more of a constricting issue. Not only was he sporting a hard-on which would make this position difficult, but the tightness of the jeans made it next to impossible.

Penelope noticed his difficulty although, because of his folded position, she missed the real issue that Colton had. She laughed lightly. "Sorry, yoga isn't meant to be done in jeans."

Colton just frowned and concentrated on the moves. "Don't worry about it. Obviously, I wasn't thinking ahead when I came over here today." He continued working through the poses, surprised at how heavy he was breathing and how much effort they really took. Penelope made them look effortless, but they were much harder to do than they looked.

They flowed together through the sequence several more times before Penelope finally stopped them. "I think you've had enough for today. What do you think about yoga now?"

Colton thought through the muscles of his body and was surprised to realize that he was much looser and more relaxed than he'd been before... with one glaring exception. "You're right. That helped."

Penelope laughed. It was a light melodious sound that reverberated all the way through his gut. "You don't have to sound so shocked about it. Every once in a while, someone else is right, even me." She rolled up the mats and turned off the radio.

Colton watched her as she moved and was suddenly aware of the graceful flow to her body he'd never noticed before. In fact there was a lot about her he'd never noticed before. Normally she wore her naturally wavy honey blond hair down, but today she had it in two braids. With the sprinkling of freckles across her nose, it made her look very young. He didn't even know exactly how old she was although he'd guess her to be close to Cassie's age since they were friends.

He rubbed the back of his neck. He needed to get laid if he was becoming tempted by Cassie's flighty friend. Normally people like her simply annoyed him. He couldn't respect a person who moved through life like it was one big party and Penelope was definitely all about the fun in life.

Honestly, that was probably his problem. He hadn't had any *fun* since divorcing his ex-wife Dianna, two years before.

Since then, he'd simply been too busy with work and finding a bedmate had required too much effort. His body was telling him that it was probably time to make that effort again. He could agree, but that person needed to be someone besides Penelope.

They walked out of the fitness center together, but when they stepped out the door, Penelope cursed, "Damn."

Colton looked across the sheets of rain coming down. It didn't rain often in West Texas, but when it did, it came in torrents. It was a good thing he was driving Chris's truck and not his motorcycle.

Penelope shrugged and pulled the hood up on her sweatshirt. "I guess I won't melt." She gave him a quick wave. "See you later, Colton."

She started off into the rain away from the parking lot before he grabbed her arm and pulled her back under the eave of the building. "Wait, don't you have a car?"

She shook her head. "No, it was a nice morning, so I walked."

"Let me give you a ride home."

Her eyes brightened at the offer. "Thanks, I'd appreciate that. It's not far. I live in those new lofts they built on the other side of campus." Colton nodded that he knew where she was talking about.

As they approached the big black truck, she said, "This is Chris's isn't it?"

Colton nodded. "I usually drive a motorcycle, so I've been using his truck to get him to his appointments."

As he drove, he could feel her eyes on him periodically. He knew she was thinking something through, but she didn't say anything more until they arrived at her building. That was fine with him. He didn't want to talk about the situation with his siblings.

"Colton, do you want to come up for some coffee or tea, or maybe even a beer? I know things are stressful at Cassie's. I get the idea you still aren't as de-stressed as you need to be. Why don't you come up and relax for a while? We can just hang out and relax, I promise."

Colton looked at her for a moment contemplating her offer. She was right. He wasn't ready to head back to Cassie's yet. "I'd like that. Thanks Penelope."

Entering her loft, Colton whistled low and looked around the spacious apartment. "This is nice."

"Thanks. Make yourself at home. There's beer in the fridge. Help yourself to whatever you want." She waved her hand toward the kitchen as she continued walking through the apartment. "I'm gonna go change out of my sweaty clothes. I'll be right back."

Colton grabbed a beer and looked around the loft more seriously. Based upon Penelope's personality, he would have expected her place to be filled with lots of thrift shop castoffs, but that's not what he saw at all. Throughout the loft, the floors were a rich worn mahogany and Penelope had done her best to set them off. A mix of antiques flanked warm traditional pieces. The couches were slipcovered in white canvas, but touches of Penelope were there with a startling bouquet of vibrant throw pillows. The art on the walls ranged from modern to impressionistic and all of it was colorful and full of life.

Not surprisingly, since Penelope ran a bookstore, there was an entire exposed brick wall with bookshelves overflowing with books. Colton stepped over to those to peruse the titles. She had all the expected bestsellers and popular authors. There was also a section of larger paperbacks that looked more worn than the others, which made him curious. He picked up one to thumb through it and was surprised to find some heavy-duty erotica. He was so caught up reading it he didn't hear Penelope come back into the room.

Penelope leaned down in front of Colton, tilting the book so she could see the title. "Hmm, Shayla Black's *Surrender to Me*." Colton could feel his cheeks heat in embarrassment. She quirked an eyebrow at him, enjoying his discomfort. "I could see you as a Dom." She nodded as she walked into the kitchen area to grab her own beer. Suddenly the blood that had been suffusing Colton's cheeks rushed to other areas as he had a flash of Penelope tied up, naked, and doing his bidding.

Colton hastily re-shelved the book, cleared his throat, and moved to change the subject. "I really like your place. You've done a nice job with it."

Penelope gave him a soft smile. "Thanks. This is my oasis and I love it. I was lucky to sign a lease while they were still constructing the building. The risk turned out to be worth it."

Colton nodded as he looked around again. "Do you know if there are any units open?"

Penelope shook her head. "No, and I've heard the waiting list is really long to get one. Like I said, I was lucky." She looked at him seriously as if pondering something, and became distracted by the swelling on the side of his face. "Does that hurt?" She gently reached up and placed her fingers, cold from grasping the beer bottle, against the bruise.

Colton sucked in a breath at the shock of her touch on his throbbing face. "No," he said in a low voice as he looked into her eyes, "I'd actually forgotten about it."

Penelope looked at him with concern in her eyes, which was nice. He started to reach toward her simply wanting to touch her, feel her, but then she said, "Was it Chris?"

That was enough to break the pull Colton felt toward her and he stepped away. "Yeah. He's having some issues controlling his temper and me being in his space all the time isn't helping." Colton shook his head and walked over to the windows. He looked out over the campus, watching the rivulets of rain drip down the tall window panes. "I need to move out. It's not working having all three of us living together."

"I know things have been tense. Cassie's mentioned it." Penelope hesitated as she watched him. "Colton, you could move in here."

He swung around and looked at her with his eyes wide. "What? Why?"

He glanced back over at her erotica section of her bookshelf, which caused Penelope to give a nervous chuckle.

"Jeebers! Seriously? You're such a guy. I'm not asking you to move in for sex games. You're so not my type." She gave an exasperated shake of her head. "Get your mind out of the gutter. My last roommate just moved out without any notice. The loft is a two bedroom. It was never supposed to be just me living here. Honestly, you'd be helping me out because the rent is too much for me to be able to afford by myself if I plan to eat too."

Her voice lowered to a whisper which made Colton nervous, "I'll tell you a secret. I like to eat." She smiled at him mischievously. "Seriously, it would help me out. You've just gotten back and this would give you some time and space." She waved him down the hall. "The room is empty. Go take a look at it. It's the second door on the right. Each bedroom has its own bathroom so we wouldn't even have to share there."

Colton looked at her thoughtfully and then moved down the hall toward the spare bedroom. He thought about the scene which had occurred at Cassie's house this afternoon, as he looked around the large room. This could be a good solution. He knew he couldn't continue on at Cassie's house, but could he survive Penelope?

Maybe he'd misjudged her. He'd always seen her as flighty, but he hadn't seen any signs of that today. He'd honestly had a good time with her this afternoon and she'd helped him to relax. Besides, they weren't talking about a relationship or a commitment here. They'd just be roommates. He felt a flash of concern about his attraction to her, but that just meant he needed to get laid. His body was simply telling him that it'd been too long. He could keep things purely platonic between them.

Besides, Chris needed this. They needed to be able to continue to work together. Colton was the one who got him to all his appointments. It certainly wouldn't help Chris's frame of mind if they were fighting all the time. Chris's need in this had to be the priority. They used to be close. Maybe if he gave him a bit of space at Cassie's house, they could find their friendship again and Chris could start to truly heal.

Decision made, Colton walked back into the living room.

He reached out to shake her hand. "If you're sure, I'll take it."

Penelope gave him a glowing smile and grasped his hand. "Welcome, roomie. When would you like to move in?"

"Is this weekend too soon?"

Penelope shook her head. "Sounds perfect."

Chapter 3

He had a gift. His mother had always said so.

He turned off the cell phone with a glow of self-satisfaction. All the pieces were falling into place after so much planning and work. The final bit of the puzzle was almost where it needed to be before he proved to them all just how damn good he was. He'd prove it to them. With this final move, they'd know.

He was the puppet master and they were his harlequins, dancing according to his commands. They didn't even know who held the strings. Soon they would realize who really had the power here. And that power was invigorating. He closed his eyes and savored the thrill. He'd beat them all and they didn't even know it yet. He couldn't wait to show them. They'd all underestimated him and they would regret that. Someday soon.

Yes, he definitely had a gift. Now he just needed to decide when and how he'd let them unwrap it.

Chapter 4

Penelope pulled her classic VW Bus into the parking spot in front of the little boutique restaurant. Her mother phoned fifteen minutes before, insisting that she meet her for breakfast, although Penelope was already on her way to the bookstore. Luckily, Aunt Alix was opening this morning which left Penelope free to meet her mother. It was odd for her to summon Penelope on a Thursday morning, when Penelope knew that her mother would normally be busy with University business.

As she crawled out of the Bus, she was thankful she'd actually worn a skirt today. It was a flippy little number her mother couldn't find too much fault in, but then she caught sight of her scuffed cowboy boots. Never mind, her mother was going to have a conniption when she saw her. With a sigh, she had to admit that certainly wouldn't be anything new.

Penelope was thirty years old and at least twenty-nine of those years had been spent under the disapproving eye of her mother. There wasn't anything she could do about it now, so she simply squared her shoulders and prepared for the battle that breakfast with her mother would bring.

As she entered the restaurant, she glanced around with an appreciative eye. She didn't know how her mother did it, but she always found the best little restaurants. This was a determinedly feminine choice. The dining room was filled with quaint little tables set up for two to four people, all painted shabby chic white. Throughout the room were gorgeous chandeliers…an eclectic mix of aged bronzes and painted fixtures which sparkled and shimmered in the soft morning light.

Penelope spotted her mother watching her with pursed lips and disapproving eyes. Obviously, she'd already noticed the cowboy boots. Penelope worked to calm the roiling of her stomach. You'd think after all this time she'd be accustomed to facing her mother's disapproval.

When she reached the table, Penelope leaned down and gave her mother's cheek a soft kiss in greeting. "Hello, Mother. You're looking well this morning." And she truly was. At the age of 72, Anna Pruitt should be enjoying her retirement, but both her parents continued to work and teach at Texas Tech. They said surrounding themselves with students kept them young, and Penelope would have to agree. Both her parents looked at least a decade younger than their actual age.

"Good morning, Penelope. You look…" Her mother looked her up and down, trying to come up with the right word. Penelope cringed internally. Her mother was going to completely lambast her. "…interesting."

Uh oh. That was almost a compliment by her mother's standards. She never held anything back in deference to her feelings. Suddenly, Penelope was worried. What was going on?

"Have you done something new with your hair?" Her mother looked at her critically. "That messy look seems to be so in right now."

Okay, now Penelope knew something was up. Her mother always hated her hair when she left it down. Always. Not that she didn't realize that was a dig, because it absolutely was. But her mother was never that subtle with her criticisms.

Unfortunately, there was a whole protocol in dining with her mother and diving right into a discussion about why she called did not fit those parameters. Penelope tried to settle her jumping nerves and looked over the menu. After they'd ordered, Penelope settled into small talk. "I didn't even know this place was here. It's cute. I like it."

Her mother nodded distractedly. "Yes, Denise Morgan's daughter opened it last year. She's such a model daughter. She does all this," her mother waved her hand over the dining room, "and she's married with two small children. She also sits on the Junior League Executive Board. She's always so put-together and such a benefit to the community."

Penelope sighed internally. Denise Morgan's daughter was obviously everything her own mother wished she could be. She chose to ignore the hurt that inflicted and instead took a sip of her tea. They settled into an uneasy silence which was finally interrupted when their waitress brought them their food.

"Have you heard from Dad lately?"

"Yes, his trip to Europe has gone rather well." Her father was an Economics professor at Texas Tech. This semester, he was working on behalf of the University in a cooperative program with several international Universities on a Global Economy symposium. "He should be back this weekend."

Penelope nodded her head. "That's good. And how are things in the Anthropology Department?" Her mother was the head of the Anthropology department of Texas Tech and took her job very seriously, not that anyone ever considered anthropology to be anything less than serious. Growing up, Penelope had certainly tried, but her mother had never found her antics humorous. For some reason, she didn't find it funny when the eight year old Penelope removed all the erect penises off her priceless fertility statue collection.

Her mother studied her for a moment, before hesitantly speaking. "That's actually why I asked you here today."

Finally, it was time for the true reason for her summoning. Penelope steeled herself and searched her mother's face, waiting. "Yes?"

"The anthropology department is facing some difficulties. As more and more funding is cut throughout the University systems, there are fewer opportunities for our research and, as you know, our field research is vital to our programs."

Penelope nodded. She knew all this, but had no idea how any of this had to do with her.

"There's an important archeological dig happening on the border between Belize and Mexico. The signs are already there that this is a discovery which none of us have ever seen before." She looked earnestly at Penelope. "It's going to mean a lot to the anthropological world."

Penelope nodded, "I could see that." But she was still confused as to why her mother was trying to sell her on the importance of this dig.

"The gentleman in charge of the dig is Dr. Damon Lopez. He's a brilliant archeologist who works for the National Explorer Society. This weekend, he's going to be in town, and this is our chance to get the University in on the dig. Saturday night, the University is hosting a reception in his honor and I hoped you would serve as his escort for the night."

Penelope followed the conversation just fine, until the very end. "Wait. What? His escort?" She gaped at her mother in disbelief. Her mother normally tried to keep Penelope as far away from her professional life as possible. Penelope had been a source of embarrassment to her parents her entire life, especially when it came to their professional careers. Also, in her experience, both anthropologists and archaeologists tended to be elderly, kind gentlemen who weren't exactly thrilled with her flamboyant style. In short, they were all a lot like her parents. This just didn't make any sense.

Her mother looked at her guiltily, so Penelope honed in on a single phrase. "You said escort." She felt a sinking all the way to her toes. She knew her mother didn't respect her, but surely it didn't go this far. The shock reverberated through her system. She lowered her voice to a whisper, both from the hurt and in a play for a bit of privacy in the quiet dining room. "You're not actually pimping me out, are you?"

"Penelope, no!" Her mother shrieked in outrage.

Okay, thank goodness she'd read that one wrong. "Well, then I don't understand."

"I'm sorry. I'm not explaining this very well. Dr. Lopez is brilliant, but he's also a bit avant-garde. His methods are unusual." Her mother pursed her lips. "He's a lot like you, in that he does his own thing, his own way. He's also around your age, so I thought it might be amenable to both of you. The department doesn't have many on staff who are his age and demeanor. We want him to be comfortable here." At Penelope's smirk, she watched her mother's color rise. "You know I don't want you to make him *that* comfortable, although I have to admit some grandchildren would be nice."

Penelope felt her mouth drop open. Her mother had never mentioned grandchildren before. Seriously, what had gotten into her this morning?

"If you don't want to do it, I completely understand, but I hope you'll at least consider it. As a favor to me. From what I understand, Dr. Lopez is very attractive."

Penelope looked at her mother and debated internally. "You realize, if I agree to this, you're not allowed to say a thing about what I wear, what I say, or how I act."

"But…"

"Not a single word, Mother. I know how to behave. I promise I won't embarrass you, but neither will you embarrass me by questioning any of my actions. Agreed?"

Her mother gave a short nod of acquiescence.

"Fine, then I'll accompany your Dr. Lopez. You said Saturday night, right?"

Her mother nodded again, looking relieved. "I'll have my assistant send you all the pertinent information and the University will provide you with a car and driver for the night."

"That's not necessary. I can pick him up in the Bus."

Her mother visibly shuddered. "No, that's not the kind of impression the University wants to give him."

"Mother," Penelope said in a warning voice, "there's no reason that we can't use my Bus."

"Please, Penelope, this is the only other thing I ask. Please use the driver service."

Penelope looked hard at her mother, but finally relented. Besides by using the University driver, she could make use of the bar at the reception if she needed to, and knowing University receptions like this one…she was definitely going to need it.

Chapter 5

By the time Penelope made it into the bookstore, she was over an hour and a half late. She rushed in the door to find things quiet and her Aunt Alix drinking coffee and reading at the front desk.

She looked up from the book she was reading as Penelope walked into the store. "Good morning, dear. How was breakfast with your mother?"

Her mother and Aunt Alix were sisters, but they were nothing alike. In fact, it had been at least six years since they'd even spoken to one another. Alix was fourteen years younger than Penelope's mother, Anna, and decades apart in attitude especially when it came to Penelope. Growing up, Aunt Alix had been Penelope's refuge, friend, and support system when faced with the overwhelmingly strict edicts by her parents. Unfortunately it was Aunt Alix's strong support of Penelope which also caused the sisters' rift six years earlier.

College was a particularly stressful time in Penelope's life. By that point in time, she'd learned to assert her own will against her parents, but standing up for herself took its toll on her mentally. She learned methods for relieving her stress…yoga and writing.

It started as something seemingly innocent, but her writing started taking a darker turn when she started writing BDSM erotica. It had actually been Alix who led her to finding that avenue. A late night filled with girl talk, way too much wine, and more than a bit of curiosity led them to a website filled with artful erotic images that Penelope couldn't let go of mentally. The stories followed shortly thereafter. Unbeknownst to Penelope, Alix submitted them for publication and they were bought.

Her alter ego, Celeste DeMarco, was born. Penelope wrote the stories. Aunt Alix acted as the author to protect Penelope's identity. Her parents had no idea that Penelope was actually Celeste DeMarco.

Being older southern conservatives, her parents never would have understood or forgiven her for doing "that kind" of writing. Celeste DeMarco was a huge secret. They'd gone on that way for three years before it all came crashing down and Penelope's parents found out about Celeste DeMarco. Alix never told Penelope's secret, that she was actually the author of the books. Instead, she covered for Penelope. Alix claimed Celeste DeMarco as her alter-ego and it cost Alix her relationship with her sister, Penelope's mother. Alix insisted it was no big loss because they'd never gotten along, but that didn't keep Penelope from feeling horrible about the entire situation.

Over the years, Penelope wanted to confess all to her mother, but Alix wouldn't allow it. She swore she'd never speak to Penelope again if she did that. It was a risk Penelope couldn't take. She needed her aunt in her life.

The situation wasn't all bad though. As she looked around Raider Readers, pride filled her. Her royalty checks from the novels paid the start-up costs of the bookstore. Another secret. As far as her parents knew, that was also Alix's doing. In reality, instead of being her partner and backer for the store, Alix was simply an employee. The store was adjacent to the campus in a historical colonial-style house, which was rezoned as commercial property. She'd left the original, gorgeous bones of the house intact…the wood paneling, the different rooms, the decorative woodwork and moldings, the many fireplaces, and the sweeping staircase. A gorgeous old mahogany bar was converted to act as their front desk and check-out counter. The front counter was nestled into the curve of the staircase so it was the first thing you saw when you came into the store.

It was here that Alix sat now, waiting for an answer.

"Breakfast was fine. Strange, but fine." She gave her Aunt a mischievous look. "She needed me to do a favor for her, so now I think I'm going to have my mom in my debt. That could be useful."

Alix smiled in agreement. "Without a doubt, but what in the world did she need you to do?"

"The University has some bigwig coming in that they want to impress, but it sounds like he's younger and hipper than your typical Anthropology dweeb."

Alix muttered, "Isn't everyone?"

Penelope giggled. "She wants me to serve as his escort to a party Saturday night." Penelope eyed her aunt, waiting for her reaction.

"Escort?" Alix's eyes widened in shock. "I know I haven't seen my sister in a few years, but I find it hard to believe that she's changed that much."

"I know, right? That was exactly my reaction. But she swears she doesn't want me for *that*." Penelope rolled her eyes. "Honestly, after all these years of disapproving of my 'wild ways,' now my mom wants to use them to impress this guy. It sounds like he's pretty unorthodox. If nothing else, it should be fun to see how my mom relates to a colleague who has more in common with me than her."

Penelope looked around the quiet store. "Thanks for covering for me this morning. Is there anything happening around here that I need to know about?"

"We got a box of ARC's and promotional swag in. I put it on your desk."

"Okay, good. When does Hannah come in next? She'll want those ARC's so she can start reading them."

Hannah was another employee at Raider Readers and she worked as their blog mistress. She read the Advanced Reader Copies of books that were coming out and posted reviews as well as giveaways, release dates, and other pertinent information on the blog for the bookstore.

"She's supposed to be in tomorrow afternoon."

"Good. She can go through them then." There was a customer in the New Fiction section and the monitors showed someone else upstairs in the Science Fiction section. "It looks like you have everything under control here." At Alix's nod, she said, "I'm going to go catch up on some paperwork in my office. Holler if you need me."

Chapter 6

"Colton! I come bearing food. Can I interest you in some pizza?" Penelope yelled down the hall as she set the pizzas on the table. She didn't hear a response so she walked down the hall to Colton's room, to see how the unpacking was going.

She found him sitting on the floor, surrounded by a meager pile of boxes, looking at a photo album. His face wasn't visible, but his posture seemed sad. Slumped over the photo album, his fingers lingered lightly over a photo of a couple. That had to be a picture of his parents.

His bare feet toes were peeking out from under his folded legs. Tilting her head, she looked again at those bare toes. Why was that so attractive to her? Especially in light of the sadness that permeated the room as he looked at his parents. She knew they'd died in a plane crash through her friendship with Cassie. How hard would that have been for him to lose both parents so young?

As she leaned against the doorframe, observing him, Colton suddenly jumped up and began searching through the few boxes in the room.

"Son of a bitch!" The muscles in his back became tighter and tighter as he dug more frantically. Whatever he'd just discovered was missing, he wasn't happy about it.

She needed to give him his privacy.

As she started to slip away, he suddenly looked up at her. She was struck by the stark anger and pain shining from his eyes at that first glance, but he quickly covered it up when he realized she was standing there.

"I didn't hear you come in," he said quietly.

"I'm sorry. I didn't mean to interrupt. I brought pizza. I knew you'd be busy unpacking today and thought you could use some sustenance." She decided not to mention whatever he was looking for. It wasn't any of her business, but she couldn't ignore the lack of stuff. She looked quizzically around the room and the obvious lack of boxes and furniture. "Um, Colton, where's all your stuff?"

He gave a self-deprecating chuckle as his eyes hardened. "Obviously, you should never trust a soon-to-be ex-wife to pack up your house and put it into storage for you. This is all there is." He looked around the bare room. "I need to go shopping." He scowled at the thought.

She smiled. "I can tell you're thrilled about the idea. First, pizza. We can figure out what you need over lunch."

They headed into the kitchen and settled into chairs at the breakfast bar. Penelope gestured toward his plate. "I hope you don't mind veggie pizza. I'm a vegetarian."

"Naw, this is great. I love any pizza from One Guy. Thanks for picking it up, but I thought you were going to be working all day."

"Ah, no, that's the beauty of being the boss. I can leave when things get slow. They can call me back in if they need me, but I think you're going to need me more today." She leaned over the counter and grabbed a pad and pencil. "We have some power shopping to get done. Let's make a list."

"Thanks, but you don't –"

"Nope, no arguments. I'm going. I'm a fabulous shopper with incredible taste. You won't regret it. Besides

I have the Bus. This way you won't have to borrow Chris's truck again."

Colton hesitated as he glanced around the apartment. "Thanks, I hate shopping, so I'd appreciate the help."

"No problem. We just have to be back here by 5:00 so I have time to get ready for my date." She looked at the clock on the microwave. "We'd better hurry. We have a lot of ground to cover and not very much time to do it in. I hope you have high limits on your credit cards."

Colton shut his eyes and groaned. "It's going to be a long afternoon."

***

As Penelope flung her body onto the huge bed, she looked over at him entreatingly. "Come on. You need to lay on the bed to get a feel if it's the one for you."

The cascade of her honey-colored hair flung across the pillow sent his pulse pounding and his fingers itched to run through the soft locks. Honestly, if she'd lie in his bed all the time, it wouldn't matter what it felt like. Regardless, he wasn't sure that he could trust himself enough to join her on a bed in a public place without developing an embarrassing erection.

He scowled down at her. She had a date tonight. Maybe he should go out and find himself a distraction. Obviously his lack of a sex life was starting to affect him.

She rolled over and sat up on her hands and knees. Obviously, she had no issues making herself right at home on the furniture displays. "Look, Colt," she grabbed hold of the slats of the headboard and the thick bedpost beside it, "this would work really well for those Dom/sub games you're into. Just imagine tying someone up to the corners of this baby." She smirked up at him and he decided a good spanking might do her some good.

A wave of lust flowed through his entire body at the idea of her tied to those four bedposts, but was distracted by the sound the salesman made, which sounded way too much like a groan. From the look on his face, he was thinking the same licentious thoughts about Penelope that Colton was having. Colton reached over and plucked her off the bed as he turned to the salesman and scowled. "I'll take it and will pay whatever you need so that it's delivered today."

"No problem, sir. Let me get the paperwork started."

***

Three hours later, they were back at the loft. Colton was kicked-back in the living room sucking down a well-earned beer while Penelope got ready for her date. Thanks to her, they'd actually gotten a lot bought and he was well on his way to having a furnished room again.

"Hey, Colton, can you come help me?" Penelope was leaning out the door of her bedroom.

"Sure." He walked into her room and was greeted with the glorious expanse of her back. He sucked in a breath at the view. God, she was beautiful.

She looked at him over her shoulder. "Can you zip me up? I can't reach it to do it myself. This is a new dress and I never realized how hard it was to get into."

"No problem," he said. Even to him, his voice sounded several octaves deeper than normal. He reached to grab the zipper tab and as he started to pull it up, he caught the glimpse of something which surprised him on her right side. She had birds tattooed up her back. He could just see the full body of one and the wings of two others. He gently rubbed his fingertips over them, feeling the silky warmth of her skin. Penelope shivered at his touch.

"These are amazing."

"Thanks."

He continued to pull the zipper up her back, but was now intrigued about exactly how far those birds traversed the side of her body. As the zipper closed at the top, he could see the edge of another bird up high on her right shoulder and the word 'free' tattooed into its trail.

He traced that final bird as he said, "I have a feeling there's a story here."

She turned to him and his breath caught in his throat. She was stunning. The plum-colored dress fit her like a glove. While it completely covered her, it clung to her curves and enhanced every single one of them. Colton's mouth went dry.

"There is."

"What?" He'd lost track of what they were talking about.

"The tattoo. There's a story. I'll share it with you one night, but now I have to finish getting ready." There was a knock on the front door. "Do you mind getting that? I just have to load up my purse and grab my sweater and then I'll be out."

At his silent nod, she murmured, "Thanks, Colton."

He gave her one last lingering look before leaving to answer the door. Damn, she looked incredible.

Colton opened the door with his thoughts still lingering back in the bedroom with Penelope and the currents zinging through his system. The man standing before him was tall, although not quite as tall a Colton. His hair was dark and styled in one of those pretty-boy casual styles, meant to look easy, but took as many products to achieve as any girl's hairstyle. His warm brown eyes crinkled at the corners like he smiled a lot or spent a lot of time outdoors. Looking at the guy, it was probably a combination of the two. He was fit, but not muscular.

The guy offered an easy, but confused smile. He looked up and down the hall, then back at the door.

"I'm sorry. I'm looking for Penelope Pruitt. This is the apartment number I have for her."

"Yeah," Colton offered out his hand, "Penelope's here. She's still getting ready. I'm her roommate, Colton. Come on in. Dr. Lopez, right?"

The man took his hand and nodded. "Yup, that's me, but please call me Damon. Doctor makes me sound older than shit." He offered a friendly smile as he entered the loft. He gave a low whistle as he looked around. "Whoa, this is nice."

"Thanks." Colton nodded. "Can I offer you something to drink? I just moved in today, so I'm not sure what we have, but I'm sure we have something."

Damon chuckled. "No, I'm fine." He looked speculatively at Colton. "You said you just moved in, so are you and Penelope an item?"

Colton shook his head. "No, we're just roommates."

"So, she's single?"

"As far as I know she is."

He gave a friendly grin. "That's good to hear. I don't want to horn in on some other guy's territory and I don't get to the States very often…" He let the sentence trail off as Penelope walked into the room and said under his breath, "Oh yeah, that's really good to hear."

Colton glared at the guy. Pretty boy was not the man Penelope needed in her life. Colton froze as that inexplicable surge of possessiveness tore through him and he worked to tamp down the sudden anger. Where the hell had that thought come from?

***

As Penelope walked into the living room, her heart gave a little stutter of shock. Talk about testosterone overload. Just look at the beefcake she had in her living room tonight. Her nerves were already strumming after looking at beds all day with the incredibly built Colton. Now he stood there with another seriously hot guy. Tall, dark, and beautifully fit times two.

The difference between the two guys was marked, but they were both very nice in their own way. Where Colton was intimidating in his pure bulk and height, Dr. Lopez was long and lean. Colton was casual in his t-shirt, jeans, and those oh-so-sexy bare feet, while Dr. Lopez wore a suit that fitted his lean physique perfectly. They both had dark hair. Colton's was military short, while Dr. Lopez's style was a little longer and more careless. Dr. Lopez had a face which was completely open and friendly, while Colton was more guarded with his expressions. Right now he looked downright pissed. Had she missed something? She glanced between the two of them, but didn't see any other signs of trouble. Curious. Dr. Lopez eyed her as she approached and his eyes showed his approval. She smiled at him and offered her hand. "Hi, you must be Dr. Lopez."

He flashed a bright smile at her, but instead of shaking her hand, he lifted it slowly to his lips. He murmured, "Please call me Damon. You're even more beautiful than your mother described, Penelope." Then he brushed his lips lightly over the back of her hand. She got caught up in the depths of his chocolate eyes before Colton cleared his throat.

He frowned at her as he said, "So you two are headed to the campus?"

Damon grimaced. "Unfortunately. This is not my idea of an ideal first date when I want to impress a beauty like this." He looked over at Penelope. "It's a University function where a lot of stuffed shirts are going to schmooze me so they can intrude upon my archeological dig."

"Hey, those stuffed shirts are my parents." She appeared contemplative for a moment. "Oh never mind, you're completely correct. Maybe we can hit a jazz bar afterwards for some real fun." She looked at him speculatively.

He gave her another easy smile. "I think that sounds like a plan, but we probably should be off so that we can get the boring part of the evening out of the way."

"No worries. They can't schmooze without you there, so they can't possibly complain about you being late." She looked over at Colton. "Don't have too much fun unpacking."

Colton groaned. "Don't remind me. Although I'm not sure which is worse…the unpacking I need to deal with or the stuffed shirts you'll have to deal with. Maybe I'll just settle into the couch with one of your books." He looked speculatively toward her erotica shelf and a shiver of awareness skated through her body. Yep, way too much testosterone in this room.

"Goodnight Colton." She dragged Damon out the front door. She needed to get away from her way-too-sexy new roommate.

Chapter 7

Penelope watched Damon as they rode in the luxurious chauffeured town car. He really was very good looking. He had a casual sense about him and an easy smile which was especially appealing. "The University must think really highly of you to offer this kind of service." She gestured toward their driver.

He shrugged. "I have something they want, so they plan to keep me happy however they can. I have to admit I'm surprised by you, though. This is the first time I've had such an interesting and beautiful date provided."

She gave a self-deprecating little laugh. "That sounds like flattery, but unfortunately I know what the typical anthropologist looks like." She paused to examine him. He was so different from Colton, but she wasn't going to start comparing her dates to her new roommate. He was a roommate. Only a roommate. "I'm the one who should be surprised. You're neither old nor crusty." She winked at him. "How did you get into archaeology and anthropology?"

"Through my uncle, who does happen to be old and crusty. I grew up going on digs with him and fell in love with the life and mystery of it all. I was fortunate to make some good contacts early in life. That and a little bit of luck thrown in and now I find myself working for National Explorer on one of the most prestigious digs happening this decade."

"What's so special about this dig?"

"*El Regalo*."

"The Gift?"

He looked at her in surprise. "You speak Spanish?"

"I've picked up a little over the years, but I'm nowhere close to fluent. And that still doesn't explain what makes this dig so important."

"First, let me tell you a story. There's a legend in the Mayan culture about the God of Rain, Chac. It's said he was a benevolent God who fell in love with a human woman. She didn't return his love and instead she fell in love with a farmer. She bore that farmer two sons. When Chac found out, he was enraged and sent a flood which killed her sons while they were working in the fields. Immediately, Chac regretted his actions and sent the woman a gift to try to make up for her sons' deaths. The gift was a golden garden... full of flowers and plants made from pure gold, but it was too late. The woman committed suicide because her grief over the loss of her sons was so great. When the farmer saw the gift Chac sent, he spent the next twenty years burying the golden garden under layer upon layer of dirt."

"But it's just a legend, right?"

"Correct, but as we study archaeology and anthropology more and more, we've come to realize that all legends are based loosely upon some grain of truth. We're seeing signs this new site could very well be El Regalo, the Golden Garden from the legend. The site is a building which was obviously buried on purpose. The first artifacts out of it have been golden flowers." She could see his passion about his work glimmering in his eyes.

"Oh wow. That sounds amazing."

"It is and I'm hoping, as we dig, we'll be able to figure out the true story behind the legend." His chocolate brown eyes sparkled with excitement. "It's all about figuring out the mystery and finding the treasure."

"So you're just an adult treasure hunter," she teased him.

"You got it, darling. The hard part is finding the 'X' and I've got it this time." He gave her a cocky smile and grabbed her hand. "I think we've arrived." He nodded toward the building where they'd parked. "Are you ready to go accept the schmoozing?"

"They want to schmooze you, not me."

"Aw, but that's the perk of being my date. You get schmoozed purely by happenstance. That and you're on the arm of the best-looking guy in the place."

"Modest, too, aren't you?" She smiled at him as he pulled her out of the car.

"Modesty has nothing to do with it, darling. I'm simply stating fact." He winked at her as he smiled, flashing his very sexy dimples.

Guys with dimples were her favorite type, so why did her thoughts keep straying to the roommate she'd left at home who hadn't flashed a dimple yet? She worried at her lip with her teeth. She may just have a problem here.

Chapter 8

Penelope let herself into the bookstore bright and early Sunday morning. The store would open for a few hours in the afternoon, but Sunday mornings were her time to catch-up on all the managerial tasks which needed to be done, from scheduling to bookkeeping.

As she sat down to her desk, she mused over the previous night's date with Damon. After they'd left the party, she'd taken him to a cozy little bar where they could sit at a table in front of the stone fireplace. They'd had a wonderful time chatting and getting to know each other. They got along famously and she'd been excited for the distraction from Colton. Damon was the type of guy she normally dated. They hadn't lacked for topics of discussion the entire night, but when it came to the end of the evening, the kiss between them fell flat.

Oh, there'd been nothing wrong with the kiss. Damon was an excellent kisser, but the zing just wasn't there for her. She'd gotten more turned on when Colton zipped up her dress at the beginning of the night. That was the problem. She couldn't get involved with Colton. He was everything she didn't want in a guy. He was too serious, too by-the-book, too straight-laced. Plus he was her best friend's brother and Cassie wouldn't take it lightly if things ended badly between them. No, she was looking for someone exactly like Damon, someone who knew how to have fun.

Maybe she'd just had an off night. Luckily Damon was in town for the next week, and they'd made plans to get together again. He was supposed to call her this afternoon to finalize things, which gave her an idea.

She picked up the phone and dialed a number she hadn't called enough lately.

"Hello, Rocking M Ranch," the masculine voice answered.

She smiled. She loved all the guys out on the Martin Ranch, but Thomas was still her favorite. Even though things didn't work out for them when they dated, they'd stayed friends in the years since. "Well, hey there sexy."

"Penny! What are you doing calling me this early on a Sunday morning? Are you coming out to visit us soon?"

"I am. That's actually why I called. I have a friend in town who I thought might enjoy a true Texas ranching experience."

"So he's not from around here?"

"No, he's an archeologist here negotiating a deal with Texas Tech to get some students to come work with him on his dig."

"An archeologist? Really? That doesn't sound like your normal fare. Where's his dig located?"

She laughed. "You know me well, but he's a nice guy. The dig is on the Mexico/Belize border."

"Does he ride?"

"I have no clue. It was just a spur of the moment idea, so I thought I'd run it by you."

"Penny, you're always welcome to bring anyone out you want. We appreciate all you do for the ranch and want to keep you coming out as much as possible."

"Thanks, Thomas. I'll let you know when we head that way. Regardless of whether he comes out with me or not, I'll be out sometime this week to exercise some of the horses."

"Sounds good, Penny. I look forward to seeing you."

"Bye, Thomas." She disconnected the call.

A few years back, when she'd been doing the research on ranching for her Celeste DeMarco series, she'd discovered the Rocking M Ranch. Owned by Michael Martin and run by him and his four sons, she'd come to love the family and the ranch.

But now she had work to do with her other passion, the bookstore. She sat down at her desk to sort through the piles of paperwork Alix left for her. One whole pile pertained to her writing as Celeste DeMarco. It included current contract negotiations, income statements, and the trickling of fan mail that came in. In this day and age, most people resorted to the internet for those sorts of things, but there were still fans who appreciated the written word of a letter. Unfortunately, the majority of those who still wrote physical letters happened to fall under the category of crazy... religious zealots and old-fashioned conservatives who viewed her writing as glorified pornography or worse.

This pile definitely had a few of those in it, but there were also a few fan letters. There were a couple from women who thanked her for spicing up their married lives. She always liked those. One letter from a prison librarian who stated her books were always among the most popular among the inmates. She had to chuckle at that one.

When she turned she noticed another pile of ARC's waiting for Hannah. They seemed to be receiving more books than normal lately. She hoped Hannah had the time to handle them all, but it had been a while since she'd done one of the reviews. Maybe she would take something home to read and distract her from her new roommate.

The night before, thoughts of Colton sleeping just a few yards away had kept her awake for hours. She wondered if he slept in the nude, whether he slept on one side of the bed, or whether he sprawled over the entire space. She needed a diversion.

As she thumbed through them, one book caught her eye, ***The Gift of Serendipity***. The cover was shades of dark purple and grey. In silhouette, there was an outline of a couple in a deep embrace. She flipped the book over to read the back copy.

Serendipity had come into her parents' lives very late and unexpectedly.
That wasn't the only thing unexpected about Serendipity.
She had a very special gift.
Unfortunately before she learned how to control it, that gift killed her parents.
Now she's just trying to protect the world.
And Blake is just trying to protect her.
In a world that doesn't understand magic, they're both fighting against the odds.

Inserted into the book was a PR flier. She pulled it out. Across the top it said, '**Abilene Authors...*a new kind of AA feeding your addiction for books.***' She giggled. That was cute, definitely catchy. She looked back at the book and yep, the author was listed as Abilene Authors. Hmm, that was different. She flipped through the book. It seemed like a normal fiction book, but was written by a group?

Looking back at the flier, there was a paragraph called *About Abilene Authors.*

```
Abilene Authors is a like-minded
group of writers based out of West
Texas. Our members range from students
to homemakers to active duty military.
As writers we know that writing takes
time, but as a group, we're impatient.
```

So we decided to combine our writing talents to create works of fiction you will want to read…right now. The goal: write good books, fast, with an output of six to nine books a year. We self-publish and do everything from the writing and editing, to the formatting and cover design. As a group, we work together to create a work of fiction we can be proud of and hope our efforts create a book you want to read.

She smiled. She liked the sounds of this group and liked to support local independent authors whenever she could. Abilene was another Texas town located one hundred seventy-five miles to the east of Lubbock. If the book was any good, maybe she could have them come to the store for a signing.

As an added bonus, the book sounded entertaining. A good, mysterious, dark romance. It was just what she needed to distract her during the late nights from Colton sleeping just a few feet away from her.

***

Penelope walked into the loft just as Colton and Jake, Cassie's fiancé, shook hands saying something about a partnership. They were both wearing shit-eating grins and seemed very pleased with whatever they'd been discussing.

"Hey guys." Penelope glanced between the two of them. "Partnership?"

Both guys grinned again, but Colton answered, "Yep, you're looking at…" He looked at Jake. "We don't have a name. We have to call ourselves something."

"Yep, we do, but now I have to go see Cassie. Email me and I'll think on it." Jake turned and rushed out the door.

Penelope stood at the door as he disappeared down the hall. "Bye Jake," she called after him. She looked over at Colton. "What's his rush?"

He looked pained. "He has time for one more booty-call with my sister before he has to head back to Arizona." His mouth curled down in displeasure and Penelope laughed.

"You know, Cassie's 28 years old. She's been having sex for years."

"No, no, no, no." He raised his hands to press them to his ears. "I realize you're a friend of Cass's, but in no way, shape, or form are you ever allowed to talk to me about my sister's sex life."

He shot her such a disgruntled look that Penelope couldn't help the giggle that slipped out.

"I'm serious, Penelope. I can't live here if we can't have that simple rule. Let's call it Colton's Life Rule #1… No talking about my sister's love life." He looked at her sternly. "If we can't abide by Colton's Life Rules, then I can't live here."

Penelope raised both hands in surrender and said laughingly, "Okay. I get it. No talking about Jake and Cassie's hot and heavy sex-life."

He looked pained, so she took pity on him. "Just kidding. I promise, no more." She made the motion of zipping her lips and throwing away the key and then gave him a considering smile. "I didn't realize there were going to be Life Rules when I invited you to move in here. Are there any others I should take note of right now?"

He still had a pinched expression on his face. "I think I'm forever mentally scarred by the need for the first one, so I can't think of any right now."

"Good to know. Let me know if that changes." She gave him another smile. "So tell me about this new partnership. Does this have anything to do with your unemployment?"

"As a matter of fact, yes. We're going to start a flight company, offer a jump school, charter services, and hopefully do some contract work for Homeland Security."

Penelope's face broke into a huge grin and she leapt into his arms to give him a huge hug. Colton was obviously not a hugger, since she felt him stiffen under her arms. If he was going to be her roommate, he'd have to get used to it. She liked to hug. "Colton that's incredible. What a perfect solution for you guys. Is Chris in on it too?"

Colton cleared his throat and she felt something else start to stiffen within her embrace. Time to let go of the big guy. She stepped back from him to give him his space and tried to hide her grin.

"Yeah, we want to include Chris. We haven't talked to him about it yet though, so don't mention it to anyone until we get a chance to approach him, okay?" He gathered the papers he'd spread across the table, in obvious discomfort from Penelope's embrace. Colton looked up at her and caught her perusal of him. He cleared his throat. "Well, I'm going to go to my room and do some more research."

"Okay. See you later."

It was several hours later when Penelope was reading that the idea came to her. She went running to Colton's bedroom door and yelled, "Mad Rob," grinning like a banshee.

Colton looked up at her like she'd grown two heads. "What did you just say?"

"The name for your company, Mad Rob. It's perfect. Jake Madsen plus Chris and Colton Robertson:

Mad Rob. It has a piratical spin to it which is so perfect here in this town. They love pirates here with the Texas Tech Red Raiders. You see pirate flags everywhere on game days."

Colton watched her and very slowly a grin spread over his face. "You're right, it's perfect. You're brilliant. Thanks."

Chapter 9

Penelope was running late the next morning. Colton had already left for the day as she exited the loft and ran into a guy in the hall about to knock on their door. He had an envelope in his hand.

"Can I help you?" He was a young guy in a wrinkled uniform and he wasn't in near the hurry she was.

"I have a delivery for Colton Robertson."

"He's not here right now. Can I sign for it? He's my roommate."

"Sure, I guess." He shoved his clipboard at her. "Just sign his name, okay?"

She rolled her eyes at him and didn't take the pen. "I don't think that's the way it's supposed to be done."

"I don't care. They don't pay me enough to come back here." He nudged the pen at her again.

She looked down at her watch again. "I'm late and I don't have time to argue with you. Fine, I'll sign it." She snagged the pen from him and started signing Colton's name. "You're lucky I'm trustworthy and will actually give this to him. Not everyone's like that."

"Yeah, whatever." He turned and walked down the hall toward the elevators.

Penelope shoved the envelope in her bag. She didn't have time to wait and headed toward the stairs.

A couple of hours later, she was working at her desk in her office at Raider Readers when Hannah walked in. "Hey, Hannah. What are you doing here? I didn't think you were on the schedule today."

She wore dark glasses and her long dark hair hung heavily over the sides of her face. She appeared to look everywhere in the room but at Penelope, when she said, "I'm not working. I just came by to pick up this week's ARC's to read for the blog."

Penelope was puzzled. Hannah was usually all smiles. She tried to get a closer look at her as she pointed over to the shelves along the wall. "I put them over there so they were out of the way."

Hannah nodded her head and went to grab them. As she reached forward, Penelope noticed a grimace of pain cross over her mouth. She also held her body more stiffly than normal. Alarmed, Penelope came around the desk to intercept her before she could escape the room. She pulled off Hannah's sunglasses and couldn't curtail the gasp as she saw the bruising all around her left eye. "Oh my God, what happened?"

Hannah wouldn't meet her eyes when she said, "I was in a bar Saturday night when a fight broke out. I was simply standing in the wrong place at the wrong time."

Penelope gently reached up and lifted Hannah's hair, which caused Hannah to wince. The bruise was shades of blues, greens, and dark purples and spread from her eye all the way across her temple and up to her hairline. She'd obviously tried to cover it with makeup, but the bruising was too bad and couldn't be covered. "Hannah, this is bad. Has a doctor seen it? Were the guys responsible arrested?"

Hannah wouldn't meet her eyes as she mumbled, "It's fine. It actually looks worse than it really is. Listen, I have to go." She lifted the books gingerly and then moved quickly out of the room. "I'll start sending you the reviews on these tonight."

"Hannah, wait."

Hannah looked up at her with leery eyes.

"Don't worry about the books tonight. I know you have to have a headache to go along with that." She gestured toward the bruise. "Just rest tonight." She looked closely at Hannah until she was forced to meet Penelope's eyes. "Are you sure you're okay?"

Hannah nodded jerkily, gingerly pushed the glasses back on, and moved out of the store as quickly as she could, clutching the stack of books to her chest.

Penelope followed her out of the office and into the store. Jon, one of the store employees glanced up as she approached. "Was that Hannah?"

Penelope nodded and looked thoughtful as she watched the closed door. She turned to Jon and asked, "Hannah hasn't ever mentioned if she's dating anyone has she?"

He shook his head. "She's not dating anyone that I know of. Is she okay?"

Something wasn't right there. That seemed to be more serious than getting tangled up into a bar fight. Hannah was young. It would be so easy for her to get mixed up with the wrong kind of guy. "I'm really not sure," Penelope responded. "Can you let me know if you hear anything?"

"Sure."

"Thanks."

As she settled back into her office and paperwork, Penelope was distracted by her worry over Hannah. She mindlessly opened the mail and sorted it when she opened a letter which began,

> Don't think you can dictate to me. We're divorced now and I will not be bullied.

Penelope stopped reading and her eyes flew to the bottom of the letter, where it was signed by Dianna Cassidy. She glanced back at the open envelope. Damn, she'd accidentally opened the envelope that had been delivered for Colton. This was from his ex-wife.

Penelope closed her eyes and rested her head into the palm of her hand. What a fabulous way to make a good impression on her new roommate, accidentally opening his very private mail. Penelope groaned. What a stupid thing to do. She resisted the urge to read any further, although her curiosity was killing her. She'd respect Colton's privacy.

***

The next day, Penelope was enjoying a nice Italian dinner with Damon when Hannah called. "Penelope, hi it's Hannah. I'm sorry to bother you."

"No problem." She sent a look of apology to Damon for interrupting their dinner. "What's wrong? Are you okay?"

"No, I'm fine, but I looked through the books I took home last night and I think I'm missing one. You didn't happen to put one somewhere else in the office did you?"

"Oh, Hannah, I'm sorry. That other book completely slipped my mind. One of them caught my attention so I set it aside. I'll do the review on it, so you don't have to worry about it."

"Umm," Hannah stuttered for a bit and Penelope could hear stress in her voice when she said, "But I need to read that one. I was looking forward to it."

"It's okay, Hannah. I know I don't do the reviews very often, but I promise you I remember how to do it."

She gave a self-effacing chuckle. "You can read the book after I finish with it, but without the pressure of having to analyze it. I know it's been a long time since you had the chance to just read a book for fun."

"But I don't think—"

Penelope could hear the stress in Hannah's voice, which she had a feeling had nothing to do with a missing book. "What's this really about? Did something else happen last night?"

She heard a sudden intake of air and what sounded like a sob come across the phone.

"Hannah, is someone hurting you?"

Hannah's voice croaked. "No. No, I'm fine. I have to go," The line went dead.

Penelope frowned as she shut off her phone.

"Is something wrong?" Damon asked her.

"I think one of my employees is in a bad relationship. She's acting odd and I'm starting to worry about her."

"Is there anything I can do?" The sincerity in his voice pulled her from her worry.

"Oh no. Thanks though and I'm sorry I let the phone call interrupt our dinner." She smiled at him apologetically. "I think you were just about to tell me how your meeting went at the University."

He gave a sigh as he ran his fingers through his hair. "I'm really not sure. Your mother runs a strong department, but I'm just not sure that we're going to be able to find an accord so we can work together." He grimaced. "I'm just not sure they can deal with my restrictions and I know I don't want to deal with theirs."

"But doesn't bringing in a University help both of you?"

"Absolutely it does, both in funding and trained labor but," his eyes took on a distant look as he thought about his project, "El Regalo has secrets to reveal and I'm just not sure I want to share them with anyone else." He gave her a slight grin. "That sounds very egotistical of me, doesn't it?"

"No, not at all. This is your life's work. I can completely understand you want to be in control of it. Knowing my mother the way I do, I think you have a good reason for your concerns."

He looked at her speculatively. "Okay, I have to ask, but try not to take offense."

"Uh oh, should I be concerned?"

He smiled at her. "No, but I just don't get it. I've met both your parents and you're nothing like them. Where did you come from?"

Penelope gasped and then laughed out loud. "Honestly, I think they wonder that same thing all the time." She smiled at him. "They had me late in their lives. Mom was 42 and Dad was 45 when I was born. I think they thought they were going to create a miniature version of themselves so they were pretty shocked by me, too. I spent the first years of my life trying to conform to their ideals, but I just couldn't fit into that mold and it was really painful to try. Finally, I decided I just had to be me."

"How old were you?"

Her smile was self-deprecating as she said, "Thirteen. The typical age when every girl decides she doesn't want to live in the shadow of her parents' ideals. It's all rather cliché, isn't it?"

"Maybe, but I like that you're your own person." He reached across and took hold of her hand and caressed it softly.

Penelope looked at his strong hands and willed herself to have some reaction to what he was doing, but there was nothing. This is how she imagined it would be to try to be romantic with her brother if she had any brothers. No chemistry. She looked up at Damon who watched her thoughtfully. He was such a nice guy and incredible looking, so why in the world didn't she feel any chemistry with him? Could it have something to do with her way-too-sexy new roommate?

He gave a soft smile then said, "This isn't working is it?"

She looked down at their joined hands. "No, but I don't understand why. You're a good-looking guy and we get along great. God, I'm so sorry."

"No, don't be sorry. Actually, I'm relieved. I hoped it wasn't just me. But I have a good time with you, so can we stay friends? I'm still in town for another week and I'd like to spend more time with you…just as friends."

"Absolutely! In fact, I wanted to see if you wanted to go out riding with me one day this week."

"Like on a horse?" He looked uncomfortable with the thought.

She laughed. "Yeah, that's what I was thinking."

"Hmm, I'm really not much of a horse kind of guy."

"Okay, it was just an idea. How about this? One of my other friends is having a birthday party Saturday night. Do you want to go with me?"

"Are there going to be any other hot single girls there?"

She laughed. "Probably."

"Okay, I can do hot single girls much better than horses." He looked relieved. "Yeah, I'd love to go."

Chapter 10

The next morning, Penelope was standing in the kitchen when Colton came into the room. She looked like she had rolled out of bed and moved to the coffee pot as a matter of habit. She was definitely not awake yet.

He chuckled quietly. He didn't want to disturb her. Mornings were not her specialty. She might bite, although now that he considered it that might not be such a bad thing.

"Mornin'," she grumbled.

He just smiled at her as he poured himself a cup of coffee. "How was your date last night?"

She slumped into one of the barstools at the edge of the kitchen and her eyes sunk back to half-mast. Penelope nodded and gave a non-committal grunt.

Colton chuckled. "I'm sure Dr. Lopez would appreciate that glowing report." Personally, he was thrilled with it.

"It was fine. Fun." She glowered at him as he continued to laugh at her. "It's not nice to laugh at those who aren't awake yet."

"Sorry." He tried to hide his smile. "But that does bring up a good point, what are you doing up this early?"

"I need to get some work done for a book-signing we have coming up, so I wanted to go into Raider Readers early."

"Is it an author I know?"

"You read a lot so probably, but I can't tell you who yet since the contract's not finalized. That's part of the reason I need to get to work. Also, I need to get going on the publicity for the event. What are you up to today?"

"I'm taking Chris to his doctor's appointment and then planning to talk to him about Mad Rob." He shook his head and thought about it for a moment. "At least that's the plan. We'll see what kind of mood he's in first." He hated how unpredictable Chris had become. He missed his friend. Before this happened, Chris had always been someone he could count on. Now he could hardly even talk to him without sending Chris into a rage.

She gave him a sorrowful look and reached over to touch his arm. "He's going to get better. It's just going to take a bit of time."

"I know." He tried to ignore the tingles running from her hand, innocently touching his arm, straight to his groin. "I'm trying to be patient. I just want my brother back."

"Give him time." She rubbed him from wrist to elbow. "Speaking of time, I better go take my shower so I can get to work." She started to walk away, but then turned around with a sheepish look on her face. She went over to the counter and pulled out an opened envelope. "I'm sorry. This was delivered the other day as I was leaving late for work. I accidentally mixed it in with my work mail and opened it. I only read the first couple of lines. I'm sorry. I honestly didn't mean to invade your privacy. I promise, I'm not that roommate."

He looked down at the envelope. This had to be the response he was waiting for from Dianna. He gritted his teeth and tried to keep his emotions in check. No reason to scare his new roommate with his issues with his ex. "No problem. Don't worry about it."

"Again, I'm sorry, Colton."

He gave a clipped nod as she turned to head down the hall. He couldn't resist watching the gentle sway of her hips under her short robe as she moved down the hallway. He dropped his head to his chest. He took deep breaths as he tried to calm down his libido. She'd simply touched his arm and he was ready to take her up against the wall. He was in such trouble. He had enough woman issues just dealing with Dianna. Besides it looked like Penelope was dating Dr. Lopez. She was off-limits. His brain knew it. Now he just had to convince the rest of his body.

***

Penelope arrived at Raider Readers with her mind still occupied with Colton. One thing was sure, her body couldn't survive many more mornings with him looking so sexy and half undressed. She could just work later in the evenings rather than meet up with him in the kitchen. She barely functioned before 9:00 AM on a normal day, but throw in a lust inducing dose of Colton and she didn't stand a chance of any brain activity happening for several hours.

She was at the bookstore a full hour and a half before opening time, so was surprised when she found the door slightly ajar. Penelope frowned. Alix hadn't mentioned anything about coming in early today.

She pushed the door inward, but didn't see anything amiss, so she called out, "Alix, are you here?" The front desk was right by the door and the register didn't look like it had been touched. She continued into the store. Whoever was here, it had to be one of her employees. A burglar would have gone immediately to that register.

A grinding noise from the New Fiction room startled her, but as she entered the doorway to investigate, she realized it was just the rumbling of the heater starting up. It was always noisier early in the morning.

She jumped as a sudden single bang pounded from above. Her office was on the second story of the old house. Alix probably just hadn't heard her when she called so she started up the stairs. "Alix? Hannah? Jon? Who's in here?" She glanced around warily at the top of the stairs, but she still didn't see anything out of place. When she got to her office doorway, the light was off and she couldn't see a sign of anyone having been in there since she'd left the night before. Weird.

Maybe they simply hadn't pulled the exterior door tightly when they closed the night before. Thankfully, it looked like the store was fine, but she'd have to talk to everyone about it to make sure it didn't happen again. But that didn't explain why the hair on her arms was still standing straight up. She needed to get all the lights on in the building so she could check all the rooms. There were too many dark corners right now for her to feel completely comfortable in the space.

With one last look around upstairs, she started to head back down to the first floor so she could turn on the lights and lock the door properly before she set to work. She didn't need anyone walking in on her before opening time. She was jumpy enough already.

She'd made it down two steps when she felt the presence behind her. She turned quickly, but only caught a glimpse of a dark figure before hands roughly pushed her and she tumbled down the curved staircase.

Chapter 11

Colton stared down at his ringing cell phone and grimaced as he glanced around surreptitiously. He'd forgotten to turn it off when he brought Chris in for his appointment, but it was Penelope so he was going to answer it. The nurse sitting at the front desk flirted with him earlier, but now she glared at him. He tried to look repentant as he mouthed 'sorry', pushed the talk button, and slipped out the door of the office.

"Hey, Penelope."

"Colton, are you still at the hospital?" Something was wrong. Her voice was weak and shaky.

His heartbeat raced as alarm set in. "Yes. What's wrong? Are you okay?"

"I'm fine, but I need a ride home. I'm in the ER. Can you come by and get me before you leave?" He could hear her sniffling like she'd been crying.

"I'll be right there." Colton took off at a run down the hall before he remembered Chris. He barreled back into the office and toward the reception desk. "My brother is Chris Robertson. When he comes out, can you tell…"

"Colton." Chris hobbled down the hall on his crutches. "What's wrong?"

"Penelope's hurt. Are you finished?" Colton, who never got rattled, sounded frantic even to his own ears.

"Yes. Where is she?"

"ER. Let's go."

Colton tried to rein in his impatience at the slower pace he had to maintain because Chris was on crutches. When they finally arrived at the ER department, he rushed over to the reception desk. A woman, with a very sick-looking toddler, talked to the nurse manning the desk and Colton frantically looked around the room trying to find a glimpse of Penelope.

Chris reacted to the impatience strumming through him. "Calm down, Colt. You said she called, right?" At Colton's nod, he continued, "So she's not in that bad of shape. Just tone it down a bit."

Colton swiped a hand through his hair. "You're right, but goddamn, she sounded upset and she's here somewhere. I didn't even find out what happened, how bad she's hurt." He glared at the receptionist who still talked to the frazzled mother. "What's taking so long?"

He looked around the active ER again, and spotted a familiar face coming out of a curtained area. A ball of dread developed in the pit of his stomach. He turned to Chris. "Can you wait here and see if you can find out where she is? I see someone who may know something, but I don't want to lose our place in line if he's not here because of Penelope."

"Sure." Chris looked over at the man curiously.

Detective Brian Barnes had been the lead detective with Cassie's stalking and subsequent kidnapping the year before. Colton had a sinking feeling that his presence here wasn't a coincidence. Colton caught up to him right before he got to the ER entrance. "Detective Barnes?"

Brian had been in the process of dialing on his cell phone when he turned at the sound of Colton's voice. His face lit up with recognition and he held his hand out to shake hands. "Colton, how are you doing? Are you here because of Penelope?"

"Yes, but I was hoping you weren't. I haven't been able to find out anything yet. Is she okay? What happened? Where is she?" He glanced back at the curtained area where the detective had just exited.

"She's okay, which is lucky since someone pushed her down the stairs of her bookstore."

Colton scrambled to understand what had happened. He raised a shaky hand to thread through his hair. "Who would do that? Are you sure she's okay?"

"Yes, she has some stitches, is really bruised, and upset. So far, it appears to just be a random break-in, but we're investigating." He gestured towards the curtained area. "Why don't you go see her for yourself? She's alone, so she'd probably appreciate the company while she waits to be discharged."

Colton was already headed that way. He signaled to Chris as he walked that he'd found her. He took a deep breath to calm his rattling emotions as he reached up to pull the curtain aside.

When he walked in, her eyes were closed. There was a bandage on her forehead. She was extremely pale and he could see purple shadows under her eyes. She was dressed and he could see blood where it had dripped on her shirt, probably from her forehead. He continued his perusal of her body and noticed a string of angry purple bruises from her wrist, which was wrapped, on her left arm up to where they disappeared under the edge of her sleeve.

He took a shaky breath and reached out to touch her cheek. She was so still and pale. When his fingertips grazed her cheek, her eyes flew open. Colton couldn't miss the flash of fright before she realized it was him, and then her eyes filled with tears.

"Shh, it's me. I'm sorry. I didn't mean to startle you. Are you okay?" He spoke to her quietly and didn't recognize the guttural sound of his own voice.

She gave a quick nod and then closed her eyes, the grimace of pain visible on her face. She swallowed hard and he perused the ugly bruise on her forehead. "Are you feeling nauseous?" After basically raising the twins, he could spot the signs of nausea and knew how to react quickly. He'd learned that lesson the hard way because invariably, Chris and Cassie always came down with the flu at the same time. They'd never managed the art of making it to the toilet on time.

She whispered, "Yes," and Colton reached over to grab a bedpan.

"Here you go." He laid it in her lap.

She murmured a quiet, "Thanks," but didn't open her eyes.

He watched her swallow convulsively several times before she seemed to gain control over the nausea. She finally opened her eyes again and gave him a weak smile. "I'm sorry I dragged you down here."

He reached for her hand, the one that wasn't wrapped and bruised, and rubbed it slowly. "Hey, no problem. What good is it to have a roommate if you can't count on him to give you a ride home when someone decides to use you as a bowling ball?"

She started to say something more, but at that moment a nurse came bustling in to give her medicine. The nurse raised her eyebrows at Colton, but focused on Penelope. "How's your pain now on a scale of one to ten?"

"Probably around an eight and a half, as long as I don't move." She gave a weak smile.

"Okay, that's to be expected." She prepped Penelope's arm for the shot. "I'm going to give you an injection right now that will give you some immediate relief. The doctor will give you a prescription so you'll have some more painkillers at home. You have a lot of bad bruising and the pain is going to get worse before it gets better." She turned to Colton. "Are you going to be the one driving her home and taking care of her?"

"Yes." He nodded and ignored the glimpse of tears and sudden tension coming from Penelope.

The nurse nodded. "Okay, good. The doctor will have some instructions for you too."

After the nurse gave the injection and left the room, Penelope turned to him. "You don't have to take care of me. I can go stay at my mom's for a few days." She grimaced, but he didn't know if that was from her pain or the thought of going to her mother's. He knew they didn't have the best relationship.

"Obviously you can do whatever you want, but I don't mind taking care of you. It's one of the benefits of having an unemployed roommate. I can be at your beck and call for as long as you need it. That way you can stay in your own home where you're already comfortable."

"Thanks Colton. I appreciate it." Her words were starting to slur a little bit so he assumed the pain meds were taking effect. "A sexy roommate at my beck and call. I like that idea. Does that mean I can make you my love slave?" She gave him a sloppy grin and he tried to ignore the surge of lust that shot through his system at her words. Those meds were fast-acting.

"Only if you can remember you said that when the drugs wear off." He brushed a soft kiss across her cheek as she shut her eyes. She'd fallen asleep. He settled back into the chair beside her bed, but didn't let go of her hand. He just sat there and watched her and thought about what happened. He still hadn't heard the full story and didn't even know the full extent of her injuries. But right now, he was fine just knowing she would recover.

Chris looked in to check on them, but settled with his e-reader out in the waiting area while they waited for the doctor. They sat there like that for another thirty minutes before the doctor came in. Penelope stayed asleep, as Colton received her home care instructions and heard the extent of her injuries.

Her left side took the brunt of her fall. She had a sprained wrist and also extensive bruising up and down that side which included three badly bruised ribs. The ribs and her wrist needed to stay wrapped for the next week just to help give support to them. She had fourteen stitches high on her forehead where they thought she'd hit one of the spindles of the banister somewhere in the fall. The doctor said she didn't have a concussion showing on the scans, but instructed Colton to keep an eye out for the symptoms just in case. Overall she was extremely beat up, but incredibly lucky because it could have been so much worse.

They were free to go. He had all her paperwork, she just had to sign it, but first he had to get her awake. He gently nudged her shoulder, "Hey sleeping beauty, it's time to take you home."

"Colton?" She looked up at him in confusion, her eyes dulled by the drugs.

"Yeah, it's me. Are you ready to go home?"

She nodded at him before swinging her head around. "Is Brian still around?"

"Detective Barnes? Did you remember something else from the attack?"

"No, I just wanted to borrow his handcuffs. You did promise to be my love slave." She leered at him.

He grinned at her. All her words slurred together and he knew she would be mortified if she actually did remember this later. Personally, he hoped she did remember and would still want to pursue the idea.

The nurse who brought the wheelchair into the cubicle smirked at him and he felt a blush rise up his face. She'd obviously overheard Penelope's statement.

He chuckled. "Sweetheart, right now let's just get you home. We'll figure the rest of it out later."

While the nurse worked to get Penelope into the wheelchair, Colton rushed out to tell Chris what was happening. Then he went to pull the truck around to the door.

As he drove up, Colton frowned at Penelope. She sat in the wheelchair with her chin planted in her right hand. Her eyes were closed and she was extremely pale. Just that small amount of movement looked like it had sent her pain level back up if the grimace on her face was any indication.

He jumped out and went to help her climb into the high cab. As she stood up, he saw a flash of pain cross her face. He leaned in close to her ear. "Pen, I'm going to pick you up slow and easy so maybe this won't hurt as much, okay?" She gave a quick nod. "Grab me around my neck so that I'm holding you on your right side."

He reached under her legs and eased her into the cab of the truck until she was in the middle of the bench seat. He held her there for a moment inhaling the honeysuckle scent from her hair. "Are you okay?"

"Yeah, thanks," she murmured.

Chris slid in beside her while Colton went back around to the driver's side.

"Thanks guys for hanging around and waiting for me." Penelope spoke and held her body very stiffly like she was afraid to move a muscle for the pain it might cause.

Chris turned to her and surveyed the bruises spanning her left side. "Why don't you lean over here and see if you can't use me as a cushion and relax a little bit? "She looked at him warily for a moment before he said, "I promise I won't bite."

"Okay, it's worth a try."

"Darling, you're hurting my feelings. Usually the girls are begging to cuddle with me." Colton was surprised by the flirty tone in Chris's voice. Chris had always been a flirt, but he hadn't heard anything even close to teasing come out of Chris since they'd gotten him back. Maybe all they needed was to find a way to get the focus off himself and onto someone else. Although he'd be happier if that someone else wasn't Penelope.

Both men watched her silently while she worked to get comfortable. Finally she seemed a little bit more at ease, so Colton put the truck into gear.

They weren't five minutes down the road, before it was obvious that Penelope had drifted back to sleep. Her head quickly sunk onto Chris's lap. Colton looked over at him. "Do you mind if we stop at the pharmacy before I take you home so I can pick up her pain medicine? I don't want to have to leave her home alone later."

Chris looked down at Penelope's hair spread over his lap and grinned cockily at Colton. "It's been a long time since I had a beautiful lady in my lap. You can take as much time as you want."

Colton literally growled at Chris. It was as much of a surprise to him as it was to Chris that he was feeling this proprietary of her.

It wasn't long before Chris looked at him knowingly. "So that's the way it is with you two, huh?" He took another look at Penelope in front of him. "I never would have put the two of you together."

Colton spoke through gritted teeth. "We're not together, but you need to keep your hands to yourself. She's hurt. I'm simply her roommate and taking care of her."

"Uh huh," Chris said in a tone which said he wasn't buying this story one little bit. He cleared his throat as he looked over her multiple bruises. "Did you ever get the full story about what happened?"

Colton glanced down at her again and clenched his jaw. "No, but you can fucking bet I'm going to find out who did this to her and they will never be able to touch her again. No one is allowed to hurt her like this."

Chris's eyes widened at the menace in Colton's voice.

They pulled into the parking spot. "I'll be right back."

"We're not going anywhere." Chris just grinned at him like the cat that swallowed the canary.

Colton ground his teeth, but shut the truck door gently behind him. He needed to get this done so he could get Penelope home and in her comfortable bed. He didn't like her sprawled all over Chris. Wasn't that an eye-opener? But he didn't have time to dwell on it right now.

Penelope still hadn't stirred when Colton drove up to the front of Cassie's house. She was still sprawled all over Chris's lap. Chris gently nudged her to get her moving. Penelope didn't truly wake up, just looked at him with disoriented eyes. He unclipped her seat belt and turned her so she was facing the back of the seat and could resume the same position on Colton's lap without hurting her injured side.

She settled right back into Colton's lap and slipped back into sleep again.

Colton looked up at him as Chris said, "You can thank me later. Just don't get in a wreck going back to your place since she's not seat-belted any longer."

Colton gave a short nod. "Thanks. I'll call tonight. I know Cassie will be worried about her so I'll call her once I get the full story from Penelope."

Penelope never stirred after they dropped Chris off. Colton debated driving around simply to let her sleep, but knew she'd be more comfortable at home in her own bed. Nevertheless, when they pulled into the parking spot, he sat there for a while watching her sleep. Her soft skin was so pale against the bruises on her forehead. Reality pounded at him. She could have died today. He gently settled his hand into the silky strands of her hair and took a deep breath. She was okay.

He spoke softly. "Penelope, we're home." He brushed the hair gently off the side of her face.

She opened her eyes slowly and looked up at him from his lap. Her green eyes were a bit clearer than they'd been when they left the hospital, but her freckles stood in stark contrast to her pale skin. She started to sit up, so Colton reached down to help her.

"Thanks." Her voice was husky with sleep.

"Hang on. Let me get around to the passenger door and I'll help you get out, okay?"

"Kay."

When he got around to the other side, he crawled into the truck with her and set up to lift her back into his arms.

She pressed her hand to his chest. "I'm sorry I've been so much trouble today. I think I can walk now."

He cupped her chin so she would meet his eyes. "Pen, you aren't any trouble at all. I'm just glad I'm here so I can help. Let me get you out of the truck and then we'll see how you feel about walking." He gently picked her up and felt her sharp intake of breath when he grazed her bruised left side. He lowered his head to her hair and inhaled her honeysuckle scent as he cradled her against him. "I'm sorry."

"Don't worry about it. I'm just going to be sore for a few days, but I won't break. Why don't we try that standing and walking thing now?"

"Are you sure? I don't mind carrying you."

"I'm sure. As much as I like this whole sweeping me off my feet thing, I think I can handle it on my own this time."

"Okay." Colton gently lowered her down, but kept a hand around her in case she needed the extra support.

It was slow moving, but they made it to the apartment and Penelope did it with just a bare amount of support from Colton.

As they shuffled into the living room, he looked at her to gauge how she was doing. Surprisingly, she didn't seem as pale as she was before. "Do you want to go lay down in your bedroom or would you prefer the couch?"

"I think the couch would be good for now."

"Okay." He helped lower her until she sat on the couch. "Wait right here. I'll be right back."

He took off down the hall to her room where he grabbed her big fluffy bed pillow, the book off her nightstand, and throw blanket to help her get comfortable on the couch.

As he tucked her into the couch, she looked up at him and smiled. "You're just a great big old marshmallow under that sexy, stern male exterior aren't you?"

"Now don't you start spreading nasty rumors. I have a reputation to uphold." He looked at her with a bemused smile.

She grinned at him. "My lips are sealed, but seriously, thank you, Colt."

"If you want to thank me you can follow Colton's Life Rule #2."

"Uh oh, we have another Life Rule?"

"Yes, and this one is extremely important. In fact, I think that we may need to put it in the #1 slot."

"Ooh, this sounds serious. Lay it on me big guy."

His voice got very quiet and husky. "Penelope isn't allowed to get hurt bad enough to need the ER anymore." He brushed his hand gently over the bandage covered her forehead. "What happened this morning, Pen?"

She sucked in a harsh breath. Then she proceeded to tell him what she knew about the break-in at the store and her subsequent fall down the stairs. "It just doesn't make any sense. Why would someone break in during daylight hours? Nothing was out of place that I could see, so he must have just gotten inside when I came in. Detective Barnes said there wasn't any sign of forced entry and the alarm was disabled."

"Did you see the man leave after you fell down the stairs?" He didn't realize it until he caught her looking, but he'd been gripping the edge of the couch so tightly that he'd wrinkled the cotton canvas. He relaxed his grip and tried to calm down.

"No, I must have passed out because the next thing I remember is the paramedics coming in."

"Who called the ambulance? Was it one of your employees? Did they see anything?"

"I... I don't know," she whispered quietly as she looked at him in surprise and alarm. "As far as I know, no one else had come in yet. No one was there besides me and whoever pushed me. Maybe a customer came into the store early and found me?"

He was skeptical. "Maybe, but it's definitely something you should talk about with Detective Barnes. For now, just try to relax. You're starting to get pale again. Are you hungry?"

"No. I think I'll just take a little nap. Is it okay if I stay out here, or would you rather me go to my room?"

"Stay here. That way I can keep an eye on you. Do you want some pain medicine before you go to sleep?"

She started to shake her head negative, but Colton interrupted. "From my estimate, you're probably only about fifteen minutes away from the time when you should take it and I'm hoping you'll be asleep then. Why don't you take it now so that you aren't hurting so bad when you wake up? It will help you rest better, too."

"Yes, Mother."

Colton stood up to his full height. "The last time I checked, I don't think anyone would confuse me with your mother." He gave her a playful grin and a wink.

As he walked into the kitchen, he heard her soft murmur, "No, there's nothing remotely feminine about you."

He turned, caught her eyeing his ass, and gave her a playful grin and wink.

***

Penelope awoke to the sounds of Cassie and Colton talking quietly in the kitchen. They didn't realize she was awake and since they were obviously talking about her, she didn't feel too bad about eavesdropping.

"What did the doctor say?" Cassie's soft voice was full of tension.

"He said she'd be sore for a while, but that she's fine. She was lucky. She fell down the full length of that staircase. She could have easily broken her neck." Colton's voice had gotten gruff with concern.

"Do the police have any leads?"

"Not that I know of, but we haven't heard from Detective Barnes. I want Pen to call him when she wakes up."

"Brian's handling the investigation?"

"Yeah, I saw him briefly in the ER when he came out of her room."

"Good. He knows what he's doing. He'll catch this guy."

"I sure hope so. She was lucky this time. Next time… Well, there's just not going to be a next time is there? If I have to go with her everywhere, she'll be safe."

Cassie laughed. "You and what army? You haven't run this plan by her yet, have you?"

"No, but she'll see the wisdom in keeping me close by." Penelope could hear the frown in Colton's voice.

"Oh, dear brother, you have a lot to learn about women. Didn't Dianna teach you anything? Penelope has her own mind. She's not going to let you or anyone else slow her down, but it should be fun watching you try," Cassie said with glee. There was nothing she liked better than tormenting her brothers.

Colton growled. "I need to go get us some dinner. Can you stay here with her while I get some food?"

"No problem."

"Thanks. Her pain medicine is by the sink if she needs some more. Tell her I'll be right back if she wakes up."

"It's okay, Colt. We'll be fine until you get back, I promise."

Penelope heard the door click as Colton quietly shut it. Then Cassie said, "You can open your eyes now. He's gone."

Penelope's eyes flashed open in surprise and she turned to her friend. "How'd you know I was awake?"

"Seriously? We've been best friends for years. I always know when you're awake. You're breathing changes. How are you feeling?" She walked over watching Penelope closely.

Penelope sat up cautiously and took stock of her aches and pains. "Better, all things considered."

"Do you need any pain medicine right now?"

"No, I'm fine. Colton made me take some right before I fell asleep. He's been really wonderful today."

"I'm not surprised. Colton's always been a caretaker. There's nothing he likes better than taking charge so he can boss everyone around."

Penelope was surprised at the harshness she heard in Cassie's voice. "That's not fair. He really stepped up and took care of me today, which is way above and beyond for a roommate."

"I'm sorry. You're right. This is where we get into the idiosyncrasies of sibling relationships. Colton can't help who he is and right now he's being really pushy with Chris. I'm a little sensitive about his bossiness."

Penelope regarded Cassie thoughtfully. "The other day when I came home, he was unpacking. He was looking at photos of you all before your parents died. He wasn't that old when they died."

"No he wasn't. None of us were."

Penelope spoke softly. "You were all so young to have to deal with that. Did you immediately come to live with your grandparents?"

"It was just our grandfather. A single old man we didn't even know. He did his best, but Colton basically raised us. It was really hard for him. He was devastated by both their deaths, but especially mom's. He was so close to her. After she died, he always wore her wedding ring on a chain around his neck. He said it made him feel closer to her. He felt that by having that piece of her with him, he could help guide us in what she would want us to do."

"He took over the role of your parents. I would imagine having done that from such an early age, it's hard to just let go of that role." She tried to imagine a young, ten year old Colton taking charge and protecting his scared siblings and her heart melted. That kind of thing said so much about the man he'd become, especially when she knew what an amazing man he truly was.

Cassie rolled her eyes. "Yes, you're right. I know you're right, but that doesn't make it any easier when he gets bossy."

"Well, from what I've seen, Colton only gets that way because he cares."

Cassie got a mischievous look in her eye as she said, "Just remember you said that in a couple of days. From what I've seen here today, you have a new caretaker. He's big, protective, and doesn't understand when someone tells him no. Colton's not an easy person to move when he's decided to place you under his wings."

"Don't worry. I think we'll be fine."

Cassie just smirked at her knowingly.

***

The next morning, Penelope glared at Colton.

"Penelope, there's no way I'm going to sit back and let you to go into work today. Someone attacked you there yesterday. You're still hurt. You don't need to be there today. I won't allow it."

"Won't allow it?" She worked to keep from yelling at him. "I'm thirty years old. If you think you can keep me from heading in to do my job, you have another thing coming." She took a deep breath to try to control her temper and then regretted the action when it caused her ribs to twinge in pain. Unfortunately, Colton spotted her grimace.

"See, you can't even take a breath without it hurting. There's no reason they can't work without you today, Penelope. Just call them and check in and I promise you they'll tell you the same thing."

"I'm sure you're right, but that doesn't change the fact, the bookstore is mine. My responsibility. My obligation. My job. I'm going in today."

"Come on, Penelope. Be reasonable. You spent half the day yesterday in the ER. You need to take at least one day off."

"I did take one day off…yesterday. Today I'm going in, at least for a few hours. I promise I'm not going to overdo it. I'll be fine."

Colton looked seriously at her. "Okay, we'll compromise. You can go into the bookstore, but I'm going with you. That way if you get tired or start hurting, I can bring you home."

Penelope rolled her eyes, although she had to admit, the guy was hot when he got in full alpha-mode. She needed to write one of the male heroes in her books based on Colton. But writing about a hot alpha male and trying to live with one were totally different things. "Oh my God. You just don't give up, do you? Okay." She threw her arm into the air and then immediately regretted the action when she felt the shooting pain through her ribs. Thankfully, Colton missed the grimace she managed to hide. "Compromise it is, but I don't want to hear a peep out of you when you're bored to tears with nothing to do."

Colton winked at her. "It's a bookstore, right? I'll have hours of entertainment right at my fingertips."

"Okay, it's your day wasted. I know you have things you need to be doing for Mad Rob. We leave in thirty minutes."

She would never, ever admit it to him, but she was secretly relieved he insisted on going with her. She didn't want him to know how much the idea of stepping foot inside of her store terrified her. It was her store. Her oasis. That someone had violated that infuriated her. She hated the idea that she needed to lean on him. She was stronger than this, but the idea of Colton's big, muscular body protecting her provided her with a much needed peace of mind. She just wouldn't tell him that.

***

Overall, it had been an enjoyable morning, but that was about to come to an end. Colton closed the book he'd read while sitting in the little reading nook of the bookstore. He'd just caught sight of Penelope's pale face as she searched the shelves for a book in the main part of the store. Whether she wanted to or not, it was time for her to call it a day. She looked wiped out.

He walked up behind her to hear her talking on her cell phone. "I'm sorry, Thomas, but I was in an accident so I won't be able to come out for a couple of weeks."

Thomas? Who the hell was Thomas? Was there another guy in her life that he didn't know about?

"No, no, I'm fine." She moved some books to face out as she continued talking. "It's really nothing. Just an accident at the bookstore, but it's left me with a bum wrist which would make doing my job there difficult. I'll miss you guys, but I'll be back out as soon as I can. Thanks, Thomas." She ended the call, but her back was still to him.

Colton frowned and wondered who this guy was but that immediately fled his mind as he saw Penelope sway. He cupped the elbow on her uninjured arm to steady her. "It's time to go home."

She turned to him. He didn't like the sight of the dark bruises under her eyes on her pale face. She looked like she was going to argue, but then thought better of it. She gave a short nod. "Let me go tell Aunt Alix I'm heading out."

"Smart girl."

She glared at him. "Don't be a condescending ass."

He raised both hands in surrender. "I wouldn't think of it, sweetheart." He smirked at her.

"Pfft." She snorted in disbelief. She looked around the store with a slightly haunted look. "Do you think she's okay to be here alone? Jon's not supposed to be in for another twenty minutes."

Colton glanced down at his watch and then looked back at her pale face. "Tell you what. If you promise to go sit down in that very comfortable chair in the reading nook that I just vacated and rest, we'll stay until he gets here. I'll go tell your Aunt Alix the plan."

At her easy acquiescence about both the rest and talking to Alix, Colton worried she was hurting more than she let on. He eyed her critically as she sat down gingerly in the large leather club chair. As soon as her head hit the back of the chair, her eyes closed. Damn, she'd overdone today. He shouldn't have let her come in, but he gave an internal chuckle as he thought about what her reaction would be if he voiced 'I told you so' to that thought. Penelope was as stubborn as she was beautiful.

Shaking his head as he went, he bounded up the steps to the second floor where Alix was shelving books.

Alix looked up at him as he walked into the Reference and History room. Her eyes were furrowed with concern for Penelope. "Please tell me you've convinced her to go home and rest."

He nodded. "I have. Right now, she's relaxing in the reading nook while we wait for Jon to arrive."

"Good. Thank you for taking care of her. I know Penelope is grateful that she didn't have to go to her mom's while she recuperates. With their relationship, spending time with her mother isn't exactly relaxing for Penelope. Actually," Alix chuckled softly, "spending time with Anna isn't restful for anyone."

"I'm just glad I'm here so I can help." He looked at her curiously. It was none of his business, but he couldn't resist asking. "What happened between you and Penelope's mother?" Penelope told him they didn't speak anymore, but he had no idea why.

"That's not my story to tell, but I have a feeling Penelope will let you in on it someday soon." She gave him a wink. "You're good for her."

He smiled and chose his words carefully. "Don't get any ideas about us. We're just roommates. Pen is awesome, but it can't go anywhere beyond that."

"Hmm." She looked at him with a single eyebrow raised which made Colton want to squirm a bit. Luckily, their discussion was interrupted with the tinkling of the door as Jon walked in.

Colton turned back toward Alix. "I'm going to take her home now. Remember, no one should be here alone until they catch the guy who attacked Pen. We still don't know why he was here and he may try to come back to finish."

She murmured, "Don't worry about us. Just take care of our girl and see if you can get her to stay home tomorrow."

He rolled his eyes at her. "You obviously don't know Penelope as well as I thought if you think I could accomplish that."

"Oh, I don't know. I think you may have a better chance than the rest of us when it comes to Penelope."

Chapter 12

Penelope awoke and listened to the quiet of the apartment. She couldn't hear Colton anywhere. She glanced at her bedside clock. She'd slept for three hours straight, and her body obviously needed it because she felt much better. Colton was right. She shouldn't have gone in to the bookstore today... not that she'd ever admit that fact to him.

She gingerly rolled over and tested the aches and pains of her body. They were definitely still there, but she didn't feel like a Mack truck had run over her in the last hour anymore. The headache, on the other hand, was still fully present, even after napping the afternoon away. She'd decided when she took the pain pills at lunchtime that those were the last ones she planned to take. She may have to re-think that plan.

When she came into the living room, Colton was sprawled on the couch reading the book he'd started at the bookstore. "Hey," he said. "How are you feeling?"

"Better. Thanks. The nap helped."

"Are you hungry?"

"I think I could eat." She gave him a smile and then looked down at the coffee table. It was covered with bits and scraps of paper. "What were you working on?"

Colton scooped them up looking embarrassed. "Sorry about the mess. Just trying to figure out some of the details for Mad Rob... like what kind of planes to buy. It got kind of overwhelming, so I decided to dive back into the fictional world." He gave her a meek grin.

Who knew that big, bad Colton could look so boyish and embarrassed? She liked seeing this side of him. "Planes, as in plural? How many are you planning on buying?"

"Two. One for the jump school and then one that we can use for charter flights. We're also working a contract with Homeland Security and if that comes through, then we'll have access to a third plane too."

"Wow. You're gonna be a big business tycoon aren't you?"

"Not quite and we certainly aren't there yet. We have tons to take care of." He ran a hand through his hair. "I still haven't even managed to talk to Chris about it yet." He assessed her. "But right now, we have other worries, like what to feed you."

She smirked at him. "Yeah, I can see where that should be right up there in your worries about what to do with the rest of your life."

"Well, it certainly can be the most important thing for the next half hour." He walked up behind her and nudged her toward the kitchen area of the loft. "Let's go see what I can scrounge up for us to eat."

They had just finished their sub sandwiches... a roast beef for Colton and a veggie for Penelope, when there was a knock at the door. Colton cocked a brow at Penelope as he headed toward the door.

She answered his silent question. "I have no idea. I'm not expecting anyone."

When Colton opened the door, the first thing Penelope spotted was a huge arrangement of white daisies.

She peered behind it and spotted Damon's anxious face. He muttered a quick, "Hi, Colton," before he strode into the room toward her.

Colton gave a half-hearted wave behind Damon's retreating back and muttered a sarcastic, "Hi, Damon. Want to come in?" as he shut the door.

When Damon reached her, he set the flowers on the counter and gently grasped her chin to turn her face, brushing the hair off her forehead so he could see her bruise.

"Damon—" she started, but he interrupted her.

"I went to the bookstore and they said you'd been hurt. Fuck, that looks painful. Are you okay? Why didn't you call me? I know we haven't known each other that long yet, but I thought we were friends." He had a hurt look on his face but Penelope couldn't decide if it was in empathy for her pain or the fact that she hadn't thought to call him.

She reached up and rubbed his shoulder. "I'm okay, Damon. Really, I am. I was in and out of the ER within a couple of hours." She gestured to the beautiful bouquet of flowers. "Are those for me?" At his nod, she answered, "Thank you. They're beautiful."

She looked closer at the bouquet when she spotted a bit of gold glimmering out of the front of it. She reached over and brushed the daisies aside to reveal a beautiful golden daisy, set in amongst the real ones. It was the same size as the real daisies and the golden metal petals appeared just as delicate as real petals. She could even see the veining on the paper thin gold. "What's this?" She caressed the incredibly delicate golden flower.

He looked embarrassed as he said, "I thought you might need an extra little something to pick you up in your bouquet."

Her mouth dropped open in shock. "This isn't one of the flowers from the Golden Garden is it?"

He shook his head ruefully. "No, I wish they looked this good. From what we've uncovered they've been crushed under tons of dirt for thousands of years and will never look like this again." He touched the delicate petals lightly. "This is a reproduction that our artists created based upon what remains of the few flowers we've uncovered so far. This is what we think they looked like originally."

"Wow, it's exquisite." She examined the flower. "What are these markings?" There were tiny delicate marks etched onto the flowers which at first glance looked like a part of the veining.

Damon looked at her oddly. "You're observant, aren't you? We haven't uncovered all the mysteries of El Regalo and that's one of them. We think it's some sort of code."

He suddenly seemed uncomfortable talking about his project, which was very odd considering it was his entire life right now. Penelope looked closer at him. Damon was wearing relaxed fit jeans and a worn t-shirt. It was the most casual she'd ever seen him looking. There was an intriguing glimpse of a tattoo peeking out of his neckline and at the bottom of the sleeve on his right arm. He didn't look sloppy, but something about him gave a feel of exhaustion. There were dark circles under his eyes which hadn't been there the last time she'd seen him. She frowned.

He looked from Colton to her and then down to their dinner plates. "I'm sorry. I didn't mean to interrupt your evening…"

"You didn't. We just finished dinner. How are the negotiations working at the University?"

"I'm not here to talk about that." He brushed off the inquiry way too quickly. Penelope felt a chill of worry for him.

He turned to Colton who'd been standing off to the side watching them interact silently. He nodded back to Penelope before asking Colton, "I get the idea she's glossing over how she's really feeling, so will you tell me? How's she really doing?"

Colton gave a grimace. "Definitely not as well as she likes to think, but she's doing better." He looked critically over Penelope. "She doesn't look like she's at the edge of death anymore."

"You really know how to flatter a girl, don't you, Colt?"

He smirked at her. "Only telling it like it is, sweetheart." But then his face got serious and he growled low at her. "If she'd stay home from work like I suggested, she'd be feeling much better."

Penelope stuck her tongue out at him. Arrogant man.

He just gave her a slow smile. "And then she'd be able to act her age and not have to give into the fact that she knows I'm right."

Damon watched their by-play with interest, before he turned back to Penelope. "You need to take care of yourself. I'm holding you to your promise of taking me to that party Saturday night."

"Aw, that's right. I did promise to introduce you to some hot single ladies didn't I?"

"That you did, so I need you to be at 100%, because you know if some hot young thing wants to take me home, I'll look like a cad if you aren't feeling better." He waggled his eyebrows at her.

"Well, in that case, I promise not to get out of bed until Saturday night. We can't have my infirmity interfering with your ability to get laid now, can we?"

Damon smiled at her, but the smile didn't quite reach his eyes. "As long as your priorities are intact." He glanced down at his watch and frowned. "I better go. I have an important call coming in about thirty minutes."

He reached over and brushed the hair off Penelope's forehead once again. "Get better, Penelope...oh, and stay away from crazy robbers wanting to throw you down the stairs."

She grabbed his hand. "I will. I promise." He started to pull away, but she didn't let go.

Damon looked back at her questioningly and she could still see the shadows in his eyes so she gently asked, "Are you okay?" She didn't like to see one of her friends hurting and she definitely had the feeling that Damon was hurting.

He gave a quick nod and headed toward the door. "Just perfect. As always." He started to open the knob but had a second thought and turned back toward Colton. "Keep her safe," Damon said, and then he left the apartment.

Colton locked the door behind Damon before turning back to Penelope. He looked at her curiously. "Correct me if I'm wrong, but I was under the impression that you two were dating."

She gave a weary smile. "I know, right? He's like my perfect guy. Oh my God, did you see that tat?" She gave Colton's hard body a once-over. "You don't have any tats hidden under there, do you, Colt?"

He frowned at her and rolled his eyes, ignoring her question. "Penelope, focus. We were talking about you and Damon."

She waved a hand dismissively. "Oh yeah. There isn't going to be any Damon and me. No chemistry."

She was still looking at Colton, trying to imagine him with tattoos. It just didn't fit his persona. She shook her head to clear it and then wished she hadn't when a stab of pain shot out from her temple.

"Have you taken any pain pills lately?" Colton was already headed into the kitchen and picking up the bottle off the counter, which he brought to her with a bottle of water.

She reached up and took them from him, with a murmured, "Thanks." As her fingertips brushed his, a tremor snaked up her arm. Yep, there was that chemistry she didn't have with Damon. She glanced at Colton's lips. Would kissing him elicit more of a response than Damon's kiss had? This jittering, this moment of connection, this chemistry told her yes. As she watched his eyes darken, she knew he felt it too. Chemistry. Just why the hell did she have it with Colton, one of the most domineering, controlling, serious men she knew?

Chapter 13

He growled into the phone. "What the fuck happened? How did she get hurt?"

"I'm sorry. She showed up and I panicked. No one was supposed to be there that early. You said it would be clear."

"So you decided to hurt her? You could have ruined everything."

"I didn't mean for her to fall down the stairs. I was just trying to push her aside so I could get out of the building before she called the cops. She wasn't supposed to fall, but I called an ambulance right away."

"You called the ambulance? What phone did you use?"

"Don't worry. I used the store phone so they wouldn't be able to trace the call back to me."

He rubbed his forehead in frustration. Incompetent idiots…every single one of them. They continued to screw this all up. He should have hired a professional for the retrieval. "Okay, I'll take care of this. Just note for further operations, in no way, shape, or form is the owner of the bookstore supposed to get hurt. We need her. If something happens to her, you will pay with your life. Do you understand?"

"Ye…yes, boss." The voice that answered was shaky so he knew he'd made his point, but now he had to find another way to retrieve The Gift.

Chapter 14

Colton sat up with a start and glanced around his darkened bedroom. What had awoken him? His heart was pounding, so he knew it wasn't a natural thing. Then he heard it…a whimper coming from Penelope's room. He flung the covers off and ran out of his room toward hers.

When he came in, he could hear her muffled sobs. There was enough light coming through the window so he could see she was alone. She must be having a nightmare and the torment in her sobs tore his heart in two. He rushed to her bedside and whispered her name, but she was still asleep. He lowered his body down beside her and drew her into his arms. She immediately quieted, although she didn't wake up. She simply snuggled into his chest and sighed lightly, ruffling the hair on his chest. He felt that movement all the way down to his cock.

Damn, he was naked. Hearing her in distress, he hadn't even thought about the need for pants. He'd lay here until she settled back into deep sleep and then he'd head back to his room.

He lowered his nose to her hair and inhaled her sweet honeysuckle scent. He groaned internally. It was going to be a long night, but despite the aching in his groin, he planned to savor each moment of what he could steal of it.

She felt so right in his arms, but he couldn't do anything about that. She'd made it clear that she wasn't interested in a relationship. There was no way he would open himself up to another relationship where they both weren't on the same page. He'd done that with Dianna and it had been a disaster. Besides right now, he needed to take care of Chris and make sure he healed. His priority had to be his family.

***

Penelope awoke with her face pressed into a very sculpted, very sexy, very hard chest. And speaking of hard, something caught her eye. She glanced down his body and the tingles immediately erupted and coiled towards her core. How had Colton ended up naked in her bed? She took mental inventory of her own body. She still had a mild headache, but that was from her fall, not drinking heavily. She didn't feel other signs of anything untoward happening between them, so why couldn't she remember how he got there?

His muscles tightened and she quickly diverted her gaze from his ever-growing cock up to his face which appeared to be glowing red. Who knew Colton could blush?

His voice was gravelly with sleep. "Sorry about that." He waved the hand that wasn't draped around her down toward his groin.

She grinned at him, enjoying the fact he was uncomfortable. "No problem. It's just something that happens naturally right? You're just a healthy guy." She glanced back down, and cocked an eyebrow at him as she murmured. "Very healthy indeed."

He closed his eyes in a silent grimace while he continued to hold her. He opened them and a barrage of conflicting emotions flashed through. A shiver of awareness skated down her spine. Colton was naked in her bed and God, he looked sexy in the morning. His eyes darkened with arousal and she felt more than a little dazed by it. "Why are you in my bed?" she whispered, not wanting to break the spell.

"You had a nightmare." He spoke and his voice was just as hushed as hers.

Her nipples hardened where she was draped across his side and she wanted to rub herself up against him. She had to get him out of here before she did something really foolish. She cleared her throat as she looked down at his muscular chest. "Well I guess this definitely clears up the matter as to whether you're tattooed or not."

His chuckle was low and sexy and made her want to do really sinful things to his body. "Oh I don't know about that. From your vantage point right now, you can only see half of me." Her eyes darted back up to his face where he was once again blushing. Was he actually flirting?

"Is that an invitation?"

He closed his eyes and groaned low and deep. Intriguing. His arms tightened around her as he took a deep breath. She couldn't resist another glance down. Jeebers, Colton was absolutely huge everywhere.

He grasped her chin and lifted her face so she had to look at him. He looked into her eyes for a moment and she thought she saw a flash of regret. "As much as I would like to explore your fascination, I think we both know that would be a mistake." He swallowed hard.

A knot settled low in her belly as his rejection slammed through her body. She jerked back and quickly slid out of bed. "Um, of course, you're right." He *was* right, so why did she feel like curling up on the floor and crying? She had to get out of here. She waved her hand at him as she moved toward the door, her mortification complete. "I'll just go into the kitchen while you find some clothes."

"Penelope," he called after her, but she ignored him and fled down the hallway.

***

Colton closed his eyes. Damn, he hadn't missed the flash of hurt in her eyes. He looked down in disgust at his still straining dick. He'd wanted nothing more than to spend the morning sinking into her luscious body, but they both knew that couldn't work. They were too different. She wanted someone fun, who knew how to have a good time. That person wasn't him. He had more baggage right now than Penelope deserved. Even on a good day, he would hardly qualify as someone to have a good time with. And right now, there weren't too many good days to be found. She needed better. He just had to keep reminding his body and mind of that.

Chapter 15

Penelope looked around the coffee table at her two best friends, Julie and Cassie, in disbelief. "I can't believe Colton managed to convince you both to take the afternoon off just so you could come over here and keep me from going into work."

Cassie smirked at her. "I warned you about Colt's protective streak didn't I?"

Penelope sighed and rolled her eyes. "You did, and you were right. The man needs to take a chill pill. I swear."

"I think it's sweet. Besides it's been ages since we've had a girls' day," Julie said as she dipped another strawberry into the chocolate fondue.

Rather than arguing with Colton after the embarrassing debacle in her bedroom this morning, she'd let him think he'd won about her not going to work. She knew he had a meeting today with his friend from Homeland Security. She'd planned to simply wait and go to work when he left for his meeting. He'd obviously seen through her plan though because fifteen minutes before he left, Julie and Cassie had shown up at her door.

They'd brought strawberries, chocolates, assorted cheeses, breads, and several bottles of wine with them. Since she was off the painkillers, they decided they needed to celebrate. At least that was the official story. The truth of why they were really there was no secret. They were Colton's diversionary tactic to keep her from going to work while he was out. If she hadn't been so happy to see them, she would have been mad. But throughout the morning things had been beyond awkward between her and Colton. She could use her girlfriends right now.

Penelope frowned as she thought about the changes in their lives over the last few months. "Well, since you two went off and decided to fall in love, I've become a fifth wheel."

Julie looked at her thoughtfully. "That's not true. You know we never think of you that way. We love it when you come out with us."

"I know, but it's just kind of awkward with all this young love around." She gestured toward Cassie. "This one will have her fiancé here with her permanently in just another week." She turned back toward Julie with a grin. "And you... how are things going with Dr. Hottie?"

Julie grinned and then blushed and ducked her head. "Aaron's wonderful. He asked me to move in with him," she whispered.

"What?" both Cassie and Penelope screamed.

"When did this happen?"

"What did you say?"

"I haven't given him my answer yet." Julie's big brown eyes filled with tears.

Cassie reached over and grabbed hold of her hand. "Hey, what's wrong?"

"I don't know," Julie wailed mournfully. "What's wrong with me? He's wonderful, but it just seems too soon. We've only been dating three months. Doesn't that seem too soon?" She gave them both a desperate look. Out of the three, Julie was the cautious one.

Penelope looked at Cassie. Cassie was the one with the long-lasting relationship experience here. It definitely wasn't Penelope. She wasn't fit to give anyone relationship advice.

Cassie took the hint and took the lead in the discussion. "Hon, if it doesn't feel like it's time, then it's absolutely not. You're both still young and you're right, you haven't been dating all that long. There's no reason to rush things."

Julie whispered, "But what if I lose him when I tell him no? He's such a nice guy. I owe him better than this."

Owe. That seemed like a strange phrase to use. Penelope frowned at Julie, wondering if there was more going on here than either she or Cassie realized.

"Hey," Cassie hugged her, "if he loves you," she drew away and looked Julie right in the eye, "and from what I've seen, he definitely does, he'll be willing to wait. He's a good guy. Don't let your doubts push you apart."

Julie dashed the tears from her eyes. "You're right. God, what a drama queen, right? Everything will work out if it's meant to be. I just don't want to hurt him."

Penelope could chime in on this one. "*Chica*, you don't even know what drama queen means and you couldn't hurt a fly if you wanted to. You're worth the wait and I know Aaron knows that too. Don't sell him short. He's a doctor. He has the brains to realize what a catch you are. Actually, he obviously already has if he wants you to move in. He'll wait."

Julie looked at them both. "I love you guys and I've missed you." She drained her glass and then tipped it toward Penelope. "Fill me back up. This is our girls' party and we're not allowed to get all schmaltzy. Besides," she tipped her refilled glass back toward Penelope, "we need to hear about your sex life now."

Penelope panicked as she thought about Colton in her bed this morning. She looked at his sister Cassie. But they couldn't know about that, right? Besides nothing happened except one great big old rejection that still stung. She tried to laugh it off, "My sex life? I must have missed it because I haven't noticed it hanging around lately."

"But you're bringing someone to my party tomorrow night, right?" Julie looked at her quizzically.

"Yes, but that's just Damon."

"Just?" Cassie asked. "Isn't he the archeologist from National Explorer? What's wrong with him? Is he a typical archeology type?" Cassie scrunched up her face in distaste, which was humorous considering she held her doctorate in history, which wasn't much better.

Penelope sighed. "Actually he's perfect." She took another sip of her wine. "He's gorgeous. He's fun. He's sexy. God, you should see his tattoos, not that I've even seen all of them, but I've seen glimpses and they are scrumptious…."

"But…" Cassie led.

"But there's no chemistry. None. Nada." She shuddered and took another deep drink of her wine and got a far-off look in her eye. "It's nothing like what I feel with…" She stopped talking suddenly, looking over at the girls and flushed red. She ducked her eyes and took another drink of wine. "Never mind. There's just no chemistry, but he's a great guy and a lot of fun to be with, so we're just friends."

Cassie looked at her searchingly. "You were about to say something else."

Penelope just shook her head in denial. "Nope that's all there is. Damon and I are friends. Just friends. And I'm not involved with anyone else, so what else could there be?" Penelope clamped her lips shut realizing that she was rambling.

Cassie and Julie exchanged a look before they turned back to her as one. It was Julie who spoke up first though. "So how are things working with you and Colton living together?"

The sweat started to gather at the center of the small of her back. "Good." God, was that her voice sounding so high and squeaky? She rolled her eyes so maybe they'd believe her exasperation with Colt. "He's just really over-protective right now after I got hurt, but other than that, we're simply roommates living in the same apartment."

She looked between her two best friends, not sure she'd convinced them. They looked a bit dubious. But probably the first thing she should do to convince them is to convince herself. She wasn't quite there yet either.

Chapter 16

Colton met with his friend, Bart Matthews, in the local Homeland Security office. The meeting had gone well and Colton felt pumped about where Mad Rob was headed. It was time to bring Chris on board. He'd swung by Cassie's on his way home and convinced Chris to come over to the loft. By bringing him here, they could discuss the business and get Chris out of Cassie's house for a few hours. Something he wasn't doing enough. Besides Colton wanted to check on Penelope.

By the time they arrived at the loft, none of the three girls were feeling any pain. Both Cassie and Julie were on the living room floor seated around the coffee table, while Penelope was on the couch. All three of them were laughing uncontrollably about something. Colton bit back a smile as he observed them. They were so caught up in their conversation, they hadn't even seen the two of them walk into the apartment.

Penelope was sprawled on the couch, one leg on and one leg off. She had her right arm raised above her head as she giggled which caused her shirt to raise high on her midriff. Her ab muscles contracted as she laughed and the sight made several muscles contract in his body. He groaned inwardly. He had to get over this lust he had for her.

He must have made some sort of noise, because Penelope suddenly sat up and grinned at him goofily. She waved her hand holding a half-empty glass of wine at him. "Hey it's Colton and Chris. Look girls. Here's our resident stud right now and he brought his equally sexy brother."

All three of them dissolved once again into peals of laughter. He gave Chris a wry look. "I'm not sure I want to know what they're talking about. It may not be safe for us to be here."

Chris grinned. "I don't know. It may be fun to just join them." He looked at Penelope again before he muttered to Colton, "I hope she's not still taking painkillers."

Colton shook his head, "She's not, but she's probably going to want them again in the morning."

Cassie got herself under control first and then she glared at the other two girls. "Hey, those are my brothers. No objectifying allowed."

"Well, where's the fun in that?" Julie started pouting as she looked longingly back toward the brothers.

Penelope just stuck her tongue out at Cassie, before adding, "Right. Just because you don't think they're sexy, doesn't mean we don't. Seriously, look at them." Penelope waved a hand over at the two guys still in the doorway. All three girls turned to study them like they were measuring their dicks through their clothing.

Chris whispered under his breath, "You may be right. Maybe we should go somewhere else."

"Pshaw," Penelope said as she struggled to raise herself from the couch. She drunkenly stumbled over to the guys and then turned back to the girls and glared at them. "Stop it," she looked specifically at Julie. Then she turned back toward Chris like she was approaching a wild animal. "Don't let us scare you away." She started pulling Chris into the room. "Come on in. We can share our wine or there's beer in the fridge."

Chris looked toward Colton entreatingly. Colt finally took pity on him. "Let's just grab a beer and move to my bedroom. I have a couple of chairs in there and we can sit and talk." At Chris's nod, Colton strode to the fridge to grab the beers.

When Colton turned from the fridge, Penelope was right there. He inhaled her honeysuckle scent which went straight to his cock. "You aren't still mad at me, are you?"

She shook her head. "Un huh." She stepped forward so she was mere inches away from his chest.

He looked at her warily as he spoke softly. "Pen, what are you doing?"

She reached up and laid her palm on the flat of his abs and flexed her hand. She stepped forward another step so he could feel the heat coming off her body. "Me? You want to know what I'm doing?"

He nodded his head silently. Suddenly his throat was completely dry. His heart felt like it was pounding out of his chest. She had to be able to feel that under her fingertips.

She took the final step that put her body flush up against his. She leaned up and very slowly licked him along his neck right under his ear before she grabbed his lobe with her teeth. He shuddered.

"I'm just letting you know what you're missing out on," she seductively whispered into his ear. Then she turned and walked right back into the living room, drinking her wine, and swinging her hips as she went.

Colton had lost the ability to think. All the blood in his body had gone south. He couldn't think of a time that he'd ever been this hard in his life. He closed his eyes and tried to gain control of his body when he heard a loud, "Ahem."

His eyes flew open and locked with Chris's. The bastard was smirking at him.

"Shut up," Colton said.

"I didn't say a word."

He growled. "And if you want to keep walking, that's the way you'll leave it." He grabbed the two bottles of beer and strode down the hall ignoring the curious glances from everyone but Penelope who ignored him completely.

***

Colton watched Chris crutch his way into the bedroom. He waved his hand at the other leather club chair seated beside the one he was already sitting in. "Have a seat."

His rock-hard cock was strangling against the pressure of the zipper of his jeans. He took a long drag of his beer while he tried to get his body under control. This wasn't the way he wanted to go into this discussion with Chris. The only good news was that little reverie between the two of them had obviously amused Chris. Instead of his normal scowl, Chris's eyes were alight with humor. The bastard was laughing at him.

Trying to control his smile, Chris asked, "Do you want to talk about it?"

Colton practically growled. "No." He ran a hand through his hair in frustration and closed his eyes trying to find his ability to concentrate. "No, that's definitely not why I brought you here." He sighed deeply and grimaced. "Sorry, this isn't how I wanted to start this conversation."

Chris shook his head. "No problem." He lifted his bottle to his lips. "As long as you have more of these, we can hang out all night while you figure out what the hell you want to talk about."

"We have plenty. No problem there and I know exactly what I want to talk to you about." Colton took a deep breath. He hoped Chris accepted this idea for what it was, an opportunity for all three of them, and didn't fly off the handle. "I have a plan for a business and I want you to become a partner in it."

"Okay, I'm listening."

"We'd be equal partners: You, Jake, and me. I want us to start a flight business running a jump school and chartering service. There's more..." Colton took a deep sigh and watched Chris closely trying to judge how he was reacting to the idea. "We already have leads on a couple of planes that would work for the business and we might have access to one other one, depending..." Colton took another deep breath.

"Just spit it out, Colt. What else?"

"I have an in on a Homeland Security contract to fly one of the C-27's. If we won the contract, we would have access to one of those planes to run missions for them." Chris paled as Colton watched him. "To do any of this, we have to have two pilots...you and me."

"Just how long have you been planning this? It sounds like you've put a lot of thought into it already. Why didn't you mention it earlier?"

Chris's knuckles were white as he grasped the arms of the chair. Colton knew this wouldn't be easy for him, but he had full confidence that Chris could do this. "I wanted to make sure Jake was in and I didn't want to get your hopes up if it wasn't going to happen."

"Fuck, I'm not six years old anymore, Colton. I can handle more than a little bit of disappointment in my life, if you haven't noticed. You need to stop trying to protect me or else we won't be able to work together. You're not my dad, no matter what the circumstances were as we grew up."

Colton flinched, but tried not to let it show. "I realize that, but I'm still your older brother. I can't help wanting to protect you. You've had to deal with way more than most over the last year. You can't blame me for wanting to keep as much bad stuff away as I can. But that does bring us back to that bad stuff. If we're gonna do this, I need you there 100%. Do you think you can run missions again?"

Chris rubbed a hand over his face. When he spoke his voice was very low. "I don't know Colt. God, I want to fly again, but I just don't know. I haven't been in a cockpit since the crash. What kind of missions is Homeland Security running from Lubbock, Texas?"

"Obviously, I don't know exactly since that's classified, but I'm hearing rumblings about human trafficking as well as the normal drug issues between here and Mexico and South America. I can only assume it has to do with those. It will take a while to get everything set up and going, but to move forward, I need to know that you'll be able to fly, both mentally and physically, in three months." Colton watched him closely.

"Damn, Colt." Chris looked up at him with desolation in his eyes. He spoke quietly. "I don't know." His voice broke. "I just don't know."

"Okay, that's fair. The next question is, do you want to be? Do want to be a part of this? A partner in the company?"

"Of course, but…"

"No, there is no but to this. Chris what happened to you was awful, but it's time for you to get past it and to do that, you're going to have to work at it…both mentally and physically. For us to move forward with this, I need your promise that you'll do that."

Chris closed his eyes and looked pained, but when he opened them back up to look at Colton, he firmed his jaw and threw back his shoulders. "Okay, you have a deal. I promise I'll be ready."

"In that case," Colton reached over to shake his hand, "welcome to Mad Rob."

"Mad Rob?"

"Yep, that's the name of our new company. Mad for Madsen; Rob for Robertson. Mad Rob, it was Penelope's idea."

Chris grinned at him. "I should have guessed. So, now are you ready to talk about what's happening between you and the beautiful Miss Penelope?"

"No." Colton said through clenched teeth.

Chapter 17

Colton looked around the interior of the VW Bus uncomfortably. He was on-edge tonight and couldn't pinpoint why. He just had a crawling feeling in his gut. It was the same kind of feeling he got when things were about to go bad on a mission. But as he peered around the interior of the Bus, he admitted to himself that it could simply be because he was so far out of his comfort zone. He should have ridden his motorcycle to this party.

Six months ago, he'd been commanding troops in a warzone and now he was riding around town in a VW Bus like a damn hippy. There was even a flower vase next to the steering wheel. How had he sunk so far so quickly?

He scowled toward the front seat where Penelope sat with Damon. The bird tattoo rose tantalizingly over the edge of her shirt. She wore some gauzy concoction that slid off her shoulders to rest at the tops of her arms. It left her shoulders deliciously bare and he wanted to take advantage of that and explore exactly where those birds flew over the rest of her body.

She was definitely the gypsy leader of this bunch. He scowled again as she laughed at something Damon said and reached over to touch his arm softly while they spoke. She needed to keep both her damn hands on the wheel if she wanted to drive.

He rubbed the back of his neck in irritation. He looked around again trying to pinpoint the source of this itchy feeling. As he did so, he realized the twins were watching him with matching looks of humor. It was eerie, and damn irritating, how alike they could look sometimes. "What?" he growled at them.

Cassie was the one who responded. "Why are you so grumpy tonight? We're going to a party. You should be having fun."

He shrugged and frowned again at the front seat. "I don't know. Something just feels off."

At this statement, Chris sat up and looked at him sharply. "Off, how?"

Colton growled. "I don't know. If I knew that I would fix it." He looked around again at their surroundings as they drove into Aaron's neighborhood and then looked back at Chris. "Just stay sharp. Something doesn't feel quite right."

When they arrived at Aaron's house, everyone piled out of the Bus. Chris and Colton were the last to get out and they walked toward the front door together. Colton once again rubbed the back of his neck. It felt like they were being watched but as he glanced around he couldn't see anything out of place.

Chris looked around the quiet suburban neighborhood. "You feel it too?"

Colton gave a sharp nod. "Someone's watching us." He glanced down the street, but with the party, there were cars everywhere. There was no way to tell if there was a car there that didn't belong. "Do you see anything?"

Chris shook his head.

They were at the front door and Colton gave one final glance down the street before he entered and gave Julie a hug. "Happy Birthday, Julie."

Julie was the tiniest of the threesome that made up Julie, Cassie, and Penelope. She barely even came to his ribs when he hugged her. Her diminutive size was emphasized by her dark pixie-cut hair and expressive hazel eyes. Right now they expressed pure joy and Colton was pretty sure a lot of that reason was standing right behind her. He reached over and extended his hand to the man. "Hey, Aaron. How's orthopedics treating you lately?"

"Hey, Colton. I can't complain." He turned to Chris. "How's the knee working for you?"

"Overall, it's pretty good. It's still a bit stiff, but coming along."

Aaron looked at him sharply. "Are you doing your PT exercises? Maybe you should schedule some extra sessions with Julie?" He reached around Julie's waist and tugged her to him.

Colton watched as a flush of red spread up Chris's neck as he clenched his jaw. "Naw, my regular physical therapist is working just fine," he said gruffly and peered out over the living room.

Chris avoided her gaze so he missed the flash of hurt that crossed Julie's eyes. When she realized Colton watched her, she gave a little shrug of embarrassment. Curious.

"Thank y'all for coming. Aaron's outdone himself. There's a ton of food and drinks in the kitchen. Please feel free to help yourselves," Julie said.

Chris crutched off in that direction without another word, so Colton turned back to their hosts. "Sorry about that. He's still a little touchy about it all."

Julie's eyes were filled with sorrow as she watched Chris's back. "Don't worry about it Colton. We're all friends here, but if he ever needs my help, I'm here. I can come by Cassie's house to work with him if that would be easier."

"Thanks, Julie. I'll keep that in mind. Right now, I should probably catch up with him before he offends someone else."

When Colton found Chris again, he was sitting in a corner of the back patio scowling at something in his hands. He was completely oblivious to the trio of nurses watching him from the other side of the yard.

"Hey what do you have there?" Colton nodded at the small brightly wrapped box Chris quickly stuffed into the pocket of his jacket.

Chris avoided his eyes as he took a drink of his beer. "Nothing." He looked around the yard. "I guess doctor's pay is pretty good. Aaron has a nice place here."

"Hm-mm," Colton agreed, but he watched Chris closely.

"He's good for her. They're good together, aren't they?" Chris almost sounded like he was pleading for that to be the case.

"Yeah, they seem pretty solid," Colton said cautiously. Honestly, he'd never paid that much attention to Julie. She was just part of their large group of friends. But now, there seemed to be something more going on here with Chris. Was there a history between him and Julie?

He cleared his throat. "Chris, did you and Julie…" He trailed off when Chris's vibrant blue eyes flashed up to his. Colton couldn't miss the pain he saw there, but Chris quickly covered it.

"Naw, she's good with Aaron."

But Colton wasn't so sure about that anymore.

Chris scowled down at the label he peeled off his beer bottle and Colton nudged Chris's good leg. "Well, in that case, there are three really hot nurses over on the other side of the yard that look capable and ready to check your vitals."

Chris smiled at him, but the smile didn't quite reach his haunted eyes. He glanced over at the women in question, but just gave a quick shake of his head. "I don't think so." He looked back down at his beer bottle.

Chris's jet crash was nine months ago. In the three months since he'd been home, Colton couldn't think of him showing any interest in dating. Now that Colton thought about it, he couldn't remember Chris even flirting since he'd come home. Sure, some of that could be accounted to what he'd gone through, but flirting had always been an integral part of Chris's personality. The only time he'd seen any sign of the old Chris when it came to women was when they'd brought Penelope home from the ER and she'd been unconscious at the time. There was no risk there. He re-catalogued the list of injuries Chris sustained in his mind with growing dread.

Colton cleared his throat and lowered his voice. "Chris, is everything... I mean..." Damn, this was harder than he thought. He gestured toward Chris's groin. "Is everything working okay?"

There was no denying the bleakness in Chris's eyes before he lowered them. Damn.

Chris's voice had slipped an octave when he said, "I don't want to talk about it."

"Damn, Chris, have you talked to your doctor about it?"

He shook his head and wouldn't meet Colton's eyes. "Not recently, no."

"Well, that's the first thing you need to do. Your body has been through a ton of stress. This is liable to be perfectly normal considering your level of injuries."

Chris was already shaking his head. His voice was guttural when he spoke. "There was damage." Chris looked off over the yard and Colton watched as he clenched his hands around his empty beer bottle. "It could be permanent. They don't know. They told me to give it time." He finally looked up at Colton when he said, "It's been three months. I don't think it's going to get any better."

"Chris…"

Chris waved him off. "It doesn't matter. What's done is done." Colton sat, stunned, as Chris stood up. "I'm gonna go grab another beer. You want one?"

"No, I'm good. Want me to head in with you?"

Chris shook his head as he headed into the house. "I'll be back in a little bit."

Guilt assailed him. No wonder Chris had spent all these months so angry and frustrated. Colton ducked his head into his hands. He didn't know how to fix this. He didn't know how he could make this better. There had to be something he could do to help. His brain scrambled for a few minutes working to come up with an idea of how he could help.

There was a light touch on his shoulder and he looked up.

Penelope stood there with a concerned look on her face. "I just saw Chris and he looked really pale. Is everything okay? You guys didn't have another fight did you?"

He shook his head. "No. No fight. Not this time."

She reached down to the side of his face and gently caressed it. That single, light touch sent tendrils of fire throughout his veins. "Do you want to talk about it?"

He shook his head and stood. He slowly pulled her into his arms, letting her honeysuckle scent wash over him. Savoring the comfort of her embrace, he bent down and brushed his lips over the crown of her head.

***

Penelope didn't know what to make of this Colton. The pain was stark in his eyes. Something had obviously shaken him which had affected Chris too. When she'd passed him while coming out of the house, he'd looked almost physically ill. She'd try to stop him, but he gestured over to Colton and told her to go sit with him.

Colton's lips brushed the top of her hair and she couldn't control the shiver of arousal that snaked throughout her body. She pressed her face into his hard chest and took a deep breath of the spicy masculine smell that was wholly Colton. He was always so big, stoic, and strong. To see him shaken up like this was surprising.

She leaned back, touched the side of his sculpted cheek, and asked, "Are you sure you're okay?"

"Yeah, I'm fine." His hands brushed up her arms. He gently traced the edge of the birds where they swooped over her shoulder before he looked back at her face. Her heartbeat quickened and she found herself breathless. His gaze settled on her lips. She moistened them in nervousness. That single move seemed to shatter some resolve within him. He groaned low before he swooped in and claimed her lips.

Penelope had been kissed lots of times in her life, but never had she felt the immediate cataclysmic reaction that came from having Colton's firm lips on hers. She wanted him. She needed him. She couldn't hold back her low groan and that seemed to push him on. He reached up behind and cradled her head, deepening the kiss to near punishing. As his tongue plundered her mouth, she arched towards him. Arousal exploded throughout her body and settled low in her belly where she could feel the press of his erection.

As he lowered his hands to her ass, her arms snaked around his neck and she pressed up against his hard frame, needing more. She ran her fingers through his hair on the back of his head as he continued to explore her mouth with his lips and tongue. It was a full-on assault, but one she never wanted to end. Everything about him and this kiss felt perfect.

He groaned deep, right before he lifted his head. She raised her eyes to meet his dark blue ones which were filled with unsatiated lust. They were both breathing hard. The callous on his fingertip caressed her swollen lips. She used her tongue to draw his finger into her mouth and she lightly sucked on it. He closed his eyes, his expression one of pure torture. He muttered a deep, guttural, "Penelope…"

She watched him visibly take in a deep breath as he tried to gain control. His breath shuddered as he looked around the yard. "We can't do this here."

She admired his control because she wasn't there yet. She didn't care who was lurking. She simply wanted to partake of his body any and every way possible. Right here. Right now. But as she looked up into his shuttered eyes, she realized that wasn't going to happen. Colton wasn't the type to have wild sex in a public place.

She inhaled a deep breath. "You're right. I'm sorry." She started to turn away, but Colton grabbed her arm to prevent her from leaving.

"I'm not. I'm not sorry at all and we will finish this, Pen. Just not here." He took another deep, shuddering breath. "Let's go back inside and see if there's any cake."

As he guided her back through the doorway, Penelope worked hard to get her hormones back under control. If she couldn't have Colton right this very moment, she needed chocolate. Lots of it, right now.

***

Penelope mused, she hoped Julie had enjoyed her birthday. Several hours later, their little group was partied out. They were quiet as they walked out to the Bus. As friends to the birthday girl, they stuck around until the very end to help clean up. Now they were all exhausted and ready to head home, minus Damon. He'd managed to get lucky and left several hours before with a very attractive female doctor.

After their encounter in the backyard, she and Colton had gone their separate ways at the party. As if by agreement, they'd avoided each other the rest of the night, but there were several times Penelope caught him staring at her. Those brooding eyes following her kept her arousal level at a low simmer the entire night.

As they walked out to the Bus, she watched his tight ass move. The guy was poetry in motion and watching him move made her mouth water. She was so lost in her thoughts and fantasies that she almost ran into him when he stopped abruptly.

He swung around to them, but directed his comment to Chris. "Stay with the girls. Something's wrong with the Bus. I'm going to check it out."

They all looked over his shoulder to the Bus parked twenty feet away. Her heart clenched, but she couldn't see anything wrong at first glance. Then she saw it. The driver's side window was shattered. She could still see small sections of it dangling from the corners of the window frame.

She started to move forward, but Chris snagged her arm. "Let Colt check it out first to make sure it's safe."

"If it's not safe for us, it's not safe for him."

"He can take care of himself."

Penelope turned to glare at Chris. "Are you saying I can't?"

He shook his head. "Pen, you're not drawing me into an argument over this. You're staying here. Actually," he glanced around the quiet neighborhood, then back at Colton who was checking under the Bus, "we're going to have to call the police, so why don't we just head back to Aaron's house?"

No way. Nuh uh. "We aren't going to leave him out here all alone. Not gonna happen, Chris." She continued to watch Colton worriedly as he moved around to the other side of the Bus.

Cassie stepped into the conversation. "I agree. We need to stay together."

Chris sighed. "Okay, fine, but one of you needs to call Julie before she and Aaron get too settled in for the night." He sounded pained. "Tell them we're coming back and they should call the police to report our car's been broken into."

Cassie nodded and Penelope was relieved to see Colton walking back over to them safe and sound. She reached around his waist and pulled him into a hug when he got to them. He returned her embrace and moved the group back toward the house. "The only thing I can see wrong is the broken window. There's an envelope propped on the steering wheel, but I didn't touch it. I figure the police will want to process it."

Aaron and Julie waited for them on the porch when they got back to the house. From the looks of them, it was a good thing they'd called ahead. Julie's shirt was on inside out and Aaron's buttons were done up crooked. Aaron's face held the pinched, tension filled expression of a man who had just been cock-blocked.

Regardless of the situation, Penelope couldn't help but smile. "Sorry to interrupt guys, but you may want to go get straightened out," she gestured toward their clothes, "before the police arrive."

Julie glanced down at her shirt and glanced guiltily at Chris, looking close to tears. Both Julie and Aaron were flushed red. They were so cute together.

As they entered the house, Aaron said, "The police are on their way. Could you tell anything about what happened?" Julie snuck back to the bedroom while Aaron stayed there and re-buttoned his shirt. Penelope couldn't help but notice the guy was fit. How'd a doctor have time to work-out to maintain those kind of abs? Lucky Julie.

She looked over at Colton to see him looking at her with a single eyebrow raised. Busted. She gave him a grin and shrugged her shoulders. No, Aaron's body didn't even compare to his, but she didn't need to let him know that. The guy had way too much self-confidence already. Speaking of that big gorgeous body.... it was suddenly tucked in behind her. Colton snaked an arm around her waist and pulled her up against him. He leaned down and whispered in her ear, "I promise I can fulfill you better than he ever could."

Shock and arousal pulsed throughout her body. What the hell? What happened to the stoic Colton she'd always known? Oh, who the hell cared? This worked for her. "Is that a promise?"

He groaned low, tightened his hold on her, and she could feel his erection pressed into her back. She swallowed hard and closed her eyes in ecstasy. When she opened them again, she was looking right into the smirking faces of all her friends. Damn, a flush of heat rose up her face. She tried to free herself from Colton's grasp, but he wasn't letting go. She elbowed him gently in the stomach.

He uttered a low oath. "What the hell was that for?"

She nodded toward their friends. "I think they asked us something."

He finally let go of her, looking just as embarrassed as she felt. "What?" he growled at them.

Cassie rolled her hand at them and grinned. "No, please continue, this is fascinating. I had no idea." She pursed her lips in thought, but her eyes continued to shimmer in amusement.

Luckily they were saved from having to respond to their friends' curiosity by the ringing of the doorbell. Aaron went to answer it and ushered Officer Pete Larson into the kitchen. A round of "Hi, Pete," went around the group. They all knew him from when he'd regularly stood guard at Cassie's house while she had a stalker. He also had begun to teach self-defense classes with Julie, so he was well-known to the group.

While the men went out to examine the Bus and the note therein, the girls stayed in the kitchen. Cassie and Julie stood side-by-side with their arms crossed and looked at her.

"What?" she asked them, feeling very defensive all of a sudden.

It was Julie who spoke up. "Colton? Really? Do you think that's a good idea with you guys being roommates? I know you were flirting with him yesterday, but I thought you were just playing. This seemed to be more." She looked concerned.

"We haven't done anything but kiss." Although the promise was definitely there for more to come. But they didn't need to know that.

Cassie frowned. "Pen, Colton doesn't play. He's had a hard couple of years especially with the failure of his marriage to Dianna. I'd hate to see him get hurt again. He doesn't need you to use him. If you're just messing around, you need to find another boy toy."

Oh, God, this wasn't what she'd expected from this conversation. "Is that what you think of me?" She tried not to let the threatening tears show.

Cassie reached across to grab Penelope's hand. "Hon, it has nothing to do with what I think of you. You know I love you, but your track record with guys isn't a real great recommendation. He's my brother. I have to look out for him."

Nothing like your best friend to knock you down a notch or two. "Sure, I understand and you're right. We certainly don't want Colton to fall under my evil spell." She knew it was wrong to lash out, but this really hurt. She dashed at the tears that continued to flow and was thankful to hear the front door so they didn't have to continue with this horribly painful conversation.

Thankfully, most of the men didn't notice the tension level in the kitchen. Except for Colton... of course, he was the one who noticed her emotional state. He looked at her with concern, but she worked hard not to meet his glance.

Instead she looked at Pete who gingerly set the envelope onto the plastic he'd spread over the counter. Obviously he was trying to secure any evidence that it may contain. He even had on plastic gloves.

As he opened the envelope and spilled its contents over the plastic on the counter, a round of gasps shattered the room. A plethora of photos spilled out. They were all photos from tonight. All photos of her friends with targets drawn over their faces. There was also a note that fluttered out. The full-sized sheet was typewritten in an easily readable bold font.

```
            Return The Gift
         and no one will get hurt.
          You have until 6:00 AM.
         Do not contact the police.
   Leave it on the porch at the bookstore.
```

Oh my God. They'd already contacted the police. Penelope's gaze flew around the room in panic. Had their actions tonight already condemned one of her friends to get hurt?

Pete directed his gaze toward Penelope. "Do you know what it's talking about? What's the gift?"

Penelope shook her head, scrambling to get her brain caught up with what they were talking about. She was still focused on those photos. A huge ball of dread settled into the pit of her stomach. "I don't know." Her eyes sought Colton's. "We brought a gift tonight for Julie. It's her birthday, but I don't think…"

"What was the gift?" Pete asked her.

"It's a piece of art…photography done by a local photographer. It's a picture of an old barn."

Pete turned to Julie. "Do you mind getting it for me so I can look at it?"

She nodded. "Sure. Hang on and I'll go grab it."

When she returned with it, he directed her to place it on the kitchen table. They all stood around the table and looked closely at it.

Julie was fascinated with derelict, abandoned buildings and this photo showed one in black and white, covered in snow. Penelope liked the contrast of the light of the snow and the dark of the aged boards. There was a serene beauty to it, but there wasn't anything to it that would be worth killing people over. It just didn't make any sense.

"I don't see anything about this photo that stands out. Does anyone else?" There was a round of heads shaking.

Chris suggested, "Maybe it's something inside the frame." They took the frame apart, but that didn't yield any clues. Everything looked completely benign.

"I honestly don't have any idea what they're talking about." It was late or early depending on perspective and Penelope desperately needed some sleep to get her brain functioning again. She was worried, tired, and afraid.

"The note said we had until 6:00. God, it's already 2:00 in the morning right now, so that means whatever it is needs to be at the bookstore," she looked at the clock on the wall again. "What if we left Julie's present on the doorstep with a note saying that I don't know what they're talking about? Maybe they'd be satisfied with that." She looked over at Julie. "Is it okay if I take back your present? I'll get you another one or something else or whatever."

Julie reached over and grasped Penelope's hand. "Of course you can."

Pete nodded. "That's a good idea. We could set up someone to watch it and then just arrest them when they come to pick it up."

Penelope immediately started shaking her head. "No. They said no police and I don't want to provoke whoever this is into attacking one of my friends. If I don't press charges, there's no reason for a police presence. I'm not filing charges."

Colton came to stand by her. He reached around her waist and pulled her to him. "Pen, you're smarter than this. You know you can't let them get away with this." He laid his head against the top of hers and while she appreciated the support, she wasn't going to change her mind about this.

"No. It's a couple hundred dollars' worth of damage and a photo I can replace. That's nothing in comparison to any of your lives." She looked around the room at her dearest friends. For some reason they were being targeted and it had something to do with her. She had to keep them safe. "If that's what they want, I'm fine with it. They can have it. We can leave the photo on the porch of the bookstore on our way home tonight. They can pick it up while it's still dark and everyone will be happy." She looked around at the very unhappy faces surrounding her. She stuck her chin out defiantly. "Well, it certainly can't hurt to try and be cooperative."

Pete spoke up. "Obviously, this is your decision, but I strongly urge you to rethink this approach. They vandalized your property and now are trying to steal from you. Those are crimes." He watched her closely as he spoke. He shook his head. "You're right, though. I can't do anything about it if you don't want me to. I'll process the photos and note so we have it on file."

Penelope nodded. "Thank you and thanks for coming out here tonight. I'm sorry we wasted your time."

"It's not a waste and I hope this is the end of your issues with whoever this is, but I'll be surprised if it is."

"Ah, you're an optimist, aren't you?" She teased him facetiously, trying to lighten the tone in the room.

"Unfortunately, optimistic souls don't last long in this job."

After Pete left, they were all too tired to discuss it any longer. Penelope borrowed a sheet of paper from Aaron to write a note. She tucked it into the frame to leave on the doorstep of the bookstore. Once again, they all headed out to the Bus. This time, Colton took the keys to drive. Penelope was too tired to argue about it. She did argue it when they got to the bookstore.

***

Colton looked over at her and clenched his jaw in frustration. They both peered out the windshield of the Bus into the inky darkness of the night. "If you think I'm going to let you walk out there in the dark, in the middle of the night alone, you don't know me at all. I'll do it." He started to unfasten his seat belt

"And why is it safer for you to do it?"

"Because I'm bigger than you are," he growled at her.

"Come on guys," Cassie called from the backseat of the Bus. "Why don't you go together? Chris and I'll watch from the safety of the Bus and will call the police if either of you go down."

Colton swung an incredulous look around at her. "In case we *go down*?"

"What? It might happen and you'll have us here for backup. Right now it's," she looked down at her watch and groaned, "3:30 AM and you all are acting like you're going to sit here and argue all night. This night needs to end sometime soon, or else I'm going to be begging someone to shoot *me*."

Colton glared at her, but finally relented. He didn't want Penelope outside the relative safety of the Bus. As they walked up to the door, he hugged her close to him, trying to protect as much of her body as he could with his large frame. The close contact just served to distract him with thoughts of that incredible kiss earlier in the night. But something had changed in her demeanor since they found the note in the Bus. Since then she'd been withdrawn and quiet. No more of those heat-filled glances.

She was probably just tired. God it was late. He looked around the quiet neighborhood again. Whoever left the note, had to be watching them, but he didn't have that itchy feeling he normally got when danger was near.

While she laid the frame by the door, he looked around again.

"Think that's okay?" She gestured to how she'd propped up the photo.

"Yeah, it's fine. Let's get out of here."

Chapter 18

The phone rang and he snatched it up. "Did you get it?" Fortunately, he sounded in complete control, although that control spun away from him a little more every day. He popped another couple of antacids and swallowed them whole.

"Yeah, boss, it was on the porch just like instructed."

The relief immediately crashed through his body. Finally, something was working out the way he planned. "Good. Good. You know where to send it. I have to head out of town, so I trust you to handle this. I can trust you, can't I?"

"Yeah, we got it handled no problem. Bobby is chatting with the girl tonight to make sure there are no more screw-ups."

He tried not to picture the girl in his mind's eye. If he wanted the power, he had to accept the sacrifice. That meant punishment when someone didn't do their part. He was in control and he hired guys like Bobby to make sure it stayed that way.

He didn't want to think about what a "chat" with Bobby meant. Bobby was not a nice guy, but honestly none of the guys he dealt with anymore could be considered nice guys. But as long as they did the jobs he needed them to do, he wasn't going to question it. The entire chain had been messed up by that girl, but now it was fixed. He could breathe freely again. Things were back on track. Nothing had been irrevocably ruined… this time. There couldn't be a next time. His entire team needed to know the consequences of messing up the job.

"Okay, I'll call you when I get back."

"Have a good trip, boss."

A good trip? No, it probably wasn't going to be that. As he turned off the phone, he had to wonder, when had he become this guy? This had never been part of his original plan. He wanted the power, sure. But he hadn't realized that fear would be such a huge part of gaining that power. Now he was the guy they needed to fear.

Chapter 19

Colton stood in the kitchen and peered over his coffee cup. Penelope sat in the living room pretending to read her book. She looked exhausted. By the time they'd gotten home last night, it had been close to 4:00 in the morning. He'd awoken at his normal 6:00. Penelope wandered out of her bedroom not too long after that looking shell-shocked and exhausted.

They'd immediately gone by the bookstore to see if the gift was still there. The photo and frame were gone, but that's all there was to it. No note. No nothing. Now they were both waiting for the other shoe to drop. He agreed with Penelope. He didn't think Julie's gift was the one they'd been referring to, but he was as stumped as her. He had no idea what gift the note referred to. As he set the coffee cup down on the counter it thunked. The sound caused Penelope to jump.

Okay, that was enough. They weren't going to sit around here all day waiting for something to happen and jumping at every little noise.

He strode into the living room and took the book out of her hands. "Go get some shoes on. We're going out."

Her eyes were filled with confusion when she looked up at him and he had to resist the urge to draw her into his arms. "What if they call while we're gone?"

"Then they can call back." He lowered his voice and told her again more gently, "Go get your shoes. Come on Pen, you're going to go crazy sitting around here all day. In fact, put on your boots and we'll take my motorcycle."

She gave a sharp nod and a ghost of a smile. "Okay, that sounds fun."

When she came back into the room, she was wearing worn, fitted jeans, cowboy boots, and a brown leather jacket that ended right at the top of her very fine ass. She'd braided her hair, but already some of the curly pieces were escaping the confines of it. Once again, Colton wanted to pull her into his arms, but this time with a very different purpose in mind.

She slid her hands into her jean pockets and seemed to stiffen when she noticed his perusal.

He didn't understand what had changed, but something had. He could feel it in her every stilted glance she gave him today. Last night at the party, she'd seemed like she was right with him in where they were going. But today, there was a wall around her. It didn't make any sense. He knew the photos scared her, but he felt like this was unrelated. He needed to figure it out. He wanted them back in the same place they'd been the night before, but this time closer to a bed.

"So where are we going?"

"I need to head out to the airport to check a couple of planes that are for sale." She gave a quick nod and snagged the book she'd been reading and slid it into the interior pocket of her jacket.

He quirked an eyebrow at her. "Planning to do some reading?"

"Hey, if you get to talking planes with someone out there, I'll need something to do. Would you rather I was bored?"

"I'll do everything in my power to make sure you're never bored when you're with me."

"Hmm, is that a threat or a challenge?"

"Sweetheart, that's a promise."

***

When Penelope said yes to riding Colton's motorcycle, she hadn't taken into account how arousing it would be to have him in between her thighs with her arms wrapped around his muscular torso. This. Was. Torture. But oh, what an incredible way to die. If she flexed her fingers even the tiniest bit, she could feel his abs moving and rippling below them.

She shifted trying to relieve some of the pressure building within her, but that just exacerbated the problem. At this rate, she was going to have an orgasm simply from riding pressed up against Colton with the vibration of the motorcycle below them. Wouldn't that be embarrassing? She shifted her body again. This time, Colt grabbed hold of her hand and gave it a light kiss before pressing it back to his stomach. Instead of letting go, he continued to hold her and threaded his fingers through hers. She, honest to God, felt like she was going to ignite into flames she was so turned on.

Finally, they arrived at the airport. As soon as they stopped, she slid off the motorcycle to get her feverish body away from Colton. She quickly turned and took off her helmet, struggling to keep her libido in check. Colton moved much slower to get of the bike, but when he did, he reached over and grabbed her and pulled her to him.

Tendrils of her hair had escaped from her braid and fluttered over her face in the blowing wind. He reached down and tucked them behind her ear, before he took off his sunglasses. As he did so, she was shocked at the naked lust shining in his dark blue eyes.

He didn't give her a chance to take in a single breath before he swooped down and claimed her lips. His hard lips pressed into hers, punishing, while at the same time so erotic. The pulse of her blood settled low into her belly. His tongue searched for hers as they tangled with combined need. She wanted more of him as she clutched him to her. He obviously agreed. He pressed his groin to hers, eliciting a low moan from her.

Suddenly he stiffened and she heard a man clearing his throat behind Colton's massive back. Colton groaned and laid his forehead up against hers. "Sweetheart," he muttered, "soon we're gonna have to do this when we're not in public." He gave her a pained grin as he turned to greet the man standing behind him.

The man grinned at them unrepentantly. When you pictured a good-old boy from Texas, this man's photo could have been in the dictionary. He wore a grey felt cowboy hat and button down western shirt stretched over his massive girth that barely left room for a glimpse of the huge silver belt buckle. He had on grey ostrich cowboy boots and Levi's that rested way too low on his hips for Penelope's ease of mind.

"Sorry to interrupt y'all." She noticed he really didn't look sorry about it at all. In fact, he looked positively gleeful about it. He reached his hand out to Colton. "Are you Colton Robertson?"

Colton nodded while he shook the man's hand. "I am. I'm assuming you're Phil Jordan."

Phil nodded and directed them over to a hangar where the doors were slid open. "The two planes you want to look at are in here." He looked them both over as if measuring their ability to buy a plane. "You're interested in the Cessna Caravan and the de Havilland Twin Otter, right?"

Colton nodded and reached over to grasp her hand as they walked. Entering the hangar, Penelope was overwhelmed by the sheer size of the building. Sure, she knew hangars were big. They hold planes. Planes are big, but she was still surprised. There were several planes in here of various sizes, but other than the planes it was very clean. Almost sterile. She tried to figure out which ones were the planes they were here to see. As she glanced around, it occurred to her she knew nothing about what Mad Rob would need.

Her attention was immediately caught by a red plane over in the corner of the hangar. She noticed it caught Colton's attention too, but Phil herded them towards a plane closer to them.

"Here's the Cessna Caravan."

They stood looking at the mostly white plane. For some reason when Colton had been talking about buying planes, she'd assumed they'd be the little 4-seater planes, but this was much bigger than that. It had windows all down the side and sat low to the ground. Phil went to open the door for them and as they entered, Penelope was immediately struck by the lush comfort of it. This was the way to fly. Huge leather seats and burl wood tables were throughout the cabin. She turned to Colton and murmured, "I thought you wanted this plane for a jump school."

"We do, but we also plan to sometimes work as an executive charter as well." He reached down to the edge of the carpeting to show her the tracks on the floor. "Everything in here can come out when we use it for parachuting." She nodded as she continued further into the lush cabin.

Colton went into the cockpit with Phil and they started talking specs and engine capabilities. Penelope wasn't interested in the mechanical details so she blocked them out. She sat down in one of the leather chairs. This was so much more luxurious than she'd expected.

She pictured what she knew about the three guys running Mad Rob. Sure, they had their moments, but this level of sophistication wasn't what she saw when she thought about them living their dream. They were not suit and tie kind of guys and they definitely weren't the type to pander to the whims of the rich and powerful. She looked back out the window into the hangar. Again, the red plane in the corner caught her eye.

As the men stepped back into the cabin of the plane, Colton's eyes immediately sought her out. He gave her a searching look and she tried to give him an encouraging smile.

Phil watched their quiet interaction before he said, "I'll give y'all a few minutes to poke around. I'll be waiting for you outside when you're ready to look at the other plane."

"Thanks, Phil. We'll be out in a few minutes."

After Phil disembarked, Colton turned to her. "Well, what do you think?"

"It's really nice, but much fancier than I expected. I can't see a bunch of college kids hanging out in here." She looked around again at the lush appointments.

"Yeah, you're right. This is perfect for executive charters, but that isn't where we want to concentrate our business right now, although we do plan to do some." He looked around the interior of the plane again, scowling in thought. "Let's go see the other plane he has to show us."

When they rejoined Phil, he started leading them towards the area of the hangar with the red plane. Penelope felt a flutter of excitement, but was surprised when Colton gave an extra squeeze to her hand. Did he feel it, too?

Across the distance of the hangar, she'd just thought the plane was red, but it was so much more. The bottom of the plane was white and the top three-quarters of it was red. The two colors were separated by a black stripe which took a lightning-like zigzag right below the cockpit windows. The wings and the tip of the tail were painted shiny black. There were two propellers on the plane…each on a wing and both of these were painted with black and white stripe. The plane was gorgeous and simply perfect for Lubbock, TX where the entire town revolved around the red and black color scheme of Texas Tech. It was fun, but still classy.

She could already imagine the Mad Rob logo painted onto the tail of the plane. Did they have a logo yet? They'd need to get one soon, so they could put it on this plane.

When they stopped below the door of the perfect red plane, Phil told them about it. "The is the de Havilland Twin Otter. It's a little bit older plane and not quite as fancy, but it's been well-maintained and I think it may work for y'all's outfit." He opened the door and led them into the cabin.

This was more along the lines of what Penelope imagined Mad Rob flying, although it was still much bigger than she'd originally pictured. In fact, this plane was bigger than the first one was. The interior here was more functional rather than luxurious. There were rows of two seats on one side of the plane and a row of single seats on the other side. The grey canvas seats complemented the red and black color scheme perfectly.

When she glanced over at Colton, he looked like a kid in a candy store. His eyes were alight with excitement. A frisson of awareness snaked through her body. She liked seeing him like this…carefree and happy.

As he continued to talk mechanical details with Phil, she thought about Cassie's reaction to them last night. There was no denying they had fantastic chemistry. But Cassie was right; she didn't have staying power when it came to relationships. Normally she went out with guys who knew the score. She wasn't looking for a long-term attachment. She wanted a fun fling and most guys were perfectly fine with that. As long as both parties stayed monogamous for the duration of their time together, it was all good. It was just a matter of fact that the duration didn't usually last more than a month or two.

Would Colton want more than that? If he did, could she give him that? In her experience, guys in long-term relationships had certain expectations for how their significant other should act. Colton already had control issues. She could only see those becoming worse if they were actually involved. That wasn't control she was willing to give up. She'd tried living that way with her parents. She didn't work that way. She needed her freedom to be completely herself.

She'd been so lost in thought; she'd missed Phil leaving the plane until Colton sat down in the seat beside her. He reached over and gently grasped her chin and kissed her softly. Even this soft, gentle touch left her aching for more. She lifted her eyes to his as he released her. She could get lost in those navy blue depths.

"Hey," he said, low and soft.

"Hi." She smiled up at him. She could really fall for this guy. Wait, fall for him? No, she wasn't falling for Colton. She frowned in consternation. He was all wrong for her.

He reached up and smoothed the frown line between her eyebrows. "Why are you looking so serious all of a sudden? I'm the one sinking my life savings here."

She ignored the first question. "So you're buying it?"

He grinned widely. "I think so. I still have to make sure Chris and Jake agree, but I don't see why they won't. This is exactly what we're looking for. I told Phil to draw up the paperwork."

She didn't want to give him the wrong idea, but she was so excited for him. This new endeavor in his life meant so much to Colton and his future. She threw her arms around him. "Colton, that's wonderful. I knew as soon as I saw this plane, it was the right one for you all."

***

Dinner at Penelope's parents' house. When they got back from the airport and heard the message from Penelope's mom summoning them both to dinner, Colton's nerves went into overdrive. Meeting the parents caused most guys moments of panic, but they weren't even dating yet, so this shouldn't be an issue for him. It was the 'yet' that caused the issue here.

The more time he spent with Penelope, the more he realized he'd been wrong about her. He really liked her. He found her incredibly sexy. No, not sexy. Fuck. He was getting ready to go meet her parents. No thinking about sex. He looked longingly into the kitchen at the cabinet that held the hard liquor. Maybe one shot or five wouldn't be a bad idea for tonight.

Colton was just about to head toward that cabinet when he heard the sound of high heels walking down the hall. He turned as Penelope stepped out of the hall and his breath caught.

She wore tight black pants that hugged every curve of her long, fantastic legs. Her top was a red and white polka-dot and it shouldn't have been sexy, but with its spaghetti straps, he got to see more of those tantalizing birds of her tattoo. He really needed to find out that whole story, preferably while tracing exactly where all those birds flew all over her body.

She'd tied her wavy golden hair up into a high ponytail and tied it off with a red scarf that fluttered down her back. Wrapped around her wrist, she'd tied another red scarf so that it looked like an accessory and camouflaged where her sprained wrist was still wrapped. Makeup covered the lingering bruises which were almost completely faded anyway. She had draped her bangs to artfully hide the stitches. The entire outfit was finished off by super-high red heels with a tiny strap that buckled around her ankles.

Overall, the effect was pin-up girl worthy and incredibly sexy. He started his internal mantra of plane checklists so he wouldn't get any harder than he already was. It was going to be a long night. With her parents. And his erection. Fuck.

He smiled at her quizzical look. "You look beautiful."

"Thanks, you look pretty nice yourself."

Colton pulled the door to the loft shut and locked the deadbolt.

"I don't think you've ever met my parents before, have you?"

"No." And there went those nerves again.

Penelope gave him a sour look. "Then I probably should warn you." She hesitated. "They can be a bit much, but don't let them bother you. They're just very set in their ways. They never understood me as a child and that's affected things." She shrugged as if indifferent, but the stubborn tilt of her chin told of very different feelings under the surface of what she said. "Just don't let them get to you. The night won't last forever, right?" She gave him what he assumed was supposed to be an encouraging smile, but he felt more sick and nervous now than he had before.

They'd walked down to the parking garage as they talked, but they both stopped dead when they looked at the Bus with its broken window. They hadn't been able to get it into the shop yet. "Crap, I forgot about that," Penelope moaned.

"It's okay. We'll take my motorcycle. Just let me run back up and grab the helmets," He looked over her outfit critically and added, "I'll get your jacket."

"Thanks Colton." She turned back toward the Bus as he headed back to the elevator, but he didn't miss Pen's comment under her breath. "Arriving on a motorcycle will start the night off great. Mom's going to love it." She sighed deeply.

***

Riding to Penelope's parents' house on the motorcycle was nothing like the ride earlier in the day to the airport. That ride was pure eroticism as Colton felt Penelope's curves pressed up against him. On this ride, all he could feel was the tautness of her body and muscles.

Finally, they arrived at the gated community where her parents lived. Penelope's hair hadn't quite survived the helmet-covered ride, so she ripped out the scarf and banded it around her head, leaving her golden locks flowing in wild disarray down her back. How did women restyle so quickly like that? The stitches in her forehead caught his eye and he was happy to see that the bruising around them was virtually non-existent now.

Penelope noticed him looking at them, brushed her bangs back over her forehead, and warned him, "By the way, my parents don't know about the break-in at the store. I'm just clumsy, okay?"

He frowned at her. "Why lie?"

"It's complicated. You'll understand better after meeting them. Just try to go along with whatever I say." She looked at him tentatively and chewed her bottom lip.

He tugged her lip out from under her teeth and rubbed it gently wishing he could lick that lip. "It'll be fine. Just try to relax." He gave her an encouraging smile and linked his fingers with hers and drew her up the door.

The door swung open before he got a chance to raise his hand and knock. He got his first look at Dr. Pruitt and wasn't encouraged by the distaste reflected on her face. Her immediate focus was on the motorcycle parked in the drive behind them. She pursed her lips then turned to Colton and offered him a lukewarm smile. She didn't even try to hide her perusal and he got the feeling he didn't pass inspection. That was a first. He always made a good first impression.

Penelope introduced them. "Mother, this is my new roommate, Colton Robertson. Colt, this is my mother, Dr. Anna Pruitt."

Colton reached out a hand to shake hers. "I'm pleased to meet you, Dr. Pruitt. You have a lovely home."

"Thank you, but please call me Anna. Do come in. Penelope, your father is back in the library. You haven't been by to visit him since his return from Europe and he's missed you." The recrimination in her voice was undeniable. "Why don't you two go join him for a drink? I'll take your jackets." With one last frown back toward the motorcycle she closed the door behind them.

"Thank you, Mother. That sounds nice." As Penelope shrugged out of her jacket, Anna, who was standing behind her, gasped.

"A tattoo? Please tell me that isn't real. Tell me you haven't destroyed your beautiful skin like that. First a motorcycle and now a tattoo? Penelope, what are you thinking?" She turned to scowl at Colton like he single-handedly corrupted her daughter. He felt like laughing at the thought, but didn't think that would go over too well either.

"Mother, stop scowling at Colton. I got the tattoo months ago, long before he moved in. It's just been cold so it's been covered up and you couldn't see it. In fact, it was my last roommate, Frankie, who gave it to me. As for the motorcycle, we're perfectly safe. Colton's a good driver and we both wore helmets. There's no need to over-react. We're going to go find Dad now."

She dragged Colton down a long hall. Before they entered the room, she stopped him, took a deep breath and nodded back toward the direction they'd come. "Sorry about that."

She looked so distressed he wanted to take her in his arms and comfort her. "Don't worry about it. I'm used to dealing with angry generals. I can handle your mom. It's okay. Shall we go see if I can make a better impression on your dad?"

She laughed softly and that simple sound helped to relax him a bit. "You should be fine with him. He's definitely easier to get along with than my mother."

They entered the library. Obviously, Penelope came by her love for books naturally. The room was massive with wall-to-wall shelving full of books. Seated at a very large desk was a bearded and distinguished gentleman who had to be Penelope's father. He was so engrossed in his book he didn't even notice them come into the room.

Penelope turned to look at him with humor filling her eyes before she cleared her throat. "Daddy," she said softly.

He looked up, startled, before he realized who was in the room. He gave a glowing smile to his daughter as he stood up and reached around the desk to greet them. He was a tall man, easily as tall as Colton, but he had a lankier build. With his grey beard, mustache, and glasses, he had the professor look down. Colton would guess both her parents were in their early 60's, but they carried their age very lightly. He could only hope to look this healthy when he became that age.

As they exchanged introductions and pleasantries, her father beamed at Penelope, until he spotted her stitches. He moved closer to her and brushed aside her hair. "What happened?"

It didn't escape Colton's notice that Pen's mom saw the motorcycle and tattoo, but it was her father who saw her injury.

She deflected and waved her hand to brush the subject aside. "Aw, you know me....just clumsy. It's no big deal."

Her father looked at her with suspicion and then looked at Colton for affirmation of her story. He wasn't comfortable with that so he tried to change the subject. He looked around the room. "You have quite the library here, sir. It's impressive."

"Hmm, thank you." He wasn't buying Colton's diversionary tactic. Luckily, Anna came in and told them dinner was ready so they adjourned to the dining room. Colton sat across from Penelope at the dinner table with her parents on the ends. After several subtle stabs from her mother about everything from her manners to her life choices during the salad course, Penelope withdrew into herself. She stared down at her plate and toyed with her food. He didn't understand how a parent could treat their own child this way. Granted, it had been a long time since he had parents, but he knew that they should be supportive, especially of their adult children. Why couldn't her mother see what an amazing person Pen was and be proud of that? Why would she want to change her? Couldn't she see that Penelope was near perfect just the way she was? He gripped his fork tightly. He didn't like seeing the normally bubbly Penelope subdued like this.

The cook brought in the main course for the evening. The salmon looked and smelled succulent, but Colton frowned at Penelope's plate which held the same entrée. Surely, her own mother knew she was a vegetarian. Penelope noticed his frown and gave him a subtle shake of her head. She didn't want him to make waves, but he didn't understand why her mother wouldn't cater to her eating habits when she invited her to dinner.

Penelope looked decidedly uncomfortable toying with the salmon, so Colton decided to put some of his small-talk skills into practice, if only to divert the attention off Penelope.

He turned to Anna. "Did the University come to an agreement with Damon?"

She shook her head and frowned. "No, not yet. In fact, there was an issue at the El Regalo dig site and Dr. Lopez had to return unexpectedly."

Penelope looked up in mild alarm. "Damon's left town?"

Her mother nodded. "Yes, but he plans to be back within a week. Then we hope to finalize the details of our partnership."

Penelope suddenly jerked her focus to him and whispered, "El Regalo means the gift. That's the name of Damon's dig site. Could there be a connection?"

"Penelope what are you muttering about?" her mother demanded.

Colton grabbed onto what Penelope was saying. The note asked them to return the gift, around the same time Damon mysteriously and suddenly disappeared. Did he have something to do with it? He turned to ask Anna, "When did he leave? Do you know what the problem was?"

Anna shook her head, "No, I got the message this morning, but I'm not sure about the details of what happened." She looked at the two of them, perplexed. "Is there something going on between you and Dr. Lopez? You didn't do something to him, did you, Penelope?"

She brushed off her mother's question. "No, Mother, but he's a friend. Of course, I'm concerned about him." The frown was back between her eyebrows, but

Colton realized she didn't want her parents to know about the problems she'd been having, so he worked to change the subject again.

"So are you all privy to the author Penelope's bringing into the bookstore?" He tossed her a teasing smile, but her eyes widened in warning. Damn. He really needed to keep his mouth shut around this family. It was like traveling a field of land mines to figure out what the safe subjects were. Obviously, anything that meant something to Penelope was off-limits.

It was Anna who responded. "Hrmph. Knowing the owner of the bookstore, I'm assuming it's probably one of those trashy pornographic authors."

"Mother, that's not fair. Erotic romance is not porn."

But Anna wasn't going to be dissuaded from her tirade. "When I think about you wasting your life and what my sister has done to you. You could have been so much more than a clerk. It's such a waste of your abilities and the opportunities we gave you."

Colton's anger levels had been simmering all evening, but in the face of Anna's disgust with her daughter, he couldn't stand it anymore. "Now wait just a minute. Penelope does an amazing job at the bookstore. She…"

Penelope interrupted him. "Colton, it's okay."

"No, it's not. Has she even been in the bookstore to see what you've built there? Your bookstore is wonderful and what you've created there is a huge contribution to the community."

She looked at him gratefully with tears in her eyes and a gentle smile, before turning to her mom. "Mother, dinner was wonderful, but I think it's time for us to leave."

Her mother sputtered, "But you didn't even finish and we still have dessert to go."

Very gently but sternly, Penelope replied, "Thank you, but no, we've had enough for one evening. It's been a long day and we need to get going."

As they settled back onto the motorcycle, Penelope reached around his waist and settled her head on his back. He closed his eyes and savored the moment of closeness. "Thanks for trying to defend me, Colton."

He could hear the emotion in her voice. She'd let her mother get to her and that made him angry on her behalf. "No problem," he told her gruffly. He cleared his throat. "Are you hungry?"

He felt her nod. "Starving."

"Okay, let's go find you some food you can actually eat."

Chapter 20

Colton pulled his motorcycle up at the end of the runway outside the fenced border. Penelope looked around at the high chain link fence and the 'No Trespassing' signs posted further down. She flipped up the visor on her helmet. "Are we supposed to be here?"

He pulled his helmet off his head, got off the motorcycle and cocked an eyebrow at her. "I thought you were supposed to be the rebel in the group?" He pulled her off the motorcycle in a smooth motion and then unfastened the strap on her helmet.

She smiled at him. He really was cute when he relaxed a little bit. "Rebel meaning I'm not afraid to do my own thing. I am afraid of doing something that means I'll end up with a cellmate and playing bitch to a woman called Big Bertha."

He tilted his head, his eyes sparkling in the ambient glow off the runway lights.

"What?"

"I'm just imagining you in one of those orange jumpsuits and in a catfight."

She rolled her eyes at him. "What is it about guys and prison fantasies?"

"I don't know. I think it has something to do with stubborn women and needing to get them under control."

"Ah, yes, we're back to your Dom/sub fantasies." She winked at him. The thought of Colton dominating her in that way sent tendrils of awareness throughout her body. Tendrils that she needed to ignore if she was going to keep her distance from Colton. He was temptation personified and she definitely wanted to give into his lure.

"Well, sweetheart, a guy's gotta keep hold of his dreams."

He was dangerous to her self-control tonight. "I thought you were going to feed me. Or was that all just a ruse to lure me here?"

He reached into the saddlebag on his motorcycle where he'd stashed her veggie sub they'd picked up. Then he surprised her when he pulled out a blanket and spread it on the ground. Who knew the guy was such a romantic at heart?

As she ate, he watched her seriously. "So have things always been like that with your mom, or have things gotten worse over the years?"

She gave a bitter laugh. "No, if anything, it's actually better than it used to be." She paused and looked at him mischievously. "How old would you guess my parents are?"

"I'm guessing early 60's, although they both look really good still."

She smiled at him indulgently. "That's very nice for you to say, but you're wrong. They look amazing for their ages. Mom is 72. Dad is 75."

Colton's mouth dropped open in shock.

"I know. They were both well into their 40's when they had me. I was an accident. They both had fully established careers and a child was never in the plans for them. But they figured they were both intelligent adults and this was just another challenge for them to conquer. I was just another challenge for them to conquer." She tried not to let the bitterness bleed through in her voice. Colton reached over and pulled her to his chest so she leaned against him. She inhaled his comforting scent of masculine spice. He wrapped his arms around her and his embrace felt way more right than it should.

"So anyway, they just thought you could treat a child like an adult and that child would act like an adult. Not so much. Although I will admit, I did a pretty decent fitting into their expectations until puberty and then everything went to hell."

"What happened?"

"Like anything else, it built up over time, but the final blowout was between my mom and me when I was thirteen. Eighth grade isn't easy for girls and I was no exception. I was discovering boys and wanted to fit in at the same time I was trying to find my own identity. But mom refused to see that I needed to be something other than her little clone." She closed her eyes and thought back to that horrible day. "We were at a Geography Bee. God, I hated those things, but my parents always insisted I participate. The only intent is to show the world how smart you are. I mean seriously, it's all about ego for one kid. The winner. For everyone else, it's just a lesson in humiliation because you weren't as smart as that other kid."

She took a deep breath. "My mom left for a little bit and I was sitting in a corner backstage when a boy and his father came through. It was awful. The father threatened this kid with what would happen to him if he didn't win and what he said was horrific." Her voice broke a bit as she remembered him. "I'd always seen this kid around, but never knew him. He was shy and quiet. When it came down to the end, it was just him and me. I couldn't do it. I couldn't let him face that fate so I blew the match on purpose. My mom knew it and was irate. Losing was not an option in our household, at least not when it came to academics. That day was a turning point. I decided they weren't going to decide my fate any longer. I make my own fate."

"Do you know what happened to the boy?"

Her eyes filled with tears. "Yes, seven weeks after that, he was beaten to death by his father when he came in second at another academic contest." She shuddered. "Thankfully, by that point, I'd refused to enter any more of those things so I wasn't there, but I always felt like I should have done something more for him. I'd told my mom what I'd heard, but she was so mad at me at the time, she didn't pay attention to what I said. I should have done more to get him help."

"You can't blame yourself for that. You were just a kid, too." His voice had gone low and quiet.

"I know that. In my mind I recognize that, but you can't help looking back on those types of things and wondering. My parents had their moments where they were truly awful, but they never laid a hand on me and I definitely pushed their buttons over the years." She looked up at him over her shoulder, needing to lighten the moment. "Do you know the story of Odysseus's Penelope?"

"Noo…" he said slowly. "Surely, I've heard it, but I don't remember it."

"It's a bit convoluted, but the overall message is true. Penelope was Odysseus's wife. When he went off to war, he was gone for a long time and she had many suitors. She put them off by saying she had to finish weaving her father's funeral shroud before choosing another lover. She wove on it lovingly all day, every day and then at night she would unravel all her work. They say she's the model for loyalty and faithfulness, but I say she chose her own destiny by using her brain and making it work for her. My parents chose to name me after her so…"

She shrugged and smiled up at him, but became caught in his gaze when she met his midnight blue eyes.

He looked at her like he wanted to eat her whole. He reached around to cup the side of her face while he leaned down to kiss her. His lips were soft and searching. She thought about backing away, but couldn't deny herself just one taste of him.

He lingered. He caressed. He made her feel like she was the most treasured creature on earth. As he nibbled down her neck, she lost all track of thought besides getting closer to him. She couldn't bring herself to draw away from his allure.

Pulling him around in front of her, she tugged at the buttons of his shirt. She wanted more of him. She needed to feel more of him. Finally, she got the buttons free and reached in to explore the hard lines of his torso. Goose bumps rose over the planes of his skin while she explored with her fingertips. It wasn't enough.

Her fingertip found a hard nipple and she reached down to caress it with her tongue and teeth. He groaned deep and started his own exploration. She quickly shrugged out of her jacket without raising her mouth from his chest.

Shivers rippled over her skin as she felt him kiss the swoop of the bird tattoos on her shoulder. He lowered the strap and pulled a breast free. Her breath caught as he lifted her and took the nipple into his mouth.

"Aw, God, Colton." Her voice didn't even sound like her own anymore and he took advantage of her arousal and ripped the shirt off over her head.

She threaded her fingers through his thick, dark hair as he loved on her breasts. Caught up in the sensations, she hadn't realized he'd unbuttoned her pants until his fingers slipped under her panties and caressed her heat. She gasped as he delved in and her hips automatically thrust to him. Her body was on fire as she pulled his head back to meet her fevered kisses. Her moans echoed through the night as he continued to work her body, alternating between caressing her folds and teasing her tiny bundle of nerves. It was too much. Her nerves jumped and bunched. Completely lost in the sensation, the force of her orgasm shattered her as she screamed his name.

Her body continued to convulse around his hand and he laid her back on the blanket where he swiftly removed her shoes, pants, and panties. She laid there nude watching him as he stood and removed his own pants, his hard thick erection bobbing in the soft light from the runway. He was built like a Greek god, one intent upon conquering her. He reached into his wallet for a condom, but she took it from him.

Kneeling before him, she had to take one taste. There was a drop of moisture dangling from the tip of him and she wrapped her tongue around him to capture it. He groaned hard and low as she did so and shoved his hands into her hair. She laid kisses down the vein running the full, long length of his shaft before taking him full into her mouth. His whole body shuddered at the onslaught before he pulled her away.

His voice was deep and husky as he said, "Sweetheart, you do that much longer and I'm not gonna last."

She nodded and gave him a final lick before she sheathed him in the condom. As she lay back on the blanket, she pulled him on top of her. She wrapped her legs around his waist which lined up their bodies perfectly.

At the intimate contact, they both moaned. Colton kissed her hard before he propped up to meet her eyes. He breathed heavy and shallow and passion filled his eyes. She couldn't look away as he slid into her all the way. Oh wow. This had never felt so good before. Having him within her was heaven. She tilted her hips to meet him thrust for thrust which caused another groan to escape from him. Still his gaze never left her eyes. She was trapped by the emotion she saw there as much as she was imprisoned by his hard, pulsing body. She closed her eyes to the ecstasy of it all, but when his fingers slid between them and touched her clit, they flew open again.

"Come for me, Penelope," he commanded and she had no choice but to comply. She screamed his name and as her internal muscles captured and milked his shaft, he moaned and shuddered in his own release.

They lay there panting and tried to recover. Colton lowered his head to the side of her neck and rained little touches and kisses there. He stayed up on his elbows to avoid crushing her and she moved her hands over the muscles of his back. Even in the cool of the night, he'd developed a sheen of sweat and he shivered from her caresses. He remained within her and she wasn't ready to give up that closeness yet. She held onto him to keep reality at bay.

Slowly he pulled out of her. The glide against her swollen sex caused her to groan again. He caressed her cheek. "Are you okay?"

Words were still beyond her at this point so she simply nodded. He kissed her forehead before taking care of the condom. He laid back on the side of the blanket and pulled her into his embrace while tugging the other edge of the blanket up over them to protect them from the cool of the night.

They must have dozed because she was startled awake by a loud noise. She jerked and Colton tightened his embrace around her. "It's okay. It's just a plane coming in for a landing."

She watched as the belly of a plane flew, what felt like inches above their bodies, heading for the runway. She grinned up at him after the noise ended. "That was amazing."

"Thank you, sweetheart. I do try."

She laughed and pushed at him. "Not you, the plane." The heat rose on her cheeks. "Although you were pretty amazing, too," she said softly and he kissed her lightly on the forehead.

"Unfortunately, amazing or not, I think we need to leave our little love nest here and see about doing this on a real bed with heat, because it's starting to get cold out here."

Chapter 21

Colton rolled over and reached to drag Penelope to him, but his arm only encountered cold sheets. He pried his tired eyes open and scowled at the empty space where her delectable body was supposed to be located. Nope, she wasn't there. He ran a hand over his tired face and hair as he looked over at the clock.

He must have dozed off again. The last time he'd looked at the clock was forty-five minutes before. At that point in time, Penelope had definitely still been heating up his sheets and body.

He heard the ring of his cell phone and groaned internally when he saw the number. Impeccable timing as usual, but he was not going to let her ruin his morning.

He answered the phone, "Did you do what I told you?" He paused, listening to her stutter through a non-answer. "Well, then we have nothing to discuss. You need to do what I said or you will live to regret crossing me." He growled into the phone, cutting off her excuses, before he jammed the off button. He didn't want to push Dianna, but he was not going to give in on this.

Massaging his temples, he closed his eyes. He and Penelope had a wonderful night.

It was time to get back to that happy place, which made him wonder. Where the hell did Penelope go?

After worshipping her body all night long, it was no wonder he'd drifted off for a little bit, but why wasn't she here dozing with him? He hoped she wasn't having second thoughts. If last night had proven anything to him, it was just how compatible they really were. He never would have guessed it two weeks ago.

It was time to drag her back in here, because he wasn't ready to let her out of his bed yet. Renewed with purpose, he flung the covers off, just as Penelope walked into the room carrying a tray laden with coffee cups and food. Relief flooded him.

She paused inside the door, her eyes guarded, but she still took in the sight of his nude body with obvious pleasure. "Damn, it's just not fair that you can look so sexy after a night with hardly any sleep." Her smile bordered upon the edge of leering as she came over and set the tray on the nightstand.

He was sitting up half in and half out of bed and she came over to stand next to him. "Good morning," she said shyly, but shy was not on his agenda this morning.

He snagged her around her waist and pulled her into his embrace, noting that she held herself awfully stiff after the wonderful night they had together. "Good morning. I missed you when I woke up."

She'd pulled on one of his t-shirts when she'd gotten up. It fell to mid-thigh and now as he reached up underneath it, he was thrilled to find she'd gone commando while preparing their breakfast. He palmed the tight curve of her ass and groaned low as the blood flooded his erection once more. She twisted out of his arms laughing, but it didn't sound like her normal carefree laugh. He frowned at her, concerned with her sudden stiffness.

"You're insatiable, but you need sustenance if you plan to keep this up." She pushed him up against the headboard, but gently caressed his ever-present erection before setting the tray of food on the bed. "Besides you don't want your breakfast and most importantly your coffee to get cold."

Maybe he'd misread her. "Coffee?" He perused the tray.

She grinned at him as she handed him his cup. "I thought that might pique your interest."

"Sweetheart, nothing competes with you for my interest this morning, but I'll make do with coffee and breakfast...for now."

She crawled into the bed on the other side and snagged some juice and toast off the tray. She cleared her throat. "So, this was nice." She gestured toward the bed, looking somewhat embarrassed.

"Nice? Is that all?" His eyes sparkled as he teased her.

She flushed bright red and he almost felt bad for giving her a hard time. He reached over and tilted her chin up so he could kiss her. "I thought it was nice, too... really nice."

They ate in silence for a few moments and he tried to take measure of where she was mentally this morning. He couldn't see any obvious signs of regrets, but he got the feeling that something was off with her. He wondered what was going through her mind. Her expression became serious as he watched her eat.

"Do you have to go into the bookstore today?"

She nodded. "Yeah, I have to finalize the details about the book signing. With everything else going on, I haven't been giving it the attention it deserves." She chewed on her lip for a bit. "We never heard from them again, do you think it's over?" He knew exactly who she meant by *them*.

He shook his head. "I don't know. It just doesn't feel right. That was too easy. I'm also curious about what's going on with your buddy, Damon."

"I'll touch base with him later today and see if I can feel him out about what's going on."

"Okay. I'll take you into the bookstore. Then I'll take the Bus to get the window fixed. I don't want you leaving the store today. Just wait for me and I'll come pick you up. I also need to talk with Cassie…".

She interrupted and he noticed that her face had paled. "Listen, Colton, while this was really fabulous," she waved her hand in between them, "it doesn't make you responsible for me. I'm still a big girl and can take care of myself. Just because we slept together doesn't mean I need a keeper."

"No," he said slowly, "it doesn't. But the fact you've been targeted twice in a week does."

"There's no reason to believe there's still a threat. We haven't heard anything in at least twenty-four hours. I'll be fine."

He gritted his teeth but didn't get a chance to answer.

"Tell me if it's none of my business," she began, "I know a little bit about your marriage from Cassie, but you never talk about her. What happened with Dianna? Was that who called earlier?"

He grimaced. He hoped she hadn't heard him. His failed marriage was certainly not something he wanted to think about after a night filled with amazing orgasms. "We had unrealistic expectations from each other." He really didn't want to say anything more. His desire for a family had overridden any common sense when it came to his ex-wife. He'd been unable to see she just wanted the prestige of being a pilot's wife. She didn't understand the sacrifices his job involved, for both of them.

For his part, he'd been looking for someone to come home to and a family to call his own. He wanted to recapture that magic he'd known before his parents died. They'd been a family. A full unit. All of them against the world. Dianna seemed like a good fit until they actually got married. Then he realized he honestly knew nothing about her. It only took them six months before they mutually agreed they'd made a mistake.

Penelope nodded her head at his brief statement and a chill settled on his spine. Her eyes were suddenly devoid of all emotion. She finished off her toast, brushed off her hands, and leaned over and gave him a short kiss. "Well this has been fun, but don't have any expectations from me. I'm not someone you can fit into the mold you see for your world. I'm responsible for me and only me. Thanks though for the fabulous use of your incredible body."

Colton recoiled at the swift kick to his gut. "Now wait a minute…"

But Penelope didn't give him a chance to say anything more as she bounced up and flung her hair off her shoulders. Her voice rose an octave or two as she airily said, "You understand, we probably shouldn't do this again. We don't need any confusion about our friendship if we want to continue living together. I'll get myself to work today. No need to worry yourself. I'm not your responsibility." Then she breezed out of his bedroom and into her own.

Colton sat there stunned and wondered where the morning had gone so wrong.

***

Penelope sunk to the floor of her shower. The water hadn't warmed up yet, but she barely noticed the cold water flowing over her body. It didn't compare to the shattering of her heart. She could never get involved with someone who spoke to their ex that way. She'd learned a little something over the years. She knew better than to get involved with a dominant man. That way only meant heartache and pain for her. She needed to cut her losses now.

Unrealistic expectations is what he'd said. Yes, like wanting her to agree to his every demand. She heard the way he'd talked to Dianna. He was in full control and commanding her to do his bidding. The sheets weren't even cold before it started with Penelope. He wanted, no demanded, she do things his way without any chance for discussion.

What was it about her that made others think she couldn't do or think for herself? She thought Colton understood. She thought he knew the real her and the fact he didn't, hurt.

Cassie tried to warn her that she and Colton weren't a good fit, but Penelope just couldn't believe that could she. She ignored all the warning signs and fell for him anyway…body and soul. But regardless of how her heart was breaking, she knew she could never give Colton what he needed. He needed to be in charge and that wasn't something she could ever submit to. She couldn't mold herself around someone else's needs. It was better to end things now than to get her heart more embroiled in their liaison. Breaking it off now would just save further heartache later.

Her body still felt the lingering effects of their incredible night of passion, and she wasn't sure she would ever be able to recover from loving Colton. Right now she would be okay if she could just figure out how to live with him and return to their platonic friendship without this ravaging pain ripping through her chest.

Chapter 22

Colton pulled his motorcycle over to the side of the road so he could make a phone call. He'd been riding around aimlessly for over an hour and was still no closer to understanding where he'd gone wrong this morning. After an amazing night and some startling revelations this morning, suddenly he faced a future without Penelope in it. The knot in his gut grew tighter. He couldn't accept this, but he couldn't fix it unless he could figure out what he'd done wrong. There was one person who might be able to help. He listened to the phone ring.

"Hey big brother. What are you doing calling me so early? I thought you were a man of leisure. Shouldn't you be sleeping in and enjoying these days of freedom?"

"Hey Cassie. I need your help. Do you have any classes in the next hour?"

"No, I'm free. Is everything okay?" He could hear the concern in her voice.

"Yeah, everything's fine… well, sort of. I just need some advice. I'll explain when I get there. Do you mind meeting me at The Mocha Mermaid?"

She hesitated for a moment before answering. "Sure, I'll be there in ten minutes."

Colton beat Cassie to the coffee shop so he went ahead and ordered her non-fat latte. He'd just gotten their drinks when she walked in the door and he didn't miss the flash of panic as she looked at the baristas working behind the counter.

Damn, he hadn't been thinking when he suggested they meet here. Three months before, the stalker who kidnapped her worked as a barista here.

He enveloped her into a hug as she reached the table. "I'm sorry. I wasn't thinking. I already have our coffees. Do you want to take them somewhere else?"

Her laugh sounded brittle, but she admonished, "Don't be silly. He's not here. I know that. He's dead and I shouldn't let the memory of him keep me from my favorite coffee shop. He wins if I let his memory affect me that way."

"Have you been in here since then?"

"No, but thanks for pulling me back. I needed the push. I love their lattes and this place is too convenient for me to stay away." She turned her gaze from the counter back to him, searching. "So what's going on with you? I'm guessing this might have something to do with Penelope. Am I right?"

He grimaced. "How'd you guess?"

"You two were looking awfully close Saturday night and you do live together. It's only safe to assume that things might have progressed since then."

"Progressed and then regressed." He stopped. How did he explain the situation to his little sister without getting into his sex life? Maybe this was a bad idea, but as one of Pen's closest friends, she had to have some insight as to where her thought-process was.

He rubbed his hand over his face and thought about the conversation that fell all to hell this morning. He looked at her. "Yesterday was great. Actually better than great. We connected. We spent the whole day together and it was fucking fabulous. Well, except for maybe dinner with her parents."

Cassie stopped him, her eyes wide. "You had dinner with her parents? How did that happen? I can't imagine Penelope taking you there by choice."

"No, we were out all day and when we got home there was a message on the machine from her mother saying we were expected for dinner, both of us. I'm guessing she wanted to check me out as the new roommate."

She chuckled. "I bet that was exciting."

He rolled his eyes at her before shaking his head. "Yeah, not so much. I don't understand how parents can behave that way. Aren't they supposed to love unconditionally?"

"Unfortunately, Pen got the short end of the stick when it comes to parents. But we're getting off track. What's the issue?"

"After we left her parents' house, we went out and talked for a long time which naturally moved to other things." The blush rose up his cheeks. God, this was embarrassing.

Cassie rolled her hand. "Yeah, keep talking. I understand what 'other things' means. So I'm not seeing an issue here yet, unless," she paused and eyed him with a certain amount of dread pouring through her gaze, "…unless you had some sort of performance issues." Now she was beet red, too.

"Cassie! Fuck, no, that's not what I'm here to talk to you about. Fuck, why, if that was even the issue and believe me, it's not… Why would you think I'd choose to discuss that with you? Shit." He sunk his face into his hands wondering when he'd lost control of the conversation and if it was too late to just say 'forget it'.

"Okay, okay. Calm down. We're both going to need bleach for our brains after this talk." She reached over and pulled his hands off his head to get his attention.

"Okay so everything went fine there. Why are you freaking out?"

"Because this morning, she totally freaked out on me and I have no idea what I did wrong. It seemed fine at first. No awkwardness like I expected." He shook his head remembering back on this morning. "She brought me breakfast in bed and we were just eating it and talking."

"What were you talking about?"

"Our plans for the day. Me taking the Bus in to get it fixed after I dropped her off at work. Mundane, boring things." Cassie nodded, but a frown formed between her eyes. He continued. "Then out of the blue she asked me what happened between Dianna and me and why we got divorced."

"Okay, what did you tell her?"

"I told her that we had unrealistic expectations from each other, which we did. That doesn't seem so earth-shattering to me. It was like this wall went up for Pen though. She started acting all breezy. She thanked me for the use of my body, but we probably shouldn't do it again. All of a sudden, instead of the brilliant, confident, intelligent woman I'd spent the last two weeks with, suddenly there was this flighty, airy, party-girl that I always thought Penelope to be."

Cassie winced. "Aw, Colton, what did you do?"

"Wait a min…."

"Let's back up. When you were discussing your plans for the day, was it a discussion or were you telling her how things were going to go?"

He frowned at her as he tried to figure out what she was getting at. She interrupted him before he even got a chance to answer.

"Never mind, I know the answer to that question. You did what you always do. You dictated to her how the day was going to go. Didn't you learn anything from your visit with her parents last night?"

"I learned her mother doesn't care one bit about her feelings or wants."

"Bingo. She was raised under that extremely controlling thumb of her mother always telling her how to act, how to dress, how to think."

"I know, but…"

"There's no 'but' here. Someone telling Penelope what to do is a major hot-button for her. I know you already realize Penelope is smart, but you probably don't realize just how smart she really is. She has an IQ of over 170 and made a perfect score on her SAT's. By the way, she didn't tell me that. Her mother did. What did she do with all that brilliance? Do you know what her degree is in?"

He shook his head.

"She earned her degree in Theater Arts…acting. She did that entirely to get out from under her parents' tutelage. She has such an aversion to someone trying to bend her to their will, she'll do anything including sabotaging her own life. Why do you think she developed the party girl attitude?"

He felt more and more sick as Cassie talked, but he still wasn't quite getting the full gist of what she was saying. "I'm not sure."

"No one has expectations from the spacey, party girl. They figure she's in her own little world and leave her to it. That's all Penelope wants…to keep control of her own world. From the sounds of it, this morning you tried to take control of her world and she reacted the way she always does. That's her defense mechanism at work and this morning you triggered it."

"So how do I fix this?" There had to be a way to fix it.

Cassie looked at him and started shaking her head. "Colt, you're a control freak. I'm not sure you can fix it.

Everything about you is hard-wired to take control of the situation and move it according to your dictate. Penelope doesn't work like that. She can't work like that. Her entire life has been spent trying to pull herself out of that type of situation."

"I can't accept that."

Her voice softened. "And therein lays your problem." She reached across and grabbed hold of his arm. "Colt, you may not be able to fix this and if you try, you're both liable to get hurt even more."

As he raised his eyes to hers, she gasped. "It's too late, isn't it? You're in love with her."

Chapter 23

Penelope looked at the clock on her cell phone. Ugh, it was only 11:32. This day was never going to end. It held such promise when she woke up this morning in Colton's arms, but quickly degenerated into a clusterfuck of grand proportions.

She took the Bus in to get the window fixed, but ran into a major roadblock. The VW Bus was from an earlier era and there weren't that many parts available anymore. It meant she'd lost her transportation for the whole freaking week while they waited for a part to come in.

Hannah didn't show up for her shift so they were shorthanded at the bookstore when she already had a million and a half other things that needed her attention.

She tried to smile at the customer eyeing her from the New Fiction section, but it probably looked as bad as it felt. She felt brittle... like she could shatter at the slightest provocation. Alix kept shooting her questioning looks, but luckily they'd been too busy for Alix to corner her yet. Thank God, it was almost time for Jon to arrive so she could retreat into the corner of her office. She didn't know how much longer she could be pleasant with the customers and not burst into tears.

At that moment, the bell above the door rang and relief surged through her as Jon walked in. She only had to hold it together for a few more minutes. She gave him a tight smile and greeting as she came around the back of the desk. She was halfway up the stairs to her office when the bell rang again.

Out of habit, Penelope looked to see who entered. Her breath caught and the tears surged forth as Cassie walked in. No, no, no. She couldn't deal with this today. Not today.

Cassie took one look at her tear-brimmed eyes and rushed over to her side. She gathered her into a huge hug before Penelope could escape. Penelope couldn't say anything as the pressure on her chest suffocated her and she valiantly tried to gain control of her emotions.

"Is anyone else here besides Jon?"

She nodded and managed to croak out, "Alix."

Cassie pursed her lips and gave her a sympathetic smile. "Okay, good." She turned to Jon. "Can you let Alix know I'm taking Pen to lunch?"

"Sure," he said, watching them curiously.

"Thanks. I'll bring her back in a couple of hours."

When they got to Cassie's jeep, she pushed her into the seat and handed her a wad of tissues. Cassie patiently waited while the sobs subsided.

"I'm sorry. God, I don't usually get this emotional. It must be hormones."

Cassie pursed her lips. "Or… it could be your heart is breaking and you don't know what to do about it."

Penelope looked into the eyes of her best friend, but also Colton's sister. "So is this where you say, 'I told you so'?"

"Nope. This is where I take you out to get some good chocolate, continue to hand you tissues, and try to talk some sense into you. You know he really likes you right?"

Penelope's eyes started to tear up again as she nodded. "It seemed like it."

"There's no 'seemed' about it, Pen. He came and saw me this morning and he's just as torn up about this as you are." She waved at the pile of tissues in Penelope's lap. "Except he's more of a guy... he does it without the waterworks and emotional display." She glanced over to Penelope as she drove. "Regardless of the evidence to the contrary right this minute, I may have been wrong."

Penelope gave a bitter laugh. "How do you figure? It seems to me you were right on the mark this time."

"Maybe on the surface, but I've never seen you this torn up over a guy before. That alone tells me this is something more...maybe something worth fighting for."

"Do you really think so?" Did she dare to hope?

Cassie nodded. "At least consider it. Obviously I'm biased because both of you fall into my favorite people category, but you could find some sort of compromise to make this work. Colt's not unreasonable. Yes, he's overbearing and domineering, but he's still a good guy. Talk to him about it. Tell him what you're feeling. See if you can find some sort of middle ground."

What Cassie said made sense. Yes, it meant opening up for possibly more hurt further down the road. But when she thought about last night, Penelope's body reacted with tingles and chills even though it had been several hours since she'd seen Colton. That had to mean something. It also meant something that she wanted to pick up the phone to talk to him, even though he was the one who upset her. Already she relied on him for his friendship and support.

They pulled into a parking spot at the local cupcake bakery and Penelope smirked at Cassie. "I thought we were going to eat lunch."

Cassie feigned an innocent look. "What? They're full of cocoa beans. You're a vegetarian and beans are good for you. Besides, all those tears mean you need chocolate to revive your system. Chocolate is a known cure for dehydration from crying."

"Hmm, that almost sounded believable."

"Absolutely. If you say it with confidence, people will believe you. Trust me."

***

Feeling better after a couple of hours laughing with Cassie, Penelope returned to the bookstore, ready once again to tackle her huge to-do list. But first, she needed to be a friend to someone else.

She listened to the phone ring and was about to hang up when she heard a harried answer on the other end, "Dr. Lopez here."

"Damon? It's Penelope."

"Well, hey, gorgeous."

"Hey, yourself. I hear you had to head back to Belize without even a 'goodbye' for yours truly."

"I'm sorry, Penelope. Unfortunately, there was an emergency and I had to get back immediately."

"Is everything okay?"

"Of course, everything's fine."

For some reason, his answer didn't sound true. Maybe it was the false humor she could hear in his voice even over the phone line. She scowled and wondered what he was hiding. "Are you sure, Damon? Everything doesn't sound fine." No answer from him so she pressed on. "Listen, the reason that I ask is that Saturday night after the party, something happened."

"What happened? Are you okay?" He suddenly sounded frantic, but she hadn't told him the nature of the incident.

"Yes, I'm fine. Everyone's fine so far. There was a note on my Bus. It said I needed to return 'the gift' and no one would get hurt. But I have no idea what they were talking about. Last night it occurred to me maybe this has something to do with El Regalo."

"Hang on, Penelope."

She could hear muffled shouts. The mouthpiece on the phone was obviously covered with something but it sounded like Damon yelling at someone in Spanish.

"I'm so sorry. Please continue."

"Damon what the hell is going on?"

He sighed deep. "I wish I could explain, but I can't. This is just a very difficult country to work in and problems arise because of that. But we were talking about you and your issues. Have you had any more problems?"

"No and I'm hoping that stays the case."

"Okay, stay close to Colton. He'll keep you safe. I should be back in town sometime later this week. I'll give you a call then, okay?"

He was rushing her off the phone and she had no idea why. But with him out of the country, there wasn't a whole lot she could do about it.

"That sounds good Damon. I hope you get everything straightened out there."

"Thanks. Bye, Penelope."

Something wasn't right there. She lifted her shoulders to loosen the tension in them. She couldn't help Damon if he didn't want her to. Besides she had her own stresses to dwell on right now.

She hung up the phone and looked at the calendar on the wall. Twelve days until the book signing. And then a week after the signing, the next installment in the Celeste DeMarco series was due to her editor. Luckily, the first draft was done, but it still needed some hard polishing before it was ready for her editor. She had a lot of work to do. It was time to stop worrying about Damon and moping about Colton. They'd talk when she got home tonight.

***

Alix gave Penelope a ride home since her Bus was in the shop for the duration. Her stomach did flip-flops at the idea of seeing Colton after this morning, but she was a big girl. She could do this. She climbed the stairs to work off the cupcakes she ate for lunch and to give her more time to plan what she needed to say. First thing, she needed to apologize for the way she'd acted this morning. She cringed at the memory of thanking him for the use of his body. That was really not cool. She would suck it up and make it up to him.

As she entered the apartment, the dead quiet revealed that Colton wasn't home. She dropped her paperwork in a chair and looked around. On the counter was a single tulip with a note attached.

```
Penelope, I had to leave town and
probably won't be home tonight. I'm
sorry. I know we need to talk and hope
you will be open to that tomorrow. Last
night was amazing. I'll miss having you
in my bed tonight. See you tomorrow. -
Colton
```

Okay, that didn't sound so bad. Maybe he wasn't mad about what a shrew she'd been this morning. She really hoped he wasn't.

She changed into some comfy pj's and poured herself a glass of wine. Colton's absence gave her the perfect opportunity to work on some of her writing. She'd printed out the rough draft of ***Dominating Clint*** at the bookstore today and was ready to go at it with her red marker.

This was the third book in the series about the Hawkins family, six brothers and two sisters running a ranch in Texas. They were definitely an erotic bunch and several of the siblings had BDSM tendencies. This particular book featured Clint, who always considered himself a Dom until he met Ashley and found out he liked to submit to this Domme's rules.

Penelope had written several books about the BDSM lifestyle, but this was the first time she'd written her heroine as the Domme. It was exciting and fun for a different change of pace. She'd even bought a tell-all book from a practicing Domme to make sure she had all her facts correct. It was most definitely titillating reading and writing.

She took a sip of her wine and imagined Colton in a submissive role. She almost snorted her wine up her nose. Like that would ever happen. She might be able to calm his controlling tendencies down a bit, but she could never imagine him letting go to that extreme.

***

Colton tiptoed into the loft. He'd hated that he had to leave town so suddenly. He'd gone to San Antonio to check on a plane for sale. It was only going to be in town for a single night so he didn't have much choice if he wanted to see it. Unfortunately, the trip was a waste as the plane wasn't going to work for Mad Rob. He hadn't planned to come back tonight. But after leaving things hanging with Penelope the way he had, he couldn't stand the thought of not seeing her. He needed to know things were okay between them.

He lowered his bag to the floor just inside the door. There was still a light on in the living room so he crept in. Penelope was sound asleep on the couch. Looking at the nearly empty wine bottle sitting next to her, he guessed she wouldn't be waking up anytime soon. She'd pulled her blonde hair up into a messy pony tail and wore some horrible flannel pajamas, but a peace settled into his heart just looking at her. He was such a goner.

She had papers and books spread all over the place and one in particular caught his eye. Just what was Penelope reading? ***My Life as a Domme***. Curious now, he took a closer look at the papers surrounding her. It appeared to be a book, but she'd obviously been marking it up. Maybe she did freelance editing or proofreading on the side.

He'd already been half-hard ever since he'd laid eyes on the sleeping Penelope, but as he read a couple of the pages, his erection came on at full-force. Whoa, this was hot stuff. He looked back over at Penelope, hoping not to get caught, but this was good reading. He sat down and read a bit more. Fuck, he needed a cold shower.

He glanced back over at Penelope and thought about their issues. She was still sound asleep and her book gave him an interesting idea. Very interesting. He snuck back out of the loft to see what he could do about putting his plan into action.

Chapter 24

Penelope rode her bicycle into the bookstore the next morning. Luckily her loft was only a couple miles away so it wasn't that much of an inconvenience. She just had to watch out for the morning University traffic. It had been too long since she'd ridden. She flexed her wrist. Her fall seemed like a lifetime ago, but it was actually just a little over a week ago. Besides a bit of residual soreness, it almost felt normal. Soon she'd be able to start back with her yoga classes. She missed her normal yoga routine and the automatic stress relief it provided for her life.

And this morning she could definitely use the stress relief more than usual. When she woke up on the couch this morning, she was surprised to find she'd fallen asleep on the couch with all her writing paraphernalia around her. But even more surprising was Colton's bag by the front door.

If he'd come home, why didn't he awaken her?

The loft was empty apart from her presence. That was so weird. Why would he come home and then leave again without saying a word to her? It just didn't make any sense. She thought back to the book she'd been writing. Did he see what she was working on?

Their relationship was already on shaky ground without adding that she wrote erotica into it. Most guys would think it was hot, but they were in the south where a lot of people, like her parents, would be scandalized and outraged. Surely Colton wasn't that guy.

In fact, he'd given every indication that he liked erotica. But was there a difference in his eyes between enjoying it and doing the actual writing of it? Who knows? God, she was going to mess up her brain trying to figure out how the male mind worked. And besides, she was jumping to some huge conclusions here.

It was probably just a case that he came home, saw her asleep and didn't want to awaken her. That's the story she'd stick to. She didn't have a choice. She had too much to do to lose another day to worrying about where things stood between her and Colt.

As she entered the store, Jon called out a cheery "Hello," from the upper floor.

"Good morning," she called as she climbed the stairs. "What are you doing up here?"

He was in the Science Fiction section with mounds of books lying everywhere. He glanced up at her ruefully. "With the book signing coming up, I thought this section needed a good overhaul." He looked down at the books spilling over the floor. "It got kind of out of control."

She laughed. "So do you have a master plan here?" She waved her hand over the mess.

"Of course I do. You know, Sylvia Roberts is a huge author in the fiction world, but a lot of her fans are romance readers because she always has a love interest in her novels. I just thought we should compound on that in the store for that weekend. Every genre has books which also feature romantic story lines."

Penelope nodded. She could see where he was going on this and it was a great plan.

"So I'm going through the section and finding the sci fi books that also have romantic story lines and turning them face-out. Maybe we can get some of her readers to cross genre lines."

"I like this idea. Good thinking, Jon. You've only done the Sci Fi section so far?"

He nodded. "Yes, it takes a while, so it's slow work."

"Okay, when I get a break, I'll start doing the same in the Mystery section."

She just wasn't sure when that break was going to happen. She needed to contact the newspaper and make sure her spots were ready to go. She also needed to check with Hannah to see if the online newsletter was going to make it out today according to their plan.

She turned back to Jon. "Hey, there weren't any messages on the answering machine this morning, were there?"

"No, should there have been?

"Not necessarily, but I hoped Hannah called."

He frowned. They were all starting to worry about her prolonged absence.

They'd never heard from her yesterday. She wasn't answering her phone and she lived alone clear across town. Without a car to go check on her, Penelope was stuck worrying. Hannah was scheduled to work later this morning. Hopefully, she'd show up.

She walked around the quiet store, checking to make sure all the bookshelves were in order. The bell on the door tinkled and she felt a surge of relief thinking Hannah had made it, but it wasn't Hannah who walked in.

"Hello, Mrs. Kincaid. How are you this morning?" Mrs. Kincaid was an avid mystery reader and one of their best customers. She read several books a week and managed to introduce the bookstore to lots of new mystery authors they never would have discovered without her.

"I'm good Penelope. It's a beautiful morning. I got a call yesterday that my order was in."

"Sure, let me find it for you." Penelope went behind the counter to check their special order shelves. That was odd. There was a pile of Hannah's things there too: some of her school books, notebooks, and a small floral zipper pouch. The employees weren't supposed to leave personal items behind.

After she rang up Mrs. Kincaid, Penelope checked the clock on the computer. Hannah was officially twenty-four minutes late. She tried calling her apartment, but there wasn't an answer. When did you know you needed to file a missing persons report? It was possible Hannah was just at her boyfriend's house and decided to blow off her job for good sex. Penelope would probably believe that if Hannah hadn't been acting strange for the last couple of weeks.

She called up to Jon, "Can you come down here for a moment?"

Jon bounded down the stairs. "What's up?" He eyed the pile of things in front of Penelope with curiosity.

"I think these belong to Hannah. Do you know?"

He nodded. "Yeah, that looks like the pile of school work she brings to work on when business is slow. Where'd you find it?"

"It was under the counter with the special orders. I'm getting a bad feeling about her. I need you here as a witness because I'm going to violate her privacy and go through this stuff to see if I can find any clues as to what may be going on with her."

He nodded his agreement with her plan.

She hated to do this, but she pulled the pile of things that belonged to Hannah toward her. She flipped through the notebooks, but didn't see anything. She handed one to Jon to see if he saw something she missed. Sucking in a deep breath because she was about to breach her employee's privacy, she unzipped the small bag. There were a couple of tubes of lip gloss, some hair accessories, a few pens, and in the very bottom a little baggie full of powder. As she drew the baggie out, Jon's worried eyes met her own.

"Drugs?" he questioned disbelievingly. "I never in a million years would have guessed she was doing drugs." He shook his head as they both looked at the mysterious powder.

"Maybe we're jumping to conclusions. Maybe it's a powder supplement to add to water or something like that." She hoped that was the case. The alternative, especially considering Hannah seemed to be missing, wasn't something Penelope wanted to think about.

"I'm going to call a detective I know and maybe he can help us. I think it's time to report her missing and someone needs to determine what's in this baggie."

She reached into the bag one last time to make sure she'd retrieved everything out of it. She could feel something else in the lining of the bag, but it appeared to be sewn in, so she would leave that to the police.

She sucked in a deep breath as she dialed Brian's number. She'd never known Hannah to be anything but a conscientious, sweet employee. She found it really hard to believe that she'd gotten mixed up in drugs, but she couldn't deny the evidence sitting right here in front of her.

"Detective Barnes," he answered.

"Hi, Brian, this is Penelope Pruitt."

"Hey, Penelope. I was planning to call you today."

"You were? Why?" A ball of dread settled into the pit of her stomach.

He chuckled low at the sound of the worry in her voice. "You know it warms my heart when people get so excited about me calling."

She smiled into the phone. "Sorry, but it seems talking to you always involves some sort of problem."

"Too true. So how about you go first. Why did you call?"

"I have an employee, Hannah Porter, who seems to have disappeared. She hasn't shown up for work the last couple of days. She's not answering her phone either. I just found a bag of hers under the counter at the store and it looks like it may have drugs in it. I wasn't sure what was the best way to proceed."

"Calling me was good. I'll come over there, say…" He paused. Penelope assumed he was checking the time or his schedule. "It looks like I can be there in about fifteen minutes to process the bag and take your statement. You're at the bookstore, right?"

"Yes, we are. Thanks, Brian. I'll see you when you get here."

When Brian arrived, he processed the zipper pouch and everything in it, so he could take it in for testing. He also promised to go by Hannah's apartment to see if he could locate her or get a lead on where she was.

Finally, he turned to Penelope, "So is there anything else you wanted to share with me?"

"Umm… no?" She looked at him, confused. "Is there something else I'm supposed to share?"

He leaned back against the counter, cocked an eyebrow at her, and crossed his arms across his chest. He looked really formidable that way. "I heard you had some excitement Saturday night."

"Oh yeah," she waved her hand in the air negligently, "the break-in on the Bus. It was weird at the time, but I haven't heard anything else from the creep, so I guess he got what he wanted."

"Hmm." Brian looked thoughtful. "If anything else like that happens, I want you to call me directly. Don't just call the police station."

"Okay," she said slowly. "You can't possibly think all this is related can you? Hannah wasn't even at that party."

"The thing is, Penelope, you've had several strange things happening around here with very few clues. The only connecting thread is that they keep happening to you."

A shiver ran down her spine at the ominous sound of Brian's words.

"Not to worry you, but you need to remain aware of your surroundings and try to keep someone else with you all the time until we get this sorted. I'll be in touch."

"Thanks Brian. I appreciate you coming down."

Chapter 25

Colton worked all day to put his plan into action. He talked to Alix earlier in the afternoon and she said she would keep Penelope at the store until 6:00. She also let him know Penelope rode her bike to work. He felt a surge of disbelief at that little fact, but since he was working to convince Penelope he could curtail his controlling tendencies, he wasn't going to give her grief over it. Instead he arranged for Cassie to pick her up after work and bring her directly to the loft.

He'd also been emphatic that Cassie not come up with her. That would be mortifying for everyone involved. Now he found himself with at least thirty minutes before Penelope showed up. Everything was ready and he was nervous.

He walked around the loft checking all the little details, hoping this worked and she didn't laugh in his face. That would be humiliating.

He needed something to steady his nerves. He went first to the liquor cabinet where he poured himself a couple fingers of whiskey. Then he walked over to the bookcase to check out the books. Reading would help calm him down. The section where Penelope kept her erotica caught his eye.

He ran his thumb across the book that Pen mentioned earlier that would appeal to him, but it was another author's books which caught his eye. Celeste DeMarco. She must be good. Penelope had nine books by her. He scanned the titles of the books and pulled out a couple which looked interesting.

He took another deep swallow of the whiskey and glanced around the loft as he tucked the books under his arm. Twenty-five more minutes. He took a deep breath, lit the candles, and left the instructions for Penelope on her arrival. With one final glance at the tools he laid there, he headed toward his bedroom, unbuttoning his shirt as he went.

***

Penelope was surprised when the bell above the door of the bookstore rang and Cassie walked in. "Well hey there, stranger. I didn't know you were coming by today. Are you checking up on me to make sure I didn't slit my wrists after yesterday's emotional debacle?"

"No, I'm actually here at the instruction of my big brother." She smiled mischievously which made Penelope nervous.

"Why would Colton send you here?"

"My instructions are to load up you and your bike and take you home."

Penelope raised an eyebrow. "Hmm, I smell a rat. How did he know I brought my bike today and why exactly do I need you to take me home?"

Cassie just shrugged but there was no missing the sparkle of amusement in her in eyes.

Penelope looked back up the stairs to where Alix continued to work on the re-shelving project. "Alix has been acting funny all day, too. She's been finding odd little jobs for me to do constantly. You wouldn't know anything about that would you?"

At that, Alix's head popped out and she looked down the stairs. "Did I hear my name?" Her focus found Cassie. "Oh hey, Cassie. Are you here to take Penelope home?"

Penelope crossed her arms across her chest. "Oh yeah, there's definitely a rat here and I'm guessing his name starts with 'C' and ends with an 'n'." She glared over at Cassie again. "So how did you get roped into doing his dirty work and why isn't he here to do it himself?"

"Calm down, Penelope. He has a plan for your evening, but I don't know what it is. Remember how upset you were yesterday. Remember how much you love the guy before you maim him. He's trying to make things right, but he's still a guy. He's going to screw it up a few times along the way. Remember he's trying, so give him the benefit of the doubt."

Alix came down the stairs and smiled at Penelope, her lips twitching the entire time.

"You were in on this, weren't you?"

"Yes, my instructions were to make sure you stayed here all day while he got everything set up for you. I don't know what he has planned tonight, but I think it's going to be good."

A flutter of anticipation rolled through her body. What was he up to now? Both her friends were still smiling but their looks were verging on worried as she took in what they told her. She should keep them wondering after they both worked with him behind her back, but she was too excited to see what he had planned.

"Okay," she smiled at them, "let's go see what kind of mischief Colt's been up to today." She looked at Cassie. "My bike's around back. Alix, I'll see you tomorrow."

"Well, since it sounds like you have an exciting night planned, I'll cover for you in the morning. Sleep in, or enjoy that big brawny man doing... whatever." She waved a hand loosely as she headed back up the stairs.

Penelope gasped. Cassie just laughed and pushed her out the door.

***

As they pulled up in front of Penelope's building, Cassie stopped in front of the doors. "This is where I stop. I've been instructed under no circumstances am I allowed to come upstairs. He was pretty emphatic about that."

Penelope rolled her eyes. "He's pretty emphatic about everything." She looked worriedly up at the building then back to Cassie. "He didn't give you any hints?"

Cassie shook her head, but she gave a gentle smile. "I think it's going to be good though. Don't worry so much. Just enjoy what he has planned."

"Okay. Thanks, Cassie. I'll call you tomorrow."

"You better. Just remember, he's my brother. No details!"

All the way up the elevator, Penelope considered things. Colton was a control freak. Case in point: he didn't want Penelope to ride her bike home so he sent his sister to bring her home. Yes, most the things he did, he did out of caring, but could she live with that? Could she give up that kind of control in her life? Could she be happy later down the road when Colton was the one in charge? When he was the one making all the decisions? The answer was still no.

She took a deep breath as she reached the front door of the apartment. She didn't know what he planned here and it made her nervous. She still needed to apologize for the hurtful things she'd said to him yesterday morning. They had a lot to work out if their relationship had a chance, but the first thing she had to do was open the door.

She took a deep breath and turned the knob.

The loft was dark as she entered, with only the flicker of candlelight illuminating the space. It created eerie, but strangely romantic, shadows all along the brick walls. There was quiet, melodic jazz playing softly over the speaker system. Penelope quickly scanned the room, but didn't see any sign of Colton. She walked toward the lit grouping of pillar candles on the countertop and noticed several items sitting nearby including a note.

```
Dearest Mistress,
     Your pleasure waits in my bedroom.
Your wants are my wants. Your needs are
my needs. I am here to fulfill your
every whim, your every command, your
every fantasy. Please join me.

Your humble servant,
Colton
```

What the hell? She looked down the darkened hall, but couldn't see him at all. The only sign was a scattering of red rose petals that were strewn about the floor where she stood. They trailed all the way down the hall to the doorway of his room.

She looked back down at the items sitting with the note. A shiver of arousal slid through her. She trailed her fingers over the items. There was a black lace mask, several ties and bindings all in black except for a single blood red silky one, and a flogger. This wasn't a flogger meant to incite pain. It was a vivid red color with at least a two dozen strands of silk ribbons knotted at the ends to make up the lashes. She picked it up and ran her fingers through those silky lashes. They were incredibly soft and supple. She glanced back down the hall to the bedroom. Still no noise besides the music. He had to be back there.

She looked down at her khaki pants and white button down shirt and grimaced. Not exactly sexy going on here. Colton had obviously considered this too, though, because her black spike fuck-me shoes were out, like they were waiting for her.

Shimmying out of her pants, she thanked the fates she'd actually worn a matching sexy panty and bra set today in light pink lace. She slid into the shoes and unbuttoned her shirt, leaving it hanging open. The black lace mask, tied around her eyes and she undid her hair from its ponytail so that it cascaded in curly waves down her back. Her transformation was complete. She felt sexy and powerful.

The rose petal trail led her down the hall. The glow of the candlelight flickered out into the hall from his room. Not knowing what to expect when she stepped into Colton's bedroom, she gasped at her first glimpse of him. He was completely nude, highly aroused, and kneeling on the floor on his knees in a position of submission. The candlelight shimmered off his broad shoulders and strong thighs. A bead of sweat dripped down the hard contours of his abs. His face was directed to the floor in supplication. A flood of arousal wet her panties. Oh my. He was gorgeous and all hers for the night. She planned to enjoy this.

***

Colton heard her indrawn gasp as she stepped into the room and hoped it was a good thing. He was dying to look at her, but he knew that wasn't his position in this scenario. He needed to show her that he could give her complete control. He was already so aroused just by the idea, he wasn't sure how much he'd be able to withstand, but he'd do this for Penelope.

She'd stepped just inside the door and he flushed knowing she had to be looking at him. Please don't let her think this idea as ridiculous. He waited and still nothing from her. No movement, no sound. He continued to look at the floor as a line of sweat dripped down his back. His hands were laced behind his back and he twisted his fingers trying to keep from looking up at her.

The smell of honeysuckle reached his nose. Her smell. His erection twitched in response.

Finally, he sensed her moving as she shifted a bit more into the room. The click-clack of her heels led to his dresser where more toys were laid out.

"You have been a busy boy, haven't you?"

"Yes, Mistress." He hardly recognized his own voice it had gone so deep in arousal. "I hope it pleases you."

She hesitated and he imagined he could feel her gaze on him. "Yes, it definitely does please me." She walked over to him and stood behind him so that he could feel the heat off her body. "Would you like to look at me, Colton?" She walked around him, but didn't touch him. He followed the line of her long, toned legs as they entered his line of vision without moving his head. He wanted to lean into her. He wanted her to touch him so badly.

"Yes, Mistress. I would like that very much."

"Since you have pleased me, you may look. For a moment."

"Thank you, Mistress." He looked up at her. He didn't think he could become any more aroused than he already was, but he was wrong. So wrong. The candlelight casted a luminous glow over her skin. From this angle, the first thing he saw were those mile-long legs in those sexy heels he'd found in her closet. Her shirt was unbuttoned and loose so that the shirttails just skimmed the tops of her thighs. He glimpsed pink lace panties with matching bra that pushed her cleavage up. He just wanted to feast upon it. He licked his lips at the thought and heard her moan softly.

Finally, he met her gaze. She was wearing the black lace mask and it made her look mysterious and sexy as hell. Her jade green eyes shimmered from the slits, lit up with arousal and excitement. His relief was palpable as he took in her look. She was definitely into this game.

"You look beautiful, Mistress."

"Thank you, Colton." She walked back over to the dresser and dragged the flogger he hadn't realized she was carrying across the toys spread out there. "I had no idea you were so kinky."

"Only with you, Mistress."

Her eyes widened in surprise.

He shrugged and smiled at her. "You inspire me."

"Hmm, very nice." She picked up a blindfold. "Are you ready to play?"

He felt like he'd swallowed his tongue. "Please."

She walked over to him and stopped in front of him. Her hand brushed over the top of his hair. He could smell her arousal. She threaded her fingers through the hair on the back of his head, pulling so that he tilted his head toward hers. She leaned down and gave him a savage kiss. It was dominance at its best and damn, he loved it. She plundered and ravaged as she kissed him. Finally when they were both gasping she pulled back from him. Her lips were swollen and wet and he wanted more, but she had other plans. Quickly she stepped behind him and tied on the blindfold.

The immediate sensory deprivation was disconcerting. After it was tied on, she leaned down and whispered into his ear, "Can you see anything?" Her warm breath sent chills down his spine.

"No, Mistress, nothing."

"Good. Very good." She spent a moment licking his ear and a drop of moisture dripped from the tip of his erection.

"Is the floor getting hard, Colton?"

"I hadn't noticed, Mistress. Another hard place has stolen my ability to think."

She chuckled low and sexy. "Is that so?" She softly caressed his dick with the ribbons of the flogger, "Yes, I can see how that might become distracting. You may stand."

"Thank you, Mistress." He hadn't realized how long he'd been kneeling there until he stood and the residual pain flowed through his knees. But that thought flew out the window as Penelope's body pressed into the full length of his and she gently grabbed hold of his balls. He hissed in surprise. There was something to be said about the arousing effects of being blind. It was overwhelming. He started to reach toward her, but she immediately sensed his intention and backed away from him. He swayed toward her automatically, but her voice stopped him.

"Nuh uh, no touching. In fact, maybe we should put some of your toys to use while we straighten a few things out."

He tilted his head at her trying to catch her meaning. "Straighten out?"

"Are you questioning me?"

Oops, he'd slipped out of character. "No, Mistress." He bowed his head again. "I apologize."

"Hmm. Just see that it doesn't happen again."

"Yes, Mistress."

"Now go lie flat on the bed on your back. Raise your arms above your head and spread your legs." He felt a shiver of dread. He could sense where this was going. He wasn't sure if he was more turned on or apprehensive.

He obviously wasn't moving fast enough for her as she prodded. "Now, Colton or you will be punished."

He did as she instructed and listened for her movements in the room. She could move amazingly quiet, considering those heels she wore. The mattress dipped as she came on to the bed. He heard the sound of metal just as she grabbed his hands. Handcuffs. She leaned over him as she secured him and he desperately wanted to arch up to touch her. That was absolutely the worst part to this game. He wanted to touch her. He needed to touch her. His mouth watered at the thought and a moan escaped him.

She must have heard his desperation. She lightly draped over half his body as she checked the handcuffs which he could tell she'd threaded through the headboard. She then ran a fingernail across his pectoral muscles, while she gave his ear and neck a nibble. This was torture. The slow, highly erotic, extremely sexy kind.

She continued to explore his chest with her hands and lips as she slowly moved down his body. The anticipation was killing him.

She shifted her weight off him, just as her lips started exploring the tops of his hips. She was so close, but then suddenly she was gone. He felt another groan, this one of frustration, escape him.

"Shhh, patience. It'll be worth it. I promise." Her voice was hushed and so incredibly sexy sounding. He could come just from listening to her talk to him.

She walked back across the room. He was getting more oriented to being blind. He could tell where she was at in the room from the sound of her heels on the wood floor. What was she getting off the dresser now? He heard her coming back, but still jumped when something draped onto the top of his thigh. It slid across as she pulled it and then moved it to the other thigh. Rope maybe?

Oh who the hell cared because it was slowly sliding up to his groin area. His cock twitched once again. His balls tightened as it slid across his scrotum and slowly inched up his dick. "Please, Mistress," he groaned.

"Please what, Colton?"

It started the downward slide along his dick and his back arched of its own volition. "Penelope..." He sounded desperate, but he was beyond caring.

But then the thing, whatever it was, was suddenly gone.

"Did you forget the rules, Colton?"

He swallowed hard. "I'm sorry, Mistress. I got carried away."

She stroked his length once and it was all he could do not to shift his hips into her wonderful grasp. "I can forgive that transgression, Colton."

There was a tug on his foot and something tied around his ankle and pulled to the corner of the bed. She was tying him to the corner posts. When she had him secured, the mattress dipped again in between his legs. Suddenly there was hot breath on his balls and his breathing sped up.

"Yes, I can forgive that transgression." She was so close to his groin, he could feel the moist heat from her breath as she talked.

He had to work hard to concentrate on what she was saying. He definitely didn't have enough blood left in his brain to process correctly.

"But there's one other place where we still have an issue, Colton. Why did you send Cassie to pick me up today? I would have been fine riding my bicycle."

Wait. What? Had she asked him a question? Did she really expect to have a conversation when he was this turned on?

He could still feel her breath before she said, "I'm waiting."

Fuck, what was the question? "Um, I'm sorry?"

"Hmm, that sounded more like a question than an answer." She gave a long moist lick up the length of his dick which had his whole body shuddering in response. "Are you sure about that apology?"

He could hear her amusement in her voice. Who knew that Penelope was this sadistic? At this point, he'd agree to anything she wanted. "Yes, I'm sure."

She rewarded him by engulfing his entire length in her mouth and he suddenly stopped breathing. "Oh fuck, Penelope, don't stop. That feels incredible." He wished he had his hands free so he could run his hands through her hair. Her mouth felt so damn good. Too good. His orgasm was coming hard and he wasn't ready for that yet.

"Penelope, you need to stop. I'm going to come if you don't." Her tongue did amazing things while her hands worked the base of his shaft. The moist heat of her mouth was incredible. He tried to remember his flight checklists, but at this point he couldn't even remember what a damn cockpit looked like.

"Penelope!" He shouted as his orgasm ripped through his body. Over and over, he pressed into her mouth and she swallowed every bit as she continued to work his length.

Finally she released him, but the shudders kept rolling through his body. That had been incredibly hot. She slid down his body to release his ankles. Once they were loose, she crawled up his body, inching up from his ankles to his thighs to his groin. There was really something to be said about doing this blind. Already his dick was showing interest of getting back in the game.

As she continued to kiss her way up his body, he finally found his voice. "Thank you, Mistress."

"Um, no thank you, Colton. That was very nice and I'm glad that we agree that you made a mistake sending Cassie to pick me up today."

What? When had he agreed to that? He cleared his throat. "Is that what I agreed to under duress?"

Suddenly she was lying on top of him and he realized somewhere in there, she'd lost her clothes because this was most definitely a naked feminine body pressed up against him. His cock suddenly flared to life again, just as Penelope removed his blindfold.

He blinked as he looked into her amused, but incredibly lust-filled eyes. Oh yeah she was definitely aroused, and amused, but mostly aroused. "You are a vixen. So is this how this relationship works from here on out? You tie me up until I agree to whatever you want?" He looked down her incredibly hot body and his hips shifted up into her heat.

She closed her eyes at the sensation and he felt her moist heat just at the tip of where he could reach. He arched just a tiny bit, barely breaching her core, but it was enough to have them both moaning. Her voice was low and scratchy as she said, "Hey, it works for me."

This time it was Colton groaning as he slipped in another tiny inch. Damn, she felt so good. He closed his eyes in ecstasy. "Damn, I have to say it works for me, too." He looked back up into her eyes and was astounded at the depth of feeling he saw shining there. Again, he found himself on the verge of an orgasm and he wasn't even fully inside her yet. "Sweetheart, you need to get a condom on me now, or else we're going to have a problem." His hips lifted slightly at the same time she shifted. The combined action caused full throttle penetration that had Colton sweating. Penelope pressed her forehead to his trying to gain control. "I'm on the pill," she gasped, "and have only ever had protected sex. I'm perfectly safe, I swear."

"Me, too. I haven't had sex since my divorce and the military checks me every year. I'm clean." Her hips were already rocking before he finished his sentence. This was incredible. He'd always taken control in the bedroom so he'd never had anyone ride him this way.

He hated that his hands were still cuffed. He needed to make sure she came before him. He shifted the angle of his hips to find her g-spot. Bingo. Her gasps increased and he felt the beginning flutters of her interior muscles clenching him. The burn began at the base of his spine just as she screamed his name and her orgasm washed over him. He continued to lever into her until he was coming again.

She collapsed on his sweaty chest and he enjoyed the feel of her lithe body draped over his. He kissed her brow. Finally she looked up at him. "That was incredible." Her voice still sounded breathy.

"It was, but sweetheart, I really need you to un-do these cuffs because I desperately want to touch you."

She smiled at him as she leaned over to the nightstand for the keys. As she leaned up to let him loose, he suddenly found himself in the right place. He sucked in the tip of her nipple and was rewarded with her gasp and then an answering moan. She abandoned the cuffs, so he released her breast from his mouth. "Keep working. I need my hands back so I can do this properly."

"And he's back. Mr. Bossy."

Finally the cuffs gave and he had his complete freedom again. He took full advantage, by grabbing Penelope by her waist and flipping her onto her back, pinned underneath him. He immediately went back to sucking on one breast while he palmed the other. He lifted his head and smirked at her after she moaned. "You weren't just complaining about me, were you now, sweetheart?"

Her eyes filled with mischief. "Not me. Nuh uh. I'd never give you a hard time."

He didn't believe her, but he was already too occupied with other things to argue with her. Besides, if they'd proven anything here tonight, they'd proven their differences could be worked out and he was counting on that because he wasn't planning on ever letting her go again.

Chapter 26

He plugged his phone into his car charger and immediately it started to ring. His stomach clenched when he saw the number on the caller ID. This is what happens when you forget to take your charger on an overseas trip. After this hellacious trip, what else could have possibly gone wrong now?

He answered, "I trust my delivery made it to you."

"Is this your idea of a joke? A fucking picture and then no way to get hold of you for days? You honestly don't value your life, do you?"

A cold chill snaked down his spine as he glanced around the airport parking lot. This was not a place to be discussing this, but he had no choice. "I'm sorry sir, but I have no idea what you're talking about. What picture?"

"All your boys brought over was a picture. I want to know where my codes are? And by the way, you are now down two boys."

He swallowed hard. Nausea churned. Paul's wife just had a baby and Jason had only been 23 years old.

The beauty of the plan all along was that none of them were traceable. They were virtually infallible. As he lost more and more control, that was quickly falling apart. He felt a drop of sweat slither down his spine. How had this entire operation gone so completely wrong?

He never thought to check what the guys picked up at the bookstore. He just assumed Penelope left the correct item. Fuck! "I apologize, sir. There must have been a miscommunication. I assure you I will get this taken care of."

"And just where were you three days ago when you should have been taking care of this? I think you mistake me for someone who forgives and forgets. I assure you, I am not that man."

He swallowed hard, but worked to sound self-assured in the face of what was definitely a threat to his life.

"Again, I apologize. I was out of the country. I had no idea the boys delivered the wrong product. Let me find out what happened and I'll get back to you." At least he would once he managed to sort out what went wrong. Failure was not an option.

"Right now I'm not sure if I trust you. You better fix this, or I'll find someone who will. Is that understood? I don't think I need to remind you what happens to men in my organization who fuck up. Do I?"

"No, sir. I assure you, this will be fixed."

He hung up the phone and gritted his teeth pushing through the nausea, exhaustion, and resulting fogginess in his brain.

He dialed.

"Yeah."

"I'm back."

"Did everything go as planned, sir?"

"Not exactly. Dr. Lopez is going to need more persuading to see our side of things, but never mind about that now. We have another issue here. The Gift is still missing." He closed his eyes and leaned his forehead against the steering wheel. He hated this, but it was either her or him. In that issue, there was no contest. He would always choose himself. "It's time to send a message to Ms. Pruitt. Arrange it and be sure it's done within the next forty-eight hours. And get me my damn codes!"

Operation: Endeavor

"Consider it done."

Chapter 27

The next morning, Penelope was still reeling from the night before. They'd made love several more times before exhaustion set in and sleep claimed them. Now they were both awake, but neither was ready to enter the real world yet.

Colton had been lovingly stroking her back as she lay on his chest. He reached down and tipped up her chin so she looked at him. "So are we okay?"

His expression was so filled with tenderness, she couldn't find the words. She just nodded.

"Because we need to be okay. I don't want to change you. I want to protect you and take care of you, but not at the detriment of who you are. If I push too far, push back. I'm not going to break. I'm here for the long haul."

Penelope couldn't swallow past the lump in her throat. Her eyes filled with tears. How did she get so lucky?

"Hey, what's wrong?" His eyes went from loving to scared and concerned in the matter of a heartbeat.

She shook her head, trying to gain control of her out-of control emotions. Her throat was clogged with tears, but she had to get rid of the fear on his face. "I'm so sorry, Colton." The tears were running freely especially now as she saw something like regret flash across his face before he started to turn away from her.

"No, Colton, listen to me." She reached up to cup the side of his face. "I'm sorry for the things I said the other morning. I didn't mean them. I'm sorry I almost blew things between us."

Relief was visible on his face and she felt guilty that she'd put the need for it there. He smiled at her. "That's good." He leaned down to kiss her. "That's very good. By the way, I think we've discovered a new Life Rule."

She quirked an eyebrow. "Oh really? So this one is #3?"

"That sounds about right." His voice had gone all growly again as he nuzzled in between her ear and her neck. She was quickly deciding that was her favorite new erogenous zone. "This is Colton's Life Rule #3..." He paused for effect. "Whenever you need to get my attention and discuss my overbearing attitude, it's best to do so by tying me up."

"Ooh, I like this new rule."

"I like to think it benefits both of us."

"It definitely does, but I have a question. Does this particular rule only apply to me or does it apply to others too?"

He looked at her puzzled.

"I'm just thinking your brother and sister could really enjoy the chance to tie you up, although I'm thinking it wouldn't quite have the same effect for you."

He tackled her, while she giggled. "You are a minx, aren't you?"

It was a little bit longer before they came up for air again and only because Penelope's cell phone rang.

She fumbled a bit trying to get hold of the phone with Colton doing things to her body that were probably illegal in several states. Finally, she managed to see the screen and hissed at Colton, "Stop it. Brian's on the phone."

"Detective Barnes, how are you this morning?" God, she hoped her voice didn't sound as breathy to him as it did to her and that he couldn't hear Colton grumbling in the background.

There was laughter in his voice when he answered. "Well, since it's afternoon, I'm guessing the day is going pretty well for you."

She flushed with embarrassment.

"Ahem...well..." Honestly what could she say to that? Probably best to just ignore it. "So what can I do for you today? Do you have any news on Hannah?"

Colton sat up, looking suddenly fierce and concerned. He mouthed to her, "What?"

She turned her back to him waving him aside with a single finger raised to let him know she'd tell him in just a moment.

Brian continued talking. "Well, first I'll tell you the good news. The baggie didn't have drugs in it. It was some sort of herbal supplement, but we did find something else in the lining of the bag which concerns me."

"What?" Her stomach lurched with sudden tension.

"Unfortunately, as part of an ongoing investigation, I can't disclose that information."

"Is the investigation my case or anything to do with the bookstore?" Her stomach clenched in fear.

"No, it's not. But Penelope, I think you probably should file a missing persons report on Hannah. I think she could be in danger. It looks like she's gotten mixed up into something really bad." That was not news she wanted to hear. She closed her eyes and leaned her head into her hand. Colton's hand rubbed her back and she was glad he was there.

"Did you find out anything at her apartment?"

"No, and I asked around. Nobody's seen her for several days. If you file a missing persons report, I can do other things to see if I can track any movements by her. Do you know anything about her family? Maybe have an emergency contact in her employee files?"

"No, I checked when she stopped showing up. I don't have any other contact information for her." She shook her head as she thought back over the holes in Hannah's employee records. She hated to think that there wasn't anyone else out there missing her. "Okay, so a missing persons report. How do I go about doing that?"

"Just come down to the police station and I'll walk you through it."

"Okay. I'll be there within the hour."

As she hung up, she turned worried eyes to Colton.

"What's going on?" he asked.

Penelope filled him in on the situation with Hannah.

"Why didn't you mention all this going on before now?"

"I don't know if you've noticed," she gestured over to the toys spread all over the room, "but we've been a little preoccupied."

"I guess that's true, but I don't like the idea of one of your employees bringing trouble to you or the store." Colton frowned fiercely. "Go get showered and I'll drive you down to the police station and then to work."

She kissed him right in between his eyebrows where the skin wrinkled from his frown. "I'll accept that very kind offer." She emphasized offer, subtly pointing out that he'd just issued a command rather than a request. "I accept because the Bus is in the shop for the week and I'm out my ride, not because you just ordered me to do so." She sashayed out the hall and into her bedroom.

***

When Colton got to the bookstore to deliver Penelope, he decided to go in and see what he could find for educational material. She was surprised when he parked and turned off the motorcycle, but when she saw where he headed in the bookstore, she just grinned at him.

"What?" he said quite innocently.

"Nope, I'm not going to say a damn thing. Go explore. Have fun." Her voice lowered. "Maybe you can find some *really* interesting reading that we can discuss in depth later." She had a sparkle in her eye.

Yep, there it was. His ever-present erection was back. Would their chemistry ever reach a non-combustible stage? He sincerely hoped not. But at this point, it would be okay for it to cool down just a bit so that he could stop worrying about embarrassing himself in public. Maybe he should hang out in the history section. At least until his libido calmed down enough so he didn't look like a pervert, reading erotica in the corner of the bookstore with a hard-on.

He made it to the erotica section when Penelope disappeared into the recesses of her office. Amazing how his erection was directly tied to her presence and that evocative scent of honeysuckle which floated on the air when she was around.

He found several novels with promising premises to explore and was surprised by just how much erotic romance there was. Penelope had a fully stocked section including several copies of all the books by Celeste DeMarco, the same author she had so many books by at home. Hmm, interesting. He'd have to check out those books more closely when he got home.

Alix wandered by just as he was narrowing his choices. He flushed in embarrassment as she took the books out of his hand to examine what he'd picked out.

"I don't think..." he started, trying to pull the books back from her.

"Nonsense. There's some good stuff in this section, but there's also some that won't work for you." She looked him up and down as if judging his sexual tastes. Please, let the ground swallow him up right now.

She shuffled through the pile of books. "This is a good one," she said about the one featuring a female helicopter pilot. "This one..." she paused to peruse the back of it, "no, this one isn't for you." She re-shelved it. "No to this one and this one. I think they're really a bit too sadistic for your tastes."

Oh fuck, this was embarrassing to have Pen's older aunt going through his erotica choices.

"Ooh, you'll like this one. Perfect for you." Yep, that was the BDSM one. And nope, he was never going to ever be able to get an erection again after this scarring event. This was completely humiliating.

She handed him back the two books which she'd deemed appropriate for him and then pulled off one of the Celeste DeMarco books. But she didn't add it to his pile. Instead she held it close to her chest while she looked seriously at him. "I see what's going on between you and Penelope and I approve. I think you're a good match for her although she may not see it quite yet." She glanced back toward Pen's closed office door, with a shake of her head. "Although she seems pretty happy today, so maybe..." She looked back at him, then down at the book in her arms, as if deciding something. She quirked an eyebrow at him before asking, "Have you seen Penelope's tattoo?"

He nodded. "Yes, it's gorgeous."

"Has she told you the story behind it yet?"

He shook his head. "I keep meaning to ask, but then get distracted." Damn, there went that blush again. He was never coming into this bookstore again. He was never going to live this down.

She just smirked at him with a knowing smile. "I think you should read this one first. I think you'll find it very enlightening."

Obviously, she was trying to tell him something about Penelope, so he added the book to his pile.

***

As Colton walked out of the bookstore after paying for his books, he called Chris on his cell phone. "Hey, Chris."

"Hiya, Colton."

"Want to go grab some dinner with me?"

"Seriously? I figured you would be completely wrapped up in Penelope's arms by now."

Wait a minute. How did he know that? But then he remembered it was Chris who sent her out to the patio at the party on Saturday. He always did have good instincts.

He laughed. "I would if I could, but she's working late tonight."

"Aw, so I see where I rank in your social calendar."

"Well, hot girl vs. annoying younger brother. Was there ever really any doubt?"

Chris laughed. "I guess not."

"Is Cassie home?"

"Naw, she's working late all this week trying to get ahead so she can spend more time with Jake after he gets home on Saturday."

"Okay, so just you and me. What do you think? You up for some pizza and beer?"

"Sure. You want to come by and ride together or meet somewhere?"

"I'm just around the corner at the bookstore so I'll come by. Besides that way you can be the designated driver since you're finally driving again."

"And there we have it, the real reason why you invited me out."

Colton just chuckled. "I'll be there in a few minutes."

***

As Colton slid into the booth of the crowded sports bar, he pushed Chris's beer over to him.

"Thanks."

"No problem. How's the PT going on the leg? You seem to be moving a little bit easier."

Chris scowled at him. "It's not going as fast as I'd like, but I'm making progress. Don't worry. I'm gonna make your deadline."

Colton took a sip of his beer. "I have no doubt about that. We have a couple of meetings next week for Mad Rob, once Jake's in town. We need to go sign all the legal papers to set up ownership of the business with the lawyers and then we can take over ownership on the de Havilland." He'd taken Chris by to see the plane earlier in the week and he was just as sold on the plane as Colton.

"Good luck getting Jake out of Cassie's grasp. I swear, I've never seen her this excited before. While I'm happy for her and Jake, it's damn nauseating. I may have to come crash at your place to get away from the lovebirds for a while." Chris scowled at him. "But judging from the shit-eating smile you've had on your face all evening, I probably won't be any better off there. I need to find a place of my own," Chris muttered.

Colton hated that their happiness caused Chris pain, but he truly was at a loss about what he could do to help. He hated not having control of the situation. He should be able to help. That's what he did. He took care of their problems.

Chris took a long drink off his beer then rubbed his left thigh in agitation. "So I'm guessing things are going well between you and the fair Penelope?"

Colton couldn't stop the grin that slid onto his face again. "Yeah, I think you'd be safe in saying that."

"What's up with all this young love? It's enough to make a guy sick...or at least thankful enough to embrace his confirmed bachelorhood." Chris took another swig of his beer and a haunted look flashed across his face.

As Colton watched, he considered and pushed his own beer away. He had a feeling tonight Chris needed it more than he did, so he'd be the designated driver.

The pizza was delivered by their very attractive waitress. She was perky and definitely sending off enough available vibes toward Chris that it would be hard to miss. He hadn't even given her a second look since they placed their order. As she walked off, Colton gestured toward her. "You should get her number. She's interested." Chris didn't even give her a glance.

"Naw, I don't think so."

They were having a good time and he didn't want to do anything to change that. If Pen had taught him anything over the last couple of days, it was there were times when it was better to back off. This seemed like one of those times.

They were quiet as they watched the game on the bar TV and inhaled the pizza.

Their waitress walked up. "Can I get you guys another beer?"

He looked over at Chris. "I'm gonna just stick with one for tonight, but if you want to have more, I'll drive us home."

"Are you sure?" At Colton's nod, Chris handed his empty to the waitress. "Sure, I'll take another. Thanks."

As she walked back toward the bar to retrieve his other beer, Chris asked, "So did Penelope ever hear anything more from whoever broke into the Bus?"

"No, and it just doesn't make any sense. That took some serious planning to do what that guy did with photographing everyone as they came into the party, printing the photos, and then breaking into her Bus to leave the threatening note. Just for that art photo she gave to Julie? I'm just not buying it." Colton noticed a significant tightening to Chris's jaw when he said Julie's name. If he hadn't been watching for it, he would have missed it completely.

He took another long swig of his beer before he agreed with Colton. "Maybe he saw the cop that night and decided whatever he was after wasn't worth the heat."

Colton nodded. "I certainly hope so. We don't need any more drama with this group. It's time for some smooth sailing."

"I'll drink to that!" Chris tipped his beer at Colton before taking another drink.

Colton settled into the booth to watch the basketball game and keep an eye on his little brother. He didn't know how to help anymore besides being there to prop him up with everything he was going through.

A couple of hours and several beers later, Chris was toast.

"Damn, it's been too long since I've had more than a couple of drinks. My tolerance isn't worth shit anymore." He gave a sloppy smile at Colton's direction. He scowled back down at the beer he was currently working on. "No booze and no women. I'm not a very good bachelor, am I?" He looked back up in question at Colton, but kept talking like only one who's feeling no pain could. "Think they'll take away my man card for that? Damn, do I even have a man card when I'm not a man anymore?"

Okay, maybe letting Chris drink a few too many beers wasn't his brightest idea. He'd been hoping it would help him relax, not make him even more morose. God, he really didn't know what kind of advice to offer here, but a thought occurred to him. He looked at Chris thoughtfully and decided now was probably as good a time as any to breach this bridge.

Colton spoke quietly. "Chris, do you think maybe the issue isn't so much related to an injury as it is related to a specific person?"

Chris became perfectly still and looked up at Colton with eyes that had suddenly become guarded. Bingo.

He spoke very low and Colton could hear the edge of dread in his voice. "What are you talking about?" Chris said, rubbing his left thigh.

"I've noticed something the last few days." He took a deep breath before proceeding into this very touchy minefield. "Something happened between you and Julie, didn't it?"

There was no imagining the stark pain that flashed through Chris's eyes before he shut them and lowered his head into his hands. He ran both of them through his hair in agitation.

Colton watched as he clenched his jaw over and over again. Finally he seemed to have control and he looked back up at Colton with his eyes blazing in determination. When he spoke, his voice was firm and harsh. "No. She's with Aaron and they're good together. I died. She met Aaron. End of story."

"That's not the end of the story, because you didn't die, Chris."

Chris shook his head in denial. "In this, I might as well have. There's no discussion here Colt. Drop it, okay?"

Colton couldn't argue against those hurting, pleading eyes. "Okay, but think about what I said."

Chris gave a clipped nod. "Are you ready to go?"

"Yeah, let's head back to Cassie's."

***

The next morning, Colton was still troubled by Chris's reaction. Penelope was asleep in his bed when he got home. She settled into his arms as soon as he crawled into bed and it made his heart ache for Chris. Chris needed this in his life, but from everything Colton could see, he'd completely given up on the idea of love.

He scowled into his coffee cup.

"Hey, what did that coffee ever do to you?"

He looked up surprised to see her. He hadn't even heard her walk in. "What?"

She picked up her own cup and leaned against the counter. She tilted her head to the side as she asked him, "Is everything okay?"

He shook his head to clear the cobwebs. "Yeah. Sorry, I just have a lot on my mind. Hey listen, was Julie dating or serious about anyone before she met Aaron? Like maybe last year around this time?"

The surprise showed on her face before she shook her head. "No, not anyone I know of. Why? Are you already thinking about dumping me?" She gave a light chuckle. "Because I'm thinking things between her and Aaron are getting pretty tight. He's asked her to move in with him."

"Really?" Well damn, that wasn't good news for Chris's prospects.

"Yeah, but she's debating telling him no. She thinks things are moving too fast between them and isn't ready for that yet. I think there may be more to the story, but Julie's pretty tight-lipped about these things."

She sidled up behind him at the breakfast bar and nuzzled the back of his neck. "So why are we talking about Julie's love life when our own is so much more exciting?"

He turned on the barstool and tucked her body in between his legs to give her a thorough kiss. "I have no idea." There was a knock at the door. "Hold that thought."

There was a kid at the door holding a clipboard and package, looking bored. "Are you Colton Robertson?"

"Yes."

"Kay. Sign here." Colton signed and the kid handed him the small package. Colton sighed in relief. Finally.

He shut the door and moved into the kitchen. He wasn't going anywhere until he was sure what this package held. He ignored Penelope's curious look while he cut open the tape. Inside was a small velvet bag. Opening it, he poured out the ring into his palm. He released the breath he hadn't even realized he'd been holding.

"I wasn't sure I'd ever see this again." He was surprised to hear how gruff his voice sounded.

"What is it?"

He looked up at her and smiled. He knew his relief showed through. He finally had it back and that little thing made his mom feel closer. He closed his eyes for a moment and tightened his fist over it. He had it back. "My mom's wedding ring. Dianna was supposed to return it in my stuff, but she didn't. I wasn't sure I'd ever see it again."

He caught the flash of tenderness and her slight sniffle. "Is that why you guys have been fighting?"

He gave a terse nod. "She refused to give it back, but it's my mom's." His voice lowered to a whisper. "It's one of the few things I have that belonged to her. I wasn't sure if I was ever going to see it again." His emotions were getting the better of him and he didn't want to break down in front of Penelope. "Let me go put it away and then we can get back to our discussion."

When he came back into the room, he nuzzled up behind her neck and wrapped his arms around her from behind. "Now where were we?"

"Hmm, I like what you're thinking, but unfortunately I have someplace I have to be today. Want to give me a ride?"

"Sure. Where are we headed?" He leaned back to look over her tight worn jeans, cowboy boots, and long-sleeved tee. She had her hair done in a low ponytail and carried a baseball hat. Hmm, a bit sedate for Penelope's normal free-styling look.

She shrugged on her leather jacket and gave him a teasing look as they walked out the front door. "I think that should be a surprise."

"That's gonna be kind of tough since I'm driving," he said as he handed her the helmet out of the saddlebags on the bike.

She simply smiled at him. "Just head out toward Buffalo Springs Lake and I'll direct you from there."

"You do like to give directions, don't you?"

Her jade eyes suddenly started to smolder. Oh yeah, she definitely liked giving directions. They weren't even on the damn bike yet and he was hard again. Damn. He couldn't resist. He pulled her into his arms and dove into her mouth, but instead of those luscious breasts pressed up against him, he felt something hard and pointed.

He pulled back. "What the hell?" He reached into her jacket and pulled out a book from her interior breast pocket.

She giggled. "Sorry about that. It's my emergency reading. Do you mind if I put it in the saddlebags?"

He smiled at her indulgently. "Be my guest." He undid the buckle for her. "Still worried you're going to get bored with me?"

"Never, but it's like a security blanket for me. I don't go anywhere without a book, or two, or ten."

He closed the saddlebag and gave her a hand so she could settle onto the motorcycle behind him. "Whatever keeps you happy, sweetheart."

***

When they drove onto a ranch, Colton glanced back at Penelope to give her a puzzled look. She just smiled at him and gestured him to go on down the road.

The ranch itself was about 35 miles east of Lubbock where the caprock dropped off and the landscape drastically changed from the flat plains surrounding the city. Out here, the land ebbed and rolled in gentle hills. There was also a drastic change in the plant life. Around Lubbock, there were miles and miles of cotton fields. On the ranch, there were bushes, wildlife, and even real trees. That was something they rarely got to see in Lubbock.

When she'd first made contact with the family, there was an instant attraction between her and the second to youngest boy, Thomas. They'd connected through their mutual issues with their parents. Thomas's mother died when he was younger and he blamed his father for that loss. It made things rather touchy for him since he had to work with his father. But Thomas loved the ranch and couldn't give that up even with the conflict between the two of them.

They'd dated for about six weeks before their romance fizzled out. In that time though, Penelope became part of the family and the ranch. Still all these years later, she came out to help exercise the horses at least once or twice a month, more in the summer when she helped out with the summer camps. She loved it out here.

As they rode up on Colton's Harley, Thomas came out to greet them. He was a great looking guy, even if he wasn't the guy for her. He had on a straw cowboy hat and she could already see his ice blue eyes peering in curiosity out from under the brim. He had about two days' worth of scruff and he looked worn out. He'd obviously been working hard today. His worn boots were dusty, as were his threadbare jeans and t-shirt. She could see the sweat stains from where he'd been working out in the hot sun.

She wished she knew a girl who was perfect for him. He was, flat out, too nice of a guy to be alone and he desperately wanted a wife and family. That was a lot of the reason why they hadn't lasted. Back then, she hadn't wanted that for her life. As she looked over at Colton, suddenly she questioned all the convictions she'd held for so long. Was this what love did to a girl?

As they got off the motorcycle, Thomas walked forward looking confused, but friendly. It wasn't until she removed her motorcycle helmet that he realized who she was. When he did, his stride faltered a bit before he flashed her his trademark smile.

"Well, hey there, Penny." He scooped her up into a full-on Texas hug, which meant he lifted her off the ground and swung her around a time or two before putting her down. By that time, Colton was scowling heavily. "I didn't expect you out for at least another week. Is your wrist feeling better?"

"Hiya, Thomas. It's feeling better and healed much faster than I thought it would. I thought we'd come out and exercise some of the horses for you, if that's okay?"

"You know it is. We always love having your help and the horses have missed you. Is this your archeologist friend?"

She shook her head.

Colton stepped up and presented Thomas with his hand. "I'm Colton Robertson, Penny's *boyfriend*." He emphasized that last half in such a way that Penelope knew she was in trouble.

"Thomas Martin." As Thomas shook his hand, he looked back over at Penelope with curiosity. "Your boyfriend, hmmm? I didn't think you let any guy close enough to claim that title."

As Penelope reached around Colton to draw him closer. "I never thought it would happen, but I guess I just needed to meet the right guy."

"Ouch," he exclaimed, but the good humor in his eyes belied his words. "Hell, Penny that hurts."

She just grinned at him. "Aw, don't pretend I broke your heart. You and I both know that's not true." She just shook her head at him. "Is anyone else around? I'd like them to meet Colton."

"Dad's in the barn doctoring Lucy with Ethan."

"What's wrong with her? Is she okay?" Lucy was one of her favorite horses. She was sweet-natured and a wonder to ride, but that darn horse was always getting herself into mischief and trouble.

"Yeah, she just got into something and cut her chest up, so he's applying some antibiotic to it. She should be fine in a few days. Matthew and Scott are out working the north pasture fencing. You'll see them if you're planning to go riding. Andrew's in town doing some work for the Rangers. Maybe he'll make it back before you leave. The horses have missed you." He looked over at Colton. "Do you have much experience riding?"

"It's been a few years, but yeah, I used to ride pretty regularly."

"Okay, well in that case," he turned back toward Penelope, "why don't you put him on Thunder to start with?"

Penelope nodded. Thunder was an older gelding. He was a huge black horse that once upon a time was probably more than a handful, but he'd mellowed with age and would be a good ride for Colt. He still had enough spirit in him to be fun to ride and he could easily handle Colton's size.

"Thanks, Thomas. We'll probably see you again before we leave." She led Colton toward the barn.

As they walked, he grabbed her around the waist and tugged her toward him. "You're just full of surprises, aren't you Penny? Who would have guessed that within that VW Bus hid a tried and true cowgirl?"

"It's definitely not my natural state of being, but I've learned to love it out here."

As they entered the barn, Penelope inhaled the musty smell of hay, leather, horses, and old wood. She laughed at the pure joy of it and sharing it with Colton. She pulled him further into the dark interior as she called out, "Michael, Ethan, are you guys in here?"

"Back here," a voice called from the back corner. "Penny, is that you?"

They rounded the corner of the horse stalls and there he was coming at them, the original Marlboro Man, without the cigarettes. Michael was in his late fifty's with salt and pepper hair. He'd worked the ranch his entire life and had the physique that showed it, regardless of his age. His wife died in a car wreck when Thomas was young, so Michael basically raised all four of his boys by himself. "Hello, Michael."

Immediately he picked her up into a big hug just like Thomas had, but without the extra swing. "Well, hey there, girly. We've missed you."

When he put her down, she pulled him over to Colton. "Michael, I'd like to introduce you to Colton, my boyfriend. Colt, this is the patriarch of the Martin clan and the Rocking M ranch."

Colton reached over and shook Michael's hand and said, "It's a pleasure to meet you, sir."

"Likewise, although I'll admit, I never thought I'd see the day where this one introduced me to a boyfriend." Michael cocked an eyebrow at her and she grinned as she interlaced her fingers through Colton's. "I'd given up on that a long while ago. There may be hope for my boys to settle down yet." Michael looked him over and seemed pleased with what he saw.

Penelope smiled. "They just haven't met the right girls yet. Don't give up hope."

Ethan walked up behind Michael, brushing off his hands. "And this is Ethan, the only guy on the ranch without the Martin name. I'm not sure what he does besides cause trouble, but they seem to think he does something valuable here." She smiled at the easy-going young man who grinned at her, obviously not bothered by her teasing.

Michael added, "He may not have the Martin name, but he's definitely part of the Martin ranch. Ethan does as much work here as any of us."

"It's a good place to work with good folks running it." Ethan gave an easy smile.

"Well darling, it's awfully good to have you back. We've missed you the last couple of weeks. The boys need a female presence every once in a while. It keeps them calmer." Michael gave her shoulder a squeeze before turning back to Colton. "Nice meeting you, son. You take good care of this girl. She's a keeper and I hope we see you out here with her often."

"Yes sir. I appreciate the invitation and will take you up on that as often as Pen is willing to bring me."

After they got the horses saddled and Pen spent some time reacquainting herself with the other horses, they settled into riding a well-worn trail around the fields of the ranch.

Colton turned to her to ask, "So tell me about the Martin's and how you know them."

"Michael is the head of the Martin family. This is the ranch that's been in their family for several generations. There are four boys: Andrew's the oldest. You didn't meet him. He works on the ranch too, but he's here less than the others because he's also a Texas Ranger. Scott is the second oldest. He's a part-time paramedic with the volunteer fire department, but mainly runs the ranch with the rest of them. You met Thomas. He's third in line. We dated for a few weeks before deciding we made better friends than lovers. The baby is Matthew. Hopefully, we'll run into Matthew and Scott out here riding so you get to meet them."

"No females? No significant others?"

She gave a sad smile. "Nope, not yet, although Michael keeps hoping. He wants the boys to settle down with wives. His wife died in a car wreck when the boys were still little. Thomas was in the car with her and still has nightmares about it. I don't know the whole story, but I do know that things are strained between him and Michael because of it. He blames his dad for her death."

After riding a while, they rode up to the old homestead, which had been abandoned by the family years ago. Penelope loved the ramshackle old house with the big wide porch. She confided in him, "I have daydreams of owning a porch like this where I can watch the sunset in the evenings and rise in the morning. Me sitting out here in a rocking chair with my cup of tea and a good book."

"Is it just you or are there a few kids running around in the yard and a husband inside making dinner?"

She cocked an eyebrow at him. "Hmm, he's making dinner?"

He nodded.

She shut her eyes as the image of Colton standing at the kitchen with a boy and a girl playing in the yard with his eyes assailed her. What was she thinking? A husband and kids were not in her future. She needed to get that fantasy under control immediately. She shook her head to dispel it. "Nope, it's just me. I like the quiet and don't want a husband and kids to disturb it."

"But just imagine it… he makes dinner, they put the kids to bed, and then make mad passionate love on the swing on the porch."

"There's a swing on the porch?" Why was her heart suddenly galloping faster than this horse ever would? Why was it so easy to imagine? This was dangerous territory and she didn't need to think along these lines. These kinds of dreams would lead to heartache.

"Of course. Every porch needs a swing. I bet this one had one. Look you can see where it hung." He pointed toward the empty eyehooks in the ceiling of the porch. "It looks like the house has been abandoned for a while."

Penelope was grateful for the change of subject to less personal things. "Yeah, I don't think the Martins have used it in over fifty years. They built the other house on the other side of the ranch, closer to the highway. I just love this house though."

Colt looked over at her. "So explain to me how this happened." He gestured up and down to her riding a horse.

"I've lived in Texas my whole life and have never really been out of the city. I was working on a project…"

she hesitated, "for the bookstore, and a friend thought the Martins might be able to help me out. I fell in love with them and the ranch and have been coming out ever since. I try to come out as often as I can. They board a lot of horses, so if I can come out and ride a few of them, it leaves them to do other chores on the ranch. In the summer, I help with camps to teach kids how to ride and care for the horses. I love coming out here."

"I can tell. You've been smiling ever since we arrived."

"How can you be anything but happy when you are surrounded by all this? I'm continually amazed by how beautiful it is out here once you drop off the caprock."

"You're constantly a surprise, Ms. Penny."

"Hopefully, I stay that way. A girl has to maintain some of her mystique. Although I have to admit, I never saw you as a cowboy either."

"When I was in college at A&M, I worked part-time on a ranch. I've always managed to find some place to ride almost everywhere I've been stationed except England. I just never could find myself wanting to try my hand at riding English-style."

She giggled. "Yeah, for some reason the idea of you posting to the trot doesn't quite do it for me either. I'm glad to know that you enjoy riding because I love coming out here. I'm happy I can share this with you."

"Me too, sweetheart. Me, too."

She had another flash of Colton and her, relaxing on their own big, rambling porch. It was a disturbing one, only in the fact that it felt so right and natural.

Chapter 28

It was late by the time Colton and Penelope headed back toward Lubbock. The night was cooling off, which was a relief for Colton. He needed as much cool air as possible to deal with Penelope's wandering hands. She was obviously in a sexy mood after so much fresh air. At first, she'd just taken advantage of their position on the motorcycle by lightly tracing her fingertips along his abs, but the longer they rode, the more daring those fingers had become. As they wandered dangerously close to his ever-hardening cock, his breath hitched.

Finally they hit the edge of Lubbock and Colton couldn't drive fast enough to get back to the loft parking lot. He was ready to detonate by the time he turned the motor off. He quickly swung off the bike, got his helmet off, and waited impatiently as Penelope removed hers. He didn't miss the flash of surprise which crossed her face as he pinned her to the wall of the parking garage for a soul-scorching kiss. She was just as turned on as he was because she quickly wrapped those long legs around his hips.

Her breasts pressed up against his chest were exactly what he wanted. What he needed. He groaned low and hard as her heat pressed up against him. She was soft in all the places where he was hard and he couldn't resist the urge to push his cock against her even more.

Both of them were breathing raggedly by the time he pulled back. "Sweetheart, we need to move this upstairs before our neighbors get an X-rated show down here in the parking lot." Despite his words, he still wasn't pulling back as he fingered the snaps on her jeans. It would be so easy to strip her and pump into her right here, right now. Judging from the dazed look on her face, she wouldn't have a problem with that. either.

He took a deep breath to regain control of his arousal and gently lowered Pen's legs to the floor. "Come on. Let's move this upstairs."

Penelope licked her lower swollen lip and nodded. "Yeah. Okay."

He chuckled. She seemed a bit dazed. He liked that he could do that to her. In fact, he loved that he could do that to her. As they rode the elevator up, she began to nibble on his neck. He closed his eyes against the rapture of Penelope's warm breath on his neck and earlobe. She whispered right into his ear, "Do you know what my favorite part of making love to you is?"

He shook his head, too aroused to even speak.

"There's a moment right before you come, when I can feel your dick inside me thicken and pulse. It's like you're reaching my soul. We're standing on the edge of an incredible cataclysmic event and it's just you as deep into me as you can go. There is no better feeling in this world." Her voice was low and hoarse with emotion and desire. She gently nibbled and licked at his ear lobe.

His cock throbbed. They would be lucky if they made it past the doorway before he was inside her. He was desperate with need. Hopefully, she was just as aroused as he was, because he wasn't going to last long once he finally got inside her.

He reached up under her shirt to fondle her breast, just as the elevator dinged that they'd reached their floor.

He basically ran out of the elevator dragging Penelope behind him. He had his keys in the door. She had her hand in his pants and on his cock, when he swung open the door to the loft.

He'd been in the process of swinging around to pin her to the wall when he spotted the utter devastation within. Books were strewn everywhere, cushions shredded, chairs overturned, everything they owned, broken and flung throughout the room.

Penelope was so intent on getting him out of his pants, she didn't see it.

"Pen, sweetheart," God, he sounded like he'd swallowed rocks. He cleared his throat and tried again, this time reaching down to pull her hands out of his pants. "Penelope."

His urgent tone got through her fog of lust and she looked up at him in question. "We need to call the police. Someone's broken in." He gave her a quick, hard kiss and then set her behind him. His senses were telling him the loft was empty, but he wasn't going to risk her while he checked it out to make sure. If someone was going to try to hurt her, they'd have to come through him.

Her eyes widened in surprise as she gasped and took in the destruction of their space. "Colton? Oh my God."

"It's okay. Just stay here while I make sure whoever did this is gone. Don't touch anything, and call Brian." He quickly tucked himself into his pants and zipped up. The quick search confirmed his original thought. Whoever had done this was gone, but they'd been very thorough. Every room in the apartment was destroyed, their belongings littering every available scrap of floor-space in utter disarray.

The desolation in Penelope's eyes as he walked back into the room was heartbreaking. He felt a surge of primal anger that someone had hurt her like this. No one was allowed to hurt her. He wanted to kill someone. Slowly. Painfully.

She looked at her bookshelves where books were torn and scattered everywhere. They'd definitely taken the brunt of the assault on the loft. Her eyes filled with tears, so he lifted her chin and kissed her softly. "It's okay. It's only stuff and can be replaced."

She nodded her head. "I know. Thank God we weren't here."

He wrapped his arms around her and she shivered. He shuddered to think that she could have been here when this happened. Who the hell was doing all this? There wasn't a note this time. At least not one he'd seen. So did that mean this was related to the Bus break-in or not? And what about whoever pushed her down the stairs at the bookstore? Were all these things related or did Penelope just have really rotten luck? Maybe this was just a random break-in. He didn't think so though. Was it wrong that he wanted to pack her away someplace hundreds of miles from here? He wanted her safe. Then he would kill whoever was doing this.

He glanced back around the apartment and tried to hide his simmering anger from Penelope. "Do you see anything missing?" The TV was still there…shattered, but still there. As was the stereo system. This wasn't just a random break-in.

"It's so hard to tell, with everything tossed everywhere, but I don't think so."

There was a knock at the door. He pulled Penelope with him as he answered the door and she seemed quite content to cling to his side. It was Brian with a couple of police officers in tow, including Officer Pete Larson.

"Hi, Detective. Come on in, guys." Colton held the door open so all three could enter.

As they did so, Brian whistled low. "Whoa, they did a number on this place didn't they? Where were y'all when this happened?"

Penelope said, "We've been gone all day. We went out east of town to a ranch called the Rocking M Ranch."

"You just arrived home?"

"Yes, we called you pretty much immediately after we walked in the door. We haven't touched anything, although Colton did walk through the apartment just to make sure they were gone."

Brian nodded and looked over at the police officers. "Go ahead and start photographing things. Look and see if you can find any prints, evidence, or anything that seems out of place."

Penelope gave a harsh laugh. "Out of place? Seriously? I think you'd be better off looking for something that's in its place."

"You may be right, but you'd be surprised what kind of clues these guys might leave. I know it's hard to tell in this state, but have you noticed anything missing?"

Penelope shook her head. "But I haven't gone anywhere besides here. Would you like me to walk through the apartment?"

Brian nodded. "Yes, but make sure you don't touch anything."

An hour later, the police were through and they couldn't see that anything was missing.

Colton kissed Penelope on the top of her head. "Come on. Let's pack a bag. We're going over to spend the night at Cassie's for tonight. We'll deal with this tomorrow."

"We can't just drop in on her this late. It's after 11:00."

"Of course we can. She's my sister," he grinned at her, "but I called her while you were going through the apartment with the police officer. She's expecting us, so don't worry about it."

She started down the hall, but Colton stopped her to give her a kiss. "I know it looks bleak, but it's going to be okay. We have to go on the motorcycle so if you have a backpack, it will make it easier to carry on the bike."

"Okay, thanks, Colt. I'm so glad you're here."

***

When they arrived at Cassie's house twenty minutes later, she gave them both huge hugs. "Thank goodness you were gone when this happened."

Penelope's eyes filled with tears. She couldn't answer. She could only nod. Overwhelmed, her emotions were definitely getting the better of her. She turned to Colton and he immediately drew her against his strong chest. She just needed to cling to him and feel safe within his arms. Tonight she wasn't ready to leave that safe haven and he must have sensed that because he had kept her within inches of him all night.

She liked it. Her heart stuttered. She *liked* being able to lean on him. She *wanted* to lean on him. This went against everything she thought she knew about herself. She gingerly explored the idea within her psyche. Was she falling in love with him?

He pulled her out of her stupor when his lips touched the top of her head as he drew his hand soothingly up and down her back. He turned back to Chris and Cassie. "Thanks for letting us crash here tonight."

"Of course."

The twins had beer and pizza waiting for them, despite the lateness of the hour, and they all settled out on the patio. As they ate, Colton pulled Penelope down into his lap. He seemed to want her just as close to him as she wanted to be. She closed her eyes and laid her head on his chest while she listened to the siblings chat. So far, no one discussed the break-in although it was definitely the elephant in the room. Penelope was fine just listening to the steady, strong rhythm of Colton's heartbeat for right now.

Before she knew what happened, Colton picked her up, like a damsel in distress being rescued by her White Knight. She must have fallen asleep on his lap. He kissed her gently on the forehead as he walked down the hall. "Hey, Sleeping Beauty, let's go to bed."

"But Chris and Cassie…" she started.

"We'll talk to them in the morning. For now, let's just go to bed."

She snuggled into the warm strength of his arms. Yeah, she liked being here. She murmured a sleepy, "Okay."

***

The next morning, Penelope was still snuggled into Colton's strong embrace and she had no desire to be anywhere else. She'd been awake for twenty minutes and from the bulge growing against her belly, she'd guess Colton was waking up, too. Unfortunately, she could hear Cassie moving around in the kitchen already so there would be no finishing what they'd started in the parking garage the night before.

Colton's arms tightened around her as he nuzzled his face against her hair. "G'morning," he mumbled. "You smell and feel so good." He continued to explore down the side of her face and to her ear and neck as he reached up underneath her t-shirt to cup her breast. What he was doing felt so good and he was already so hard against her stomach. Tingles erupted throughout her body and settled low against his hardness.

She groaned low. "Colt, we can't do this. Not here. Cassie's just in the next room." Unfortunately the room they were in backed right up against the kitchen wall.

"You're right." He whispered as he lifted her shirt and closed his lips around the hard nub of her nipple. Her eyes rolled back into her head and she threw her leg over his hip to bring him closer to her. Her breathing was quickly becoming gasps.

Suddenly the crash of a breaking dish came from the kitchen, followed quickly by Cassie's curses. They'd both stiffened at the sound, but now Colton was grinning at her as he leaned over her, caging her with his body. "I guess that was our wake-up call. Get up, sweetheart, before I ravage you with both my brother and sister within listening distance. And I will work to get this," he grimaced down to his straining erection, "back under control."

She gave his shaft a slow stroke which had him moaning low. He pressed into her hands.

His voice lowered an octave when he said, "You're really not helping the situation here."

She withdrew her hand. "I'm sorry. I'll see you in the kitchen in a little bit." She slid out from underneath him.

He sat up and watched her with gleaming lust-filled eyes as she put on her robe. When she was fully covered, he glanced back down at his lap. "It may be a few minutes before I'm presentable."

Penelope just grinned and winked at him as she shut the door behind her. She was still grinning when she walked into the kitchen. On the other hand, Cassie was on the floor, cleaning up the remnants of some sort of a casserole and cursing a blue streak.

She looked up at Penelope's smiling face and scowled. "You should not look that happy with everything going on with you." But then she smiled at her, "But I forgive you for it, since that obviously means things are going well between you and Colt."

Penelope couldn't help the smile that became even wider. "Yeah, things are good with us. What about you? Jake gets in tomorrow, right?"

Cassie's eyes lit up. "Yeah, he's driving in from Arizona tonight. He should be here early in the morning. I can't wait. I'm so ready to have him here permanently. This long-distance thing is for the birds."

"Any idea when the wedding's going to be yet?"

"Not yet. We've discussed a few things, but haven't settled on a date. We wanted to get him here before we decided for sure."

"That makes sense. I know there's still a lot to get settled with setting up Mad Rob and the house and all." She looked down the hall. "Speaking of guys, where's Chris?"

"He had an early PT appointment. He told me to tell you guys that he can help later today if you need some help cleaning up."

"Thanks. We should be able to handle it. Chris seems to be doing better lately."

Cassie nodded. "He is. He still has his moments, but being able to focus on Mad Rob has been good for him. It's given him something else to concentrate on, besides everything that he's lost."

Colton walked in and immediately wrapped his arms around Penelope's waist from behind. He settled his chin on her shoulder. "Are we talking about Chris?"

Both girls nodded.

"He's gonna make it back to us. He's doing better, so now it's just a matter of time." He sounded so confident. Colton was a force to be reckoned with when he set his mind to something. She just hoped he wasn't disappointed. There was so much more healing that Chris needed to do, both body and soul. Penelope had a feeling there'd be a few more setbacks before Chris was truly on his way to a full recovery. Honestly, after all he'd been through, she wasn't so sure he'd ever be completely healed.

Cassie looked at them both before asking quietly, "So how bad is the loft?"

Colton grimaced. "Pretty bad. We'll get in there and see what's salvageable."

Penelope gasped and searched around the room for the clock. "Aww damn. I'm supposed to meet with a reporter this morning about the signing next week and I also need to pick up the Bus. I wasn't even thinking about all that last night." She looked at the clock again, then Colton. "We need to get going."

He nodded. "Go take your shower and get ready for work. I can drop you off at the bookstore. Chris should be done by then. He and I can pick up the Bus and we'll work on the loft until you're off. I didn't have anything important going today."

"Okay."

***

When Colton and Chris entered the loft, Colton was struck again by just how bad it was. He'd been hoping his memory of it was worse than it actually was. Wrong.

"Man, this sucks." Chris was good at stating the obvious.

Colton looked over at him on his crutches and the mess scattered all over the floor. He hadn't really thought this through. He started clearing paths through the living room, simply so Chris could move through the room. "Yeah, it does." He gestured to the piles of books that were shredded and tossed everywhere. "What do you think? If you sit there on the floor, can you sort through and figure out which books are salvageable and make piles of the ones that aren't? That pile of books was the thing she was most devastated about last night."

"Sure, I can handle that." He lowered himself to the floor and started piling up the miscellaneous books. "I'll just re-shelve the ones that look okay. She'll have to reorganize it again later, but at least it won't look so bad."

"Thanks Chris. I appreciate you helping with this. I think it would be completely overwhelming to stand here looking at this mess by myself. Not that it's not overwhelming anyway, but it's nice to have company. Thanks."

"No problem. I'm glad to be able to help…at least as much as I can."

Colton worked on hauling out the large pieces, like the shattered TV's, to the trash while Chris worked through the books. After the eighth trip to the dumpster, Colton stopped at the fridge for a beer break. He looked up to offer one to Chris and started grinning when he noticed Chris's nose buried in one of Pen's erotica books.

He popped the top on the second beer and walked over to see which book had caught Chris's attention. When he caught sight of the Celeste DeMarco cover, he smirked. He and Chris must have more in common than he thought. He inserted the beer between Chris and the book pages. "Find something interesting?" he asked innocently.

Chris looked up at him with a slightly stunned look in his eye. "I had no idea girls actually read this stuff." He looked back down at the text again and then looked up to Colton with a speculative look. "So, does she just read them or does she also…?" He left the question hanging as he grabbed the beer from Colton.

Colton felt himself flush. He rubbed the back of his neck. "Man, I can't tell you stuff like that."

Chris just smirked at him knowingly. "Just tell me this…does she tie you up or do you tie her up?"

"Shut up, asshole." Colton stalked back down the hall, ignoring his brother's laugh that followed him. He needed to tackle the mess in Penelope's room. He sure didn't want his smug bastard of a brother going through the lingerie flung throughout the room.

Just as he entered the doorway, he heard a final mutter from Chris, "Lucky bastard." As he took in the wisps of lacey red, black, and pink scattered throughout Penelope's room, he had to nod. He really was, wasn't he?

It took about an hour to get Penelope's clothes and shoes back into a reasonable order. Most of them hadn't been damaged. They'd just been flung all over the room. He really didn't understand the reasoning for all this. Why would someone break in to simply make a mess? They had to be searching for something, but what?

The note in the Bus had said 'the gift'…were these the same guys? Were they still looking for that elusive gift? He thought back to Pen's theory about Damon's dig site, El Regalo. Could it have something to do with that? He didn't know as much about the dig as Penelope did. He thought back to the flowers Damon brought her. They'd long since died, but she kept the golden one in a bud vase by her bed. He looked around the room, but he didn't see it anywhere in this mess. Was that maybe what they were looking for?

There was another bookcase in this room. Like the living room, the books were opened, scattered, and in wild disarray. These guys had too much fun scattering Pen's precious books. He gathered them up, sorting them as he did so. There were several notebooks here which Penelope obviously kept stored on the bookshelves. He'd picked them up and started putting them in their own pile, trying to straighten the bent and ruffled pages as he went. He was doing this when some of Penelope's writing caught his eye. Phrases like 'Rocking M' and 'ranching' combined with 'Dom', 'roping', and 'bondage' made him start to think about their trip to the ranch the day before.

Penelope said she met the Martin family through the bookstore, but what would a family ranch have to do with a bookstore unless one of the Martin's was an author? Penelope hadn't mentioned anything like that the day before. As he flipped through the notebooks, a thought occurred to him that seemed impossible. Surely not, but then he found a list of names in one of the notebooks. He rushed back out to the living room carrying the notebook and looked frantically at the bookcase trying to find it.

"Colt, what's wrong?"

"That book you were looking at earlier. Penelope has a whole bunch of books by that same author. One of the covers shows a picture of a ranch with a cowgirl tied up on the front of it. Have you seen it? The author is Celeste DeMarco."

Chris nodded and shifted down to the area of the bookcase which was already filled. "Yeah, I remember that one. That cover was hot. I can only imagine what the book is like."

Colton scanned the bookshelves looking for the book, becoming more and more convinced he was right.

Chris yelled a triumphant, "Found it!" and held the book up in the air in victory. Colton quickly snatched it and started reading the cover copy, comparing it to the notes in the notebook.

"I'll be damned. It's her." He stared at the notebook blankly, trying to process what this could mean.

"What's her?"

He glanced at Chris distractedly. He'd forgotten he was here. He looked back down at the book in his hands and then looked back up at Chris. "I'm pretty positive Penelope wrote this book." He strode back over to the bookcase and started snagging the other Celeste DeMarco books off the shelves. "Which means she wrote this one, and this one, and this one." He looked down at the pile of books in his arms. "She wrote all of these." He stared, stunned.

Chris snagged one of the books and read the story description. He looked back up at Colton with a hint of admiration in his eye. "Have I mentioned that you're a lucky bastard?"

Colton glanced back down at the books in his hands and at the piles of ruined books on the floor. Besides the TV's, they were the worst destruction in the apartment. There had to be a reason for that fact. He felt a sinking in his gut.

He shook his head at Chris. "I'm not, if these are the reason this is happening to her. What if someone has figured out who she is and fixated on her? What if this guy is a stalker trying to cover his tracks?"

Worry flashed through Chris's eyes. They both knew how dangerous a stalker could become since Chris, Jake, and Cassie had all almost died at the hands of a stalker just three months prior.

"Come on. We need to get to the bookstore and talk to Penelope."

Chapter 29

The interview with the newspaper seemed like it went really well. Penelope could only hope that would translate into good attendance numbers for the actual signing.

There was still no sign of Hannah and every day she was gone, the outlook seemed more bleak. She didn't have time to dwell on that today though.

She needed to get the blog updated about the signing. Luckily, she'd already managed to get the newsletter out and Jon and Alix were handling the store okay. Penelope probably should look into hiring someone else soon though. She pulled out her to-do list and added hiring to it. She sighed deeply. Every day it seemed like that list became more and more unmanageable. Looking at her list reminded her of something.

She picked up the phone and dialed the phone number from the information sheet.

"Yo!" A very happy voice answered.

She smiled. This was probably just what she needed today. "Hi. This is Penelope Pruitt from Raider Readers in Lubbock. I was wondering if I could speak to Tony from Abilene Authors."

"Whoa, this is Tony. No shit? You're from a bookstore?"

"Yeah, I am and I've been reading your group's book. I'm very impressed and more than a little curious about how you all do it, writing and releasing a book as a group? I wondered if I could ask you a few questions about the group."

"Dude! That would be awesome. You like the book?"

She laughed at the pure happiness coming from the guy. He sounded young. She would guess college age or maybe even high school, which made her even more curious about their group if this was their chosen spokesperson. "So how does it work?"

"Man, you wouldn't believe it. It's awesome. We've had our group for a while, but before it was just a normal writers' group. But that was before Dev Masters."

"Who's Dev Masters?"

"He's some loaded dude who's our beneficiary. He organized us and got us to writing and releasing the books. He fronts all the investment money. We provide the writing, editing, and graphic design for the covers. It's a win-win for everyone."

"Really? That's astounding. I've never heard of such a thing before."

"I know, right? The dude is revolutionary and we love it. We're getting to do what we love….write, and he makes sure that we can. For his help, we just have to work within the parameters he gives us for the books."

"Parameters?"

"Yeah, he comes up with the character names and settings, but then leaves everything else up to our creativity. It's so cool. It's like the ultimate in writing prompts and we write as a group so it gets done really quickly with that many brains working at it. It's awesome."

"You said graphic design, too. Does the group design your own covers? The cover for ***The Gift of Serendipity*** is really amazing."

"Thanks, the title was mine, but Melinda did the design. She's dope with a computer."

Penelope laughed. "Yes, she is. So, I was thinking. Sometime, I'd love to host your group for a signing. Do you think that's something you all would like to do?"

"Seriously?"

"Yeah."

"We'd love that. Just wait until I tell everyone. When could we do it?"

"Well, we're having another signing here next weekend, but let me look at the schedule. You talk to the group and we'll work something out. I'll be in touch."

"Thanks so much, Penelope. Dev and everyone are going to shit a brick."

"I'm happy to hear it. It was nice talking to you Tony."

She hung up still smiling. She loved enthusiastic authors.

Suddenly her cell phone rang. She didn't even bother to look at who was calling before answering it.

"Hello," she answered as she wrote another note onto her list.

"You didn't do what you were told to do." The voice was deep and menacing and a sudden chill raced down her spine, as she dropped her pen.

"Wha…" she wasn't given time to question him before he interrupted her.

"Now one of your friends will pay. You shouldn't have called the police and you should have returned the gift." A loud shot echoed through the phone and the blood left all her extremities. Immediately the voice came back on. "This is not a game." His voice was harsh and cruel. The line went dead.

Suddenly Penelope was shivering. Oh my God. Who had he shot? She immediately fumbled with her cell phone trying to get her fingers to work. Colton had to be okay. As she scrambled trying to hit his number on her phone, she rushed out of her office and down the stairs. No, no, no. He wasn't answering. She left a frantic message. "Colton, where are you? Call me as soon as you get this. You have to be okay. You have to. Call me."

She hit the disconnect button and called the loft. Again, there was no answer. Where could he be? Her breath was coming in gasps by the time she reached the first floor. She looked around frantically. He had to be okay. He couldn't be dead. He just couldn't be.

Alix spotted her rushing toward her. "Penelope, what's wro…"

The front door of the bookstore opened and Colton walked through it. Penelope sobbed as she launched herself into his surprised arms. "Thank God, you're okay. You're okay, right?"

She wrapped around him as tight as she could get and she felt all along his chest and neck and head to make sure he was all in one piece. She threaded her hands around behind his head and sobbed into his neck. "I thought you were dead. He shot someone and you didn't answer your phone and I was sure you were dead." Her breath hitched again as the sobs rolled out of her. She could have lost him today.

"Penelope, what the hell is going on?" He rubbed up and down her back as she tried to get her crying under control. He was here and he was fine, but someone else wasn't. She started to hyperventilate in panic.

Colton quickly strode behind the counter with her still clinging to him. He gingerly sat her on the stool by the register and yanked a bag out from under the counter which he shoved against her mouth. "Breathe, sweetheart.

You're hyperventilating. Just breathe and try to calm down." He looked at her with worried eyes.

She looked into his eyes and pressed her palm to the side of his face. Thank God, he was okay. The tears continued to roll, but she was getting herself back under control.

"Better?"

She nodded and pulled the bag away from her face. "We have to call the police. Call Brian. He shot someone. The envelope from the party with all the targets. He called me and shot someone while I was on the phone with him. I heard it happen. I thought it was you. You didn't answer your phone. Why didn't you answer your phone?" She was rambling, but she was beyond caring.

Colton searched his pockets. "I must have left it at the loft." He turned toward Chris, who she hadn't even realized was standing there, watching her breakdown. "Call Cassie and make sure she's okay. I'll use Penelope's phone to call the police and Brian." He pried it out of her frozen fingers. She hadn't even realized she was still clutching it.

As the guys talked into the phones, she thought about all the photos in the envelope that night. Which one of her friends had she just condemned to die?

"Cassie's okay." Chris told them and then turned back to his phone, punching in another phone number.

Colton hung up his phone and returned to crouch in front of her. "Brian's on his way. Are you okay?"

She nodded numbly. "One of our friends has just been shot." She looked at him bleakly.

Chris was on the other side of the counter and he looked grim as he hung up his phone. "Julie's okay, but there's been a shooting in the hospital parking lot so they're in lock-down."

"Oh no…Aaron?" she whispered.

Chris's jaw was clenched. "Maybe, but there were a lot of medical personnel at the party that night. It could be any one of them, or it could be something totally unrelated. But I don't want to leave Julie alone just in case. I'm going to head over there."

Colton nodded. "Watch your back. The shooter could still be around. Call me as soon as you know something."

***

Brian showed up at the bookstore shortly after that to take her statement. By that time, they had closed the store and moved into the reading nook. Jon left, but Alix continued to hover as Colton worked to calm Penelope down.

Colton shoved a cup of hot tea into her hands before drawing her down into his lap. Her panic was subsiding, but she was chilled to the bone. She couldn't get warm and her body continued to shiver. Colton wrapped his arms around her and held her close. Closing her eyes, she again thanked God he was okay. She didn't know what she would do if she'd lost him.

She asked Brian, "Do you know who was shot at the hospital yet?"

He looked at her, surprised. "How did you know about that situation?"

"One of our friends, Julie, works there. When we called to make sure she was okay, she told us what was happening."

He nodded. "The SWAT team is securing the scene right now. In fact, I'm headed over there after I finish here. Do you think that's related to your phone call?"

She nodded mutely and tried to swallow past the lump in her throat. "The photos from the party. That's the guy who did the shooting. That party was for Julie, our friend who works there so there were lots of hospital personnel at the party." Tears welled in her eyes again.

"Okay, let's start at the beginning. Did he call you on your cell phone or the store phone?"

"My cell." Colton handed her cell phone to Brian so he could go through the call log. "I was working on something so I didn't even look to see if there was a number listed or not."

"Do you mind if I take this? Our IT guys may be able to trace him."

"Sure, that's fine. I'll do whatever it takes."

"Thanks. Tell me exactly what he said, or at least what you remember him saying."

Penelope took a deep breath and tried to recall his exact wording. "He said I didn't do what I'd been told to do and now someone had to pay. He said I should have given him the gift and not called the police. Then I heard the gun go off." Her breathing hitched, but she continued. "He said this wasn't a game. That was it. Then he disconnected the call." She could hear his voice in her head like a nightmarish audio recording. She shivered harder.

"Could you hear anything in the background? Was there anything notable about his voice or the way he spoke?"

Penelope shook her head. "I don't think so, at least not that I remember."

"Okay, thanks, Penelope. I'll be in touch. I need to head over to check out the situation at the hospital. I really hope the victim there isn't one of your friends. Hopefully, this is just someone messing with your head as some kind of sick joke."

They walked with him to the front door. Just as he was about to leave, Colton had a thought. "Brian, on the off-chance this is one of our friends, Chris went to the hospital. Can you try to make sure that he can get in to be with our friend, Julie? If this is someone we know, she's going to be devastated and will need his support."

"Sure, I'll keep an eye out for both of them."

"Thanks, Brian."

After Brian left, Penelope turned bleak eyes to Colton. "What do we do now?"

"Let's head over to Cassie's. We can wait for word there."

***

When they arrived at Cassie's house, she met them at the door with worry-filled eyes. Colton immediately pulled her into his arms, although he continued to hold onto Penelope's hand the whole time, too. His voice sounded gruff when he said, "Thank God you're okay. Have you heard anything yet?"

She pulled them into the house shaking her head. "Nothing yet. They're reporting the shooting on the television stations, but they haven't revealed anything about the victim yet, except for the fact it's someone from the hospital. They haven't said anything about whether or not they caught the shooter." She looked back out the door. "Wait a minute, where's Chris? I thought he was with you."

"When he heard about the shooting at the hospital, he went up to see if he could be there to support Julie, just in case it's Aaron. Brian said he would do his best to get him inside the hospital to her."

Cassie's voice was quiet when she asked, "What happened today to make you think the victim is Aaron?"

The never-ending chills took hold of Penelope's body again. Colton must have felt her shiver because he pulled her within his arms once again and cradled her against his chest.

She was the one who answered though. "We don't know that it's Aaron, but we're pretty sure that it's someone from Julie's party. The guy who left the note on the Bus called me. I heard the gun go off over the phone. Whoever's been shot, they were shot because of me. This is my fault." The tears started falling down her cheeks and Colton stiffened underneath her.

His voice was low and angry. "This isn't your fault. You didn't do anything to provoke this attack. You've done everything possible to keep anything bad from happening. There's no way you're to blame for this. The guilty party is the guy who was holding that gun."

She placed her palm against his chest. "I know there's truth to that, but I still can't help but feel responsible. Somehow this all ties back to me. We have to figure out how if we're going to stop it."

Colton agreed. "We absolutely have to figure out what this guy's after and I had a couple of thoughts about that while cleaning the apartment. First, I didn't see the golden flower from Damon. Don't you usually keep that on your nightstand?"

She nodded.

"That's what I thought. I didn't see it when I was in there today, but the room isn't completely cleaned yet, so it may still be under a pile somewhere. But for now, it's missing and that might be a clue."

Penelope winced at the thought of the loft mess, but then thought better of it. What did it really matter when someone had been shot? Which brought up a point. "If they'd found what they'd wanted at the apartment, why would they have gone through with the shooting?"

"To prove a point maybe? I don't know, but you're right, that doesn't really fit. We need to find that flower and figure out if there's something more going on with Damon's project."

"I agree. I'm pretty sure he's coming back into town this weekend. I'll call my mom and find out his flight information."

Colton nodded then looked at Penelope speculatively. "There's one other possibility that occurred to me today."

"What's that?" He had a strange look in his eye that made Penelope nervous.

He watched her closely as he said, "Is it possible this could have something to do with Celeste DeMarco?"

The blood drained from her face and her eyes widened in shock. She searched his face, but couldn't get a read on him. She'd kept this secret hidden from everyone in her life for years, but within a few short weeks, Colton figured it out. "How did you find out?"

"I found some of your notes and pieced it all together. So it's true."

It wasn't a question, but she haltingly nodded anyway.

"Wait a minute," Cassie blurted out. "What are you both talking about? What does any of this have to do with an erotica author?"

Colton gave a strangled moan as his gaze swung to Cassie and he choked out, "You know who that author is?" He grimaced.

"What?" Cassie looked at them both in confusion.

Penelope was on the verge of a nervous breakdown but couldn't help the little giggle that escaped her, despite the terror and adrenaline flying through her system after all the events from the day. "I think you just broke Colton's Life Rule #1."

"Life Rule #1?"

"Yes, in his eyes, you're virginal and chaste." Penelope giggled again as Cassie rolled her eyes. "Life Rule #1 states we're not allowed to talk about anything that might burst his delusional bubble. I'm not sure, but I think you reading erotica falls into that category."

"Seriously? I don't know how I'm supposed to react to that." She turned her confounded gaze toward her big brother. "I think mainly, I'm a little disturbed that you two have discussed my sex life to the point where there's actually a rule about the discussion of it. I think we're headed into psychotherapy area." She gave Colton a look of chastisement. He had the good grace to flush in embarrassment at that.

But he quickly turned his scowl back to Penelope. "We're losing sight of the discussion. We were talking about Celeste DeMarco."

Cassie said, "I still don't understand what the author has to do with any of this. She writes incredible sexy books, but why are you bringing her up?"

His eyes never left Penelope's as he raised an eyebrow in question. "Aren't you going to answer her?"

In his eyes, she could see his dare. The secret she'd kept since college was going to come out. He was going to make sure of it.

She watched him, looking for a trace of anger, but she couldn't get a read on what he felt. "He thinks it might be important because I'm Celeste DeMarco."

Cassie's audible gasp finally drew Penelope from Colton's navy blue gaze to Cassie's shocked one.

Cassie looked at her in complete disbelief. "No way. If that were true, why wouldn't I know it? Why wouldn't you tell me?" She looked and sounded hurt as the reality set in.

"Until today," she glanced back at Colton who still watched her closely, "no one knew the truth except Alix, my editor, and my lawyer."

"Is it possible that someone else found out and this can all be traced back to some sort of stalker?" He'd slowly started rubbing up and down her back, his warm hands reassuring her he wasn't mad.

"I don't know." She shook her head and looked back over at Cassie. "My best friends never even figured it out. Why would anybody else? And even if they did what could that possibly have to do with a gift?"

"I figured it out."

"I know, but you're different. You know me. You live with me."

"You've had other roommates. Maybe one of them figured it out. What about your last roommate? You said he left suddenly. Do you think maybe there was more to that situation than you were aware of?"

"I don't think so, besides Frankie's not the type. He's a complete pacifist."

"And listen, this is another possibility… the books you write are very sexual. A lot of times, a woman giving sexual favors is considered a gift. Could he be looking for something sexual from you since you write these books?"

A chill rolled down her spine and Colton pulled her back into his embrace.

His voice was soothing as he persisted, "We have no idea what the motivation is behind all this. We need to look at all the possibilities at this point."

"You're right. This has just been a secret for so long. I'm not sure I'm ready to put it out there for everyone to know. This is why my mom and Aunt Alix don't talk any longer. Alix covered for me and claimed she was Celeste DeMarco when my mom found one of my writing contracts. She was snooping around the bookstore and it resulted in a huge blow-out between mom and Alix. My parents are too rigid about these types of things. They might be able to forgive me becoming a theater major, instead of an academic, but they'd never understand my writing erotica. So I just kept it a secret," she looked over worriedly at Cassie, "from everyone. I'm sorry."

"Sweetheart, we need to tell Brian."

Penelope nodded in agreement. "Do you really think this has something to do with the books I write? This all seems awfully serious for some erotica fiction. I mean honestly, we're talking about someone getting shot."

"I just don't know, but I think we need to look at all the angles."

Cassie had been quietly listening and absorbing their discussion. But now she looked at Penelope with curiosity and a touch of mischief. "Girl, I think we need to dish a bit about your research."

Colton launched up out of the chair and stalked to the back door. "I'm not listening to this. Have you already forgotten Life Rule #1? I'm gonna go out back to leave a message for Brian." He slammed out of the house and left both girls dissolving into laughter.

Just minutes before she had been on the verge of a nervous breakdown. This was what good friends did. They provided you with stress relief and a break to the mental stresses in life.

***

An hour and a half later, the laughter turned into tears as the call from Chris finally came. The victim was identified as Aaron. He'd been shot with a sniper rifle as he was leaving the hospital from the parking garage across the street. The shot had been to his head and he died instantly.

Of course, Julie was devastated, but she insisted she didn't want any of them coming over tonight. Chris was with her and had gotten her home. He planned to stay with her until her older sister arrived.

"It doesn't feel right for us to be here when Julie's whole world has just fallen apart." Cassie paced around the room in agitation.

Penelope agreed on one level, but she understood Julie's reasoning. "You know how Julie is. She hates to be the center of attention. Tonight she just wants to grieve by herself. Chris is with her and he knows to call us if she needs us."

"I know. You're right." Cassie looked at them as she brushed the tears from her eyes. "Will you both stay here tonight? I don't want to be alone and I don't want you out on the street tonight while this madman is still free."

Penelope looked over at Colton and nodded her assent.

He reached over to hug his little sister. He may be overbearing sometimes, but there was no doubt he loved his siblings deeply. "Sure Cass. The apartment is still a mess anyway so you'd be doing us a favor. Besides, I think we all need to stick close tonight. Why don't you head to bed and try to get some sleep. Jake will be here in the morning and things will feel better."

"For me, maybe, but for Julie, her nightmare is just beginning." Her voice was drenched in the sadness they all felt. For Julie. For Aaron. For his family. It was just such an incredible waste. He'd been a wonderful and talented man. It wasn't fair that his life had been cut so short.

Colton and Penelope watched Cassie walk down the hall. Penelope didn't even realize she was crying again until he reached up to brush tears off her cheeks. He tilted her chin up and lightly brushed his lips across hers. It wasn't a sexual kiss. It was soft and tender and filled with love. He led her down the hall into the bedroom and as they settled into bed, he wrapped his arms around her, holding her from behind. Gently, he leaned down to her ear and placed a tender kiss there.

Her tears flowed hot and heavy from within her soul. If she'd learned nothing else from today it was this: Times like these were meant to be treasured because in this life there were no guarantees that they would be there tomorrow.

Chapter 30

Colton watched Penelope and Julie work in tandem in the kitchen. The weekend had passed in a blur of tears, hugs, and cooking. Aaron's family was local, so they took over all the arrangements for the funeral and handling any family coming into town. That left Julie at loose ends. She was just the girlfriend and Aaron's mother didn't want her to be part of the process. So she did the only thing she could...she cooked. She'd taken over Cassie's kitchen and made everything from breakfast muffins, to casseroles, to desserts. Jake and Colton took turns running the items over to Aaron's mother's home.

A sniper shooting in Lubbock, TX was a rare thing. It hadn't taken the media long to sniff out that Julie was Aaron's girlfriend. His family lived in a gated community so the media hounds went after Julie. They'd taken to camping out in front of her townhouse hoping to sniff out any detail about the investigation. As a result, she'd moved in temporarily with Cassie, Jake, and Chris.

Chris being at the hospital the day of the shooting bonded the two of them. He didn't stray far from her side and hovered protectively when the others were around.

Overall the group dynamic was strained, sad, and extremely reserved. What should have been a joyous weekend, with Jake coming home, had turned into just the opposite.

For the moment, Jake and Cassie had run to the grocery store for more food ingredients, while Penelope and Julie cooked.

As Colton watched the girls work in the kitchen, he frowned. Penelope looked close to tears and this time, he didn't think it was directly related to Aaron's death. From the pained looks Pen kept throwing Julie when she wasn't looking, he guessed something happened between the two of them, but he'd missed it.

Colton caught Chris's eye and raised an eyebrow in question. Chris gave a slight shrug and subtle shake of his head, before turning back to watch the girls again. He obviously didn't know what happened between them either.

Both men saw it coming and lunged forward yelling a warning, but it happened anyway. Julie turned away from the refrigerator with an uncooked casserole in her hands, just as Penelope swung around to take a dish to the sink. The two collided which resulted in the gooey, raw egg casserole sliding down Julie's shirt and jeans.

For a moment, time stood still. They both stood there stunned as the raw ingredients slipped off Julie's body to plop to the floor. Pen was the first to recover. She scrambled over to grab a towel and started wiping off Julie's ruined clothes.

Julie forcefully grabbed hold of her hands and quietly said, "Stop. Just stop."

From Colton's position, he could see Penelope's stricken face. She whispered in a broken voice, "I'm so sorry, Julie."

Julie closed her eyes for a moment, but when they opened back up again, they were blazing in anger. "It's too late for that, isn't it?" She wasn't yelling, but the recrimination coming through her low-pitched voice hit Penelope like a physical blow, as she flinched backwards.

Everyone in the room knew they weren't talking about the casserole mess.

"I want you to leave." Julie ground out, fists clenched.

Penelope shook her head. "I'm sorry. Please let me…"

"No!" Julie finally lost it and screamed, "I need you to leave! Now, Penelope! Leave!" She sank to the floor sobbing. "Please just leave."

Penelope was crying just as hard as Julie, but Colton knew they needed to separate before one or both of them said something they'd really regret. He picked Pen up by her waist and walked out of the room with her, just as Chris made it to Julie's side and pulled her sobbing form into his shoulder.

As Colton exited the kitchen, Chris said to him, "Take the truck," and tossed his keys at him. Colton never slowed down as he caught them and carried the sobbing Penelope out the door.

***

The morning dawned soggy and overcast. It seemed appropriate for Aaron's funeral.

Ever since her confrontation with Julie, Penelope had withdrawn into herself. Colton didn't know what to do to help. She was quiet and closed-off. She'd taken to writing in her notebook, but did little else. She refused to talk to anyone on the phone. The shooter hadn't been caught, so Colton remained vigilant and at her side.

She was hurting and he didn't know how to fix it, besides simply be there for her and try to make sure the madman didn't get hold of her. They continued to sleep together, but that's all they were doing, sleeping. They hadn't had sex since before the loft had been destroyed.

As they left for the cemetery, Penelope began to fidget. Colton laid his hand across her's. "It's going to be okay," he reassured her. "Julie's grieving right now. Just give her a little bit of time and space."

"Do you honestly think it will make the difference? If they didn't know me, Aaron would still be alive today. Because of me, her boyfriend is dead. She's lost their future. How can she forgive me for that?" She looked out the truck window watching the West Texas landscape roll by, but Colton knew she wasn't seeing any of it.

"She'll forgive you because you haven't done anything that needs forgiveness. Julie knows that, but she needs someone to blame right now. Until they catch this guy, you're the only one she can focus on."

She nodded mutely, but still wouldn't meet his eye. Unfortunately, the police department didn't have any more leads than they had before the shooting. Every day that went by, Colton could feel the danger to Penelope getting closer, but he didn't know where it was coming from so they could protect her from it.

Even more worrisome, other people seemed to be disappearing without a trace from Penelope's life. Hannah was still missing and, over the weekend, Damon never showed up in Lubbock. His associates at the dig said he'd left according to schedule and the airline showed he made the flight. But from there he disappeared without a trace. There was no way to know what happened.

No one knew whether these disappearances were related or just really strange coincidences. All of it gave Colton a really bad feeling.

They pulled up to the cemetery and before they got out of the car, Colton tugged Penelope's hand up to his mouth and kissed it. "It's going to be fine."

She gave him a soft smile. "I'm so glad you're with me today. I know why Julie is so upset. I think about what she's going through." Her eyes filled with tears. "If anything happened to you, I don't know how I'd be able to go on."

He reached across and pulled her to him so he could kiss her. "Nothing's going to happen to me, sweetheart. Nothing."

She wanted to be able to believe him.

They made their way over to the chairs set up around the gravesite. The family decided to thumb their nose at the shooter by doing a graveside service out in the wide open rather than a more protected church service. The Lubbock PD was there in full-force to keep the media, unwanted guests, and random shooters away.

It wasn't enough for Colton to feel safe having Penelope there. But there'd been no dissuading her from coming to support their friend and say goodbye to Aaron. He hovered over her protectively, sharing his warmth in the cold air and hoping the bulk of his body would shield her in case anyone tried to shoot at her.

Julie sat two rows back from the family with Chris close to her side. The rest of their friends stood in the back of the gathering. As they walked up, Cassie enveloped Penelope into a big hug. Colton couldn't hear what she said, but Penelope nodded and then turned back toward him.

It wasn't raining, but there was a definite heaviness to the air that wasn't caused only by the grief. It seemed at any moment the heavens were going to open up, mourning the loss of Aaron too. During the middle of the ceremony, Colton heard Penelope gasp. He followed her gaze, his defenses immediately up and poised to drag her to the truck if need be.

A huge white butterfly had landed on Julie's shoulder. It was springtime in West Texas. It was damp and cold. There shouldn't have been butterflies out, but there was most definitely a huge snow white one on Julie's shoulder. It stood in contrast to her black suit jacket. She must have seen something from the corner of her eye because she looked over her shoulder at it. It simply sat there slowly moving its wings back and forth. By this point, almost everyone at the funeral had seen it.

It was beautiful and eerie. It sat there a full three to four minutes before it flew off. As it did, Julie watched it fly away, her eyes filling with tears. She looked to the crowd standing around the chairs. Colton could see her searching. Finally her gaze found Penelope's and she gave her a soft smile. They were going to be okay.

Afterwards, it was Julie who approached Penelope. After giving her a long, tight hug, she smiled up at Penelope with watery eyes. "Come back to Cassie's house. We're celebrating Aaron's life with margaritas and beer tonight."

Penelope searched Julie's eyes. "Are you sure you want me there?"

Julie nodded. "Absolutely."

***

After the damp and dreary morning, the afternoon turned out warm and sunny, so when the group got back to Cassie's house, they quickly retreated out to her backyard oasis, drinks in hand. It had been a while since the six of them had gotten to hang out and despite the somberness of the day, the gathering quickly dissolved into more of a party atmosphere. The drinking definitely helped with that development.

As they sat there, Colton looked around the group. Jake and Cassie were snuggled up into one of the outdoor lounge chairs. Chris and Julie sat at the little bistro table under the umbrella. Penelope leaned up against him and they both had their feet in the warm water of the hot tub.

Everyone had been drinking and relaxing together for a couple of hours so most of their group was feeling no pain.

Julie lifted her margarita glass to Jake and Cassie. "So, put us out of our misery. Let's have some fun news today. Please tell us you've set your wedding date."

Cassie was sitting in front of Jake in between his legs on the lounger and she leaned back to share a private smile with him. He could see the mischievous sparkle in his little sister's eye as she asked Jake, "Should we tell them?"

"I think we probably should, especially since it's not very far away."

They both looked back at the group and then they zeroed in on at the table where Chris and Julie sat. Jake said, "This past year has been tough and it started out with the worst thing we ever could imagine experiencing, Chris's death. Thankfully, the news of his death was greatly exaggerated." He lifted his beer to Chris who smiled and rolled his hand to keep Jake talking. "As awful as that was, it was the beginning of what brought us together. We want to be able to move through May without revisiting the sadness of that day. Soooo, we plan to get married on May 10th, the day Chris died. We want to make it into a day of celebration instead."

"Wait a minute." Julie eyes widened and her hands started flying through the air. Her OCD was showing. "Are we talking about the May 10th that's happening in just a little bit over six weeks?" She looked mortified at simply the idea of it.

"It's okay, Julie. We're going to do a very small wedding so it will be easily done."

She still looked disbelieving. "While you're finishing up the semester at Tech?" Cassie taught military history for Texas Tech University and the end of the semester was notoriously crazy, for both staff and students alike.

Cassie just nodded. "We can do it. You'll help keep me organized."

Julie was in full-blown panic mode. She stood up suddenly. "I need a paper and pen." She looked around the group as if one of them might have them handy. They all looked at her blankly.

Cassie chuckled as she waved her inside. "There's a notepad and pen in the kitchen drawer by the phone. Knock yourself out."

As Julie went into the house to gather her organizing supplies, it was Chris who commented. "That was good of you guys."

Cassie's face fell as she looked worriedly back at the back door. "It gives her something else to focus on for the near future. At least to get her through the next few weeks and maybe that will make it easier for her in the long run."

"You're a good woman, Cassie." Penelope was close to tears again.

"It's what friends do. We stand by each other when one of us is hurting. Besides, she will have me way more organized than I could ever be on my own."

Chapter 31

By Thursday, Colton, Penelope and everyone around them settled into an uneasy pattern. They were all on pins and needles waiting for the other shoe to drop but, so far, there'd been no word from whoever was terrorizing her.

Colton drove her to work every day and then hung out at the bookstore during her shifts, scowling ferociously at any customer who he felt might pose a threat. It had only been two days so far and Penelope was already at the end of her patience with his hovering.

Today was worse because she was conducting interviews for Hannah's replacement. They needed the extra help in the store for the signing scheduled on Saturday. Unfortunately, a minimum wage retail job brought in lots of people who Colton felt were untrustworthy at first sight. As she exited her office with her latest interviewee, a flighty sixteen year old who didn't even realize they still made print books anymore, Penelope felt old and just about at the end of her rope.

So when she found Colton with her next candidate cornered demanding he show him his driver's license, she lost it. The balding man looked small and terrified with Colton towering over him. The poor man's eyes were darting about as he tried to find an escape around Colton's mammoth size.

Colton ignored her arrival and continued to glare at his prey.

"Colton!" She said forcefully as she pinched his arm and dragged him behind her.

He turned his glare on her. "Ow! What?"

"Don't you use that tone with me. Stop terrorizing my customers and wannabe employees." She turned to the bald man, who still looked pale. She laid a soothing hand on his arm and gave him her most disarming smile. "I'm sorry about that. Are you Mr. Krazinski, my 2:00 interviewee?"

"Yes," he mumbled quietly, "but I've reconsidered and don't think I want to apply anymore." He scooted out around her and darted out the door.

She watched him go in disbelief before turning to glare at Colton. "Dammit, Colton. What the hell am I supposed to do now? He was the last person I had to interview."

He shrugged, but looked a little chagrined when he said, "What about the girl? She seemed nice."

Penelope rolled her eyes at him. "Sure, if my business was selling lip gloss, she would have been perfect. Unfortunately, I sell books and she doesn't even know what those are."

"Oh come on, it couldn't have been that bad."

"Seriously, Colt. She straight out asked me how old all these books are because and I quote here, 'they aren't even making books anymore, right?' He was my last hope and you just sent him scurrying out of here, peeing his pants in fright." She waved her hand at the now shut door. "You've been terrifying my customers all day and you have to stop it."

Colton nodded and she finally thought she was making some headway through his stubborn brain. "You're right. I need to take care of some Mad Rob stuff anyway, so you can just take the rest of the week off until they catch this guy. You'll be safe with me and I'll feel better when you're not here. This guy knows you work here and that makes it too easy for him to target you, so taking off for the rest of the week is the right thing to do."

Her mouth dropped open and she was pretty sure she'd never in her life been this close to literally having her head explode off her body. The man was stubborn and impossible and completely hard-headed. She was ready to do him physical harm. It didn't matter that he out-weighed her by 100 pounds of pure muscle. She was going to kill him.

Luckily, Brian returned her cell phone to her the day before. She glared at Colton as she pulled it out of her pocket and started dialing.

"Hello."

"You need to come over here and remove your big brother from my store right now before he stains my carpets." Colton narrowed his eyes at her and started shaking his head. He tried to take the phone from her which just pissed her off more. It must have shown in her eyes because suddenly he backed off with his hands raised.

Chris laughed. "He's not already bleeding, is he?"

"Not yet," she said through gritted teeth, "but he's getting real close." He reached for the phone again and she held a single finger up. "And if he tries for my phone one more time, he's going to lose a finger or five."

Chris continued to laugh, which just ticked her off more.

"You obviously don't care for his well-being at all, do you?"

"Darling, I'm just glad to know I'm not the only person he likes to drive bat-shit crazy with his control issues."

Penelope growled in frustration.

"Okay, I'm coming and don't worry, I'll bring reinforcements. We'll get the over-protective big guy back under control." He lowered his voice when he said, "I know he can be a pain in the ass, but he's only like this because he cares. You know that, right?"

She closed her eyes and sighed. "I know, which is why I called you before doing him bodily harm."

"We'll be there in five."

"Thanks Chris."

Colton continued to glare at her as she hung up the phone. He was doing a bit of growling on his own. "Do I have to remind you that some guy is intent on doing you harm?"

She rested her hand on the flat of his pecs. "I haven't forgotten. Both Alix and Jon are here. I promise not to leave the store until you get back. I'll stay away from the windows. In fact, I plan to work in my office the whole time you're gone. Just give me a few hours of space. You're smothering me." She could see the worry and hurt in his eyes and she reached up to smooth the lines between his brows. "We can't survive like this. A few hours, Colt. That's all I'm asking. I promise I'll be careful and diligent about that safety. Please."

Finally, reluctantly he nodded. "Okay, but Pen, no leaving without me by your side. Do not endanger yourself. We have no idea who we're dealing with. Someone could come in randomly off the street and kill you."

He looked back at the front door and tensed up. "No, I can't leave. It's not worth it." He shook his head. "I can't take that risk."

"Colt." He continued to stare at the door like someone was about to walk in with guns blazing. She reached up to grasp his chin so that he would turn and look at her. "Whoever this is, they need something from me. They can't get it if I'm dead. That's going to keep me relatively safe for now. Please, you have to relax." She arched an eyebrow at him. "Am I going to have to tie you up again?"

His eyes darkened at the suggestion. "Hmm, maybe." He reached down around her waist and pulled her snug up against him so that she could feel his erection while he kissed her.

They were both so caught up in the moment, they didn't hear anyone come in until a humor-laced voice asked, "I thought you said she was angry at him? That's not what Cassie does to me when she's angry."

They both turned to look into the smirking faces of their four friends. Cassie punched Jake in the arm, but he kept his focus on Colton. "So are you gonna share your secret with your friends? How do you get her from mad to passionate in five minutes flat?"

Colton looked down at her with desire before whispering in her ear, "Should I tell him the secret is rope?"

He'd forgotten who he was messing with. "I dare you to tell him and exactly how it was used." It was satisfying to watch Colton blush like that.

He grinned as he pulled her back toward him. "Behave and we'll continue this later tonight." To the girls, he sternly said, "Keep her here until I get back. No one is to go outside."

Cassie saluted him and said, "Yes, sir," before pushing him out the door.

As Penelope watched them walk out, she heard Chris mutter, "Were you actually just blushing?"

Penelope smiled to herself as she watched the door close behind them. Tonight… They hadn't had sex since Aaron was shot. They both could use the physical release from all the stress. It was an intriguing thought.

Penelope didn't realize she'd gotten lost in her daydream until Cassie waved a hand in front of her face. She turned to face her two friends. "Sorry about that. Let's go up to my office. You all can hang out there while I get some work done. I may even have a bottle of wine or two in there."

Cassie said, "You keep wine in your office?"

Penelope nodded. "Sometimes it's necessary. This week it's necessary." She reached around Julie and gave her a hug. "How're you doing?" The circles under her eyes said she wasn't sleeping and there was an aura of sadness around her.

"I'm okay, but I could really use a distraction."

It was Cassie who said, "Some girl time will do us all some good. I just need to grab one thing. You all go ahead up to Penelope's office. I'll be right up."

As they entered her office, Penelope saw the pile of books that Cassie went to get and she rolled her eyes at her. "So did you tell Julie?"

Cassie's eyes were sparkling as they all settled onto the floor around the coffee table. There was a couch, but the three of them discovered long ago that they were more comfortable hanging out on the floor. It was more relaxed for girl chat. "No, I figured it was your secret to tell."

"Yeah, sure, that's why you brought all those books up."

"Call it a little nudge."

Julie looked confused as she looked between the two of them. "What are you two talking about?" She looked down at the pile of books Cassie set on the floor in front of them and blushed. "Never mind, maybe I don't want to know."

Cassie shook her head, "Oh no, you definitely want to know this and I want to know more about how it happened." She looked back over at Penelope with a challenge in her eyes.

Penelope raised her hands in surrender. "Okay, I know when I've been beat, but we probably should open up the wine for this one." She gestured to Julie who was reading the back of one of the books with wide eyes and more than a bit of trepidation. "I have a feeling she's going to need it."

She found coffee mugs for all three of the girls and then gave Julie twice as much wine as she gave either herself or Cassie. "Drink up, oh innocent one."

Julie looked at them both suspiciously, but followed Penelope's instructions.

While Julie drank, Penelope got the phone call from Sylvia Robert's publicist which she'd been expecting all day. She relocated to her desk since she was talking business. As she listened to the publicist, Penelope felt the need to top off her own wine glass and started to imbibe more freely. She grimaced at her friends who looked at her curiously. They could only hear her side of the conversation and she honestly wasn't getting a chance to say too much.

When she hung up the phone, she let her head bang on her desk a couple of times, before taking a long swallow of wine.

"Bad news?" Cassie asked.

"That was Sylvia Robert's publicist. Sylvia's the author who's supposed to be here on Saturday. Since Lubbock has become such a hotbed of crime, she's cancelled."

"What? Can she do that this late?"

Penelope shrugged. "There's a penalty clause in her contract for cancelling so late, but it's really negligible in the grand scheme of things. The problem is that it's too late to pull back my publicity and I'm going to have customers here with no author to show to them." She closed her eyes and rubbed her forehead where a headache was beginning. "Okay, there has to be a way to make this work." She took another deep drink of her wine and laid her head back down on her desk while Cassie and Julie watched her with concern.

As Penelope laid there, the flier from Abilene Authors hanging on her bulletin board caught her eye. She yanked it down and immediately started dialing the number from it. "Please let this work," she muttered as the phone rang.

"Yo," he answered.

"Tony, this is Penelope Pruitt, from Raider Readers in Lubbock. We talked a few days ago."

"Hey, how's it hanging? Everyone was stoked when I told them about your phone call."

"Good. I hope they're really excited because I've had a cancellation by an author and hoped that maybe your group could come do a signing at my store on Saturday."

"Seriously? We'd love to come. Road Trip. Dude, that's sweet! I'm not sure how many will be able to come, but I'd guess at least four to five of us could be there."

"That would be wonderful, Tony. My next question is: Do you all have any of your books stocked?"

"Oh man, let me think. ***The Gift of Serendipity*** doesn't release for another couple of months. You have the proof copy, but we had another romantic suspense called ***Spirit Betrayed*** that released last month. It's intense."

"That sounds perfect. Do you have stock of it you could bring with you?"

"Oh yeah, no problem. We got it covered."

"Thank you so much Tony! You're really saving me by doing this at the last minute. I'm looking forward to meeting all of you. The signing is at 12:30, so if you all could be here by 10:30 that would be great. I'll send you the details and directions."

"Thanks, Penelope."

She turned back to Cassie and Julie who watched the conversation with interest and gave them two thumbs up.

"Whew, that's a relief. Although it will be interesting to see how Sylvia's fans take to this group if they're all like Tony. He's an interesting guy." She rejoined them on the floor.

"Who are they?"

"A writing group out of Abilene who write and release books as a group. It's bizarre, but from what I've read, their books are pretty good." She nodded, happy to have found a solution quickly.

Now she refocused on her girlfriends. She leaned over to pick up the books Cassie brought up. "Sorry, I got sidetracked there. I think we were about to talk about these."

She looked at Julie who radiated discomfort. "What Cassie is dying to let you know is that I'm Celeste DeMarco." She held the book up in front of her and pointed to the author's name on the cover.

"What? You write these? Seriously?" Julie looked shocked, but also a little intrigued.

Penelope nodded. "Yep."

"Now I want to know how all this began." Cassie trailed her hand over the pile of books. "You've obviously been doing it for a while."

Penelope nodded. "Since college. At first, it was purely for the shock value. Rebellion. Alix and I were playing around one night and found some erotic artistic photos. The first idea came from there." She held up her first book. "And this book was born."

Cassie took it from her hands and started reading the back cover with Julie looking over her shoulder.

"I never planned to get them published. I shared the first couple with Alix because she knew about the inspiration. She was the one who submitted them. It was a complete surprise when she came to me with the first contract. These books are how I paid for the store."

Julie looked at her curiously. "I always thought Alix loaned you the money to buy the store."

Penelope nodded. "We've just always let that impression stick. It was easier than explaining how a recent college graduate with no real income managed to buy and start a bookstore." She shrugged. "It's actually the other way around. Alix works for me."

Both girls flipped through the books, reading little sections, and taking turns looking at her with awe and a bit of disbelief.

Julie paused and looked up from a particular passage. "So," she hesitated looking really embarrassed. She looked back down at the book as she asked, "Do you do all this stuff?"

"Oh, God no!" Penelope laughed and Julie looked relieved. "I do lots of research. I'm not a prude, but some of this stuff is out there even for me. These books are all about the fantasy. I just have a very active imagination."

Penelope couldn't resist teasing Julie a bit more. "Although they do make for great inspiration in the bedroom. There are always elements from each scene that will work for just about anyone." Cassie looked intrigued while Julie looked shell-shocked.

"Does Colton know?"

Penelope nodded at Julie's question. "Yes, he's the one who blew my cover to this one." She quirked her eyebrow at Cassie. "He discovered my secret when he was cleaning up the apartment and found some of my writing notebooks. He doesn't seem to mind it too much."

Cassie snorted. "I can't imagine any guy having issues with this kind of imagination." She lifted the book with the tied up cowgirl on the front of it.

They all laughed, but Julie turned serious as she took another drink of her wine. "Seriously Penelope, this is fabulous. I admire you. You see what you want and go after it, no fear."

Penelope looked at Julie in disbelief. "Did you miss the part where no one has known about this for nine years?"

"I know, but it's not just this." She looked down at one of the books in her hands. "You live your life to the fullest and you don't let anything or anyone stand in your way. You grab onto life and live it." Her eyes filled with tears as she talked.

Cassie reached across and put her arm around Julie. "Is this about Aaron?"

She nodded. "But it's not just him. I've made so many mistakes with guys because I'm never willing to step up and take a risk. He asked me to move in with him and I told him I felt like it was too soon in our relationship." She laughed bitterly before saying, "Too soon? I had no idea our time was so short."

"Julie, you can't blame yourself for that. There's no way for any of us to know that kind of thing."

"I realize that and you would have thought I'd learned my lesson the first time."

Penelope and Cassie exchanged a look of confusion. The first time?

"I just feel so guilty. I should have told him 'yes'... to so many things. I wasn't fair to him. I should have been living with him. I don't want to fear life anymore. I want to embrace it. I don't want to have any more regrets. I want to be able to look back at my life and know I lived it like one of these heroines." She leapt up and pounded the cover of the book she was holding which showed the heroine standing in between two gorgeous hunks.

At the looks on both her friend's faces, Julie looked at the book and sank back down to the floor, blushing once again. "Okay, well maybe not exactly like the heroine in this particular book." She took another deep drink of wine and went back to examining the cover. She looked at Penelope, curiosity glowing through her hazel eyes. "You haven't ever..." She flung her hand at the cover of the book.

This time it was Penelope blushing. Both her friends looked at her in surprise, but it was Cassie who spoke in a hushed voice, "No way."

"What? It was college. I was a theater major. The parties sometimes got a little out of hand."

Cassie looked at Julie. "Who knew the theater parties were where we needed to be?"

They both looked at her with a newfound respect. "I sure didn't," said Julie.

Penelope just rolled her eyes at the two of them. "It wasn't as hot as you'd think. Honestly, I think I was just there as an excuse for two straight guys to experiment with each other." She winked at them.

"Oh wow," Julie muttered, "I've definitely been missing out."

Chapter 32

Colton locked the loft door behind him and leaned against it to watch Penelope move around the room. She was so beautiful. His gut tightened from just the sight of her. She'd left her wavy hair loose tonight and it tumbled down her back. As she reached over to take something off the coffee table, he could see the shadow of her cleavage and his hand tightened into a fist. He needed to feel the heat of her skin under his fingertips, but first he needed to get her to relax. It'd been a hell of a week and unfortunately, there wasn't an end in sight.

He could see the tension radiating off her. They'd heard from Brian earlier in the evening. They'd found Hannah's body. She'd been dumped somewhere out in the country and a rancher found her. They wouldn't know for sure until after the autopsy, but figured she'd been dead at least a week and the signs showed that she'd died at the hand of some pretty brutal violence. Brian had no idea if this was tied to everything happening with Penelope, but they were looking at all the possibilities.

Penelope wasn't taking the news well. She'd been really quiet since Brian's call. It was hard for her to accept the death of another friend, especially since it all seemed to stem from something to do with her. He didn't know what to do to ease her pain. She was hurting and it made him feel helpless that he couldn't fix it. He thought back to their fight earlier in the bookstore. Pushing definitely wasn't the way to effectively deal with her and he should know that by now.

She continued to putter around the room and he realized she wasn't looking at him. In fact, she seemed to be studiously avoiding him. He frowned at the idea and approached her slowly.

When he reached her side, she finally looked at him, but she seemed wary and jumpy. He reached below her chin and lifted it up. He caressed her lips with a soft kiss, but when her lips trembled below his, he pulled back.

He had a hand on each side of her face, holding her gently so he could look her in the eye. "Hey, what's going on? You're not still mad at me are you?"

She shook her head mutely and her eyes filled with tears again. She didn't say anything and her visible pain broke his heart. She stiffened in his arms before she whispered brokenly, "It's too much. Too much risk. You need to leave before you die, too." She tried to pull out of his arms, but he wouldn't release her. He knew what she was doing and he wasn't going to let her get away with it.

"Come on." He reached down, picked her up in his arms, and carried her down the hall to his bedroom. When they got there, he kissed her softly again., "You aren't going to get rid of me that easy. I'm not going anywhere." He dipped his head down so that they were at eye-level. "I don't know if you've noticed, but I'm in pretty good shape and military trained. I'm not that easy to kill."

She started to shake her head, but he stopped her. "If you think I'll walk away from you, then you don't know me very well. It's been a long week. Please just let me take care of you tonight."

He started to slowly unbutton her shirt but she stopped him, grasping his hand. She took it and raised it to her lips and kissed it. "I don't know how I got so lucky to deserve you. I must have been really good in a former life."

She looked up at him and the emotion in her eyes took his breath away. This was it for him. She was it for him. And unless he was reading her wrong, the feeling most definitely went both ways, but he didn't want to scare her away. Penelope was skittish when it came to relationships. He needed to keep this to himself for right now

"Aw, sweetheart, you've been great in this life and I'm the lucky one here. Now let's see what we can do about all these tight muscles." He slid her shirt off her shoulders, laying tantalizing kisses along her clavicle and lower as he went. When he had her down to just her lacy thong, he lowered her to the bed. "Turn over."

"You're not telling me what to do are you?" There was a distinct challenge in her voice, but her nipples were tight and her eyes were sparkling with arousal.

He leaned down to whisper in her ear, "You bet your sweet ass I am. Now do it." He watched her chest heave and her nipples tighten even further.

She leaned back, looked at him with a touch of mischief, and then gestured to his fully clothed body. Her voice had gone deep and sultry. "How about a compromise since you seem to have me at a disadvantage? I'll do what you say if you shed some clothing to put us on a little bit more equal ground."

He kicked off his shoes and pulled his t-shirt over his head. He saw her take in his full erection pressed against his jeans and she started to reach toward his buttons. "Nuh uh, not yet. If those come off, things will be over way too soon. First, let me take care of you. Please, Penelope." He leaned down to give her another soft kiss. "I feel like I'm not doing anything to help. Let me do this for you. Please roll over."

"Okay, but when you're done, I'm taking care of this for you." She stroked him slowly through the denim of his jeans before she rolled over on the bed.

He chuckled low. "I'll hold you to that."

He rubbed down her back, easing her tensed muscles, and quickly got distracted by her tattoo. Things were always so hot and heavy between them, he'd never taken the time to examine it closely. He did that now with his hands and his lips, brushing over the soaring birds across her body. She moaned beneath his ministrations. He followed the path of the birds from her shoulder to her hip and was surprised when he found a birdcage there. He'd never noticed it before. It was smaller than the soaring birds and had a single bird within it. It was not a happy bird, small and sickly-looking, and he had a sinking feeling in his stomach.

As he looked at the cage, she tensed up, obviously realizing what he saw. He tried to sound light as he said, "You never did explain the full story behind your tattoo. Alix mentioned something about it tying into one of your books."

She turned to look at him and he couldn't read the expression in her eyes. If he had to guess, he would say it was cautious.

"Would you tell me what it all means?"

She nodded slowly and sat up to face him, pulling a pillow onto her lap, as if to shield herself. She took a deep breath and her eyes flashed with a vulnerability he'd never seen before. He felt a premonition of dread about this conversation.

When she spoke her voice was so low, he had to concentrate to hear it. "It's all symbolic. My first book was called *Caging Lily*. It was the first thing I wrote and at that point in time I wrote purely as a form of therapy. When I started the book, my parents were unhappy with what I was doing with my life and I'd just broken up with an abusive boyfriend who wanted to control me." She smiled at the thunderous look that suddenly appeared in his eyes and immediately went to soothe him. "It's fine. That was a long time ago." She rubbed up and down his arm until he calmed down a bit.

"Back to the book... Lily, the heroine in the book, had also been in an abusive relationship... a really bad one. Her husband in the book was a tattoo artist and he tattooed her- a birdcage with a lily inside to show her that she'd always belong to him. Like I said, it was all symbolic at the time. In the book, she met a nice guy eventually and found her Happily Ever After." She rolled her hands. "You know, the way all good books and fairy tales end."

She took a deep breath. "My tattoo has a little bit of a different twist to the story. Ever since that guy in college, I've pretty much stuck with party-guys. They were all short-term guys just out for a good time. Everyone knew the score— no long term relationship expectations. But a little over a year ago, I met someone different. He was serious and intense. Things were different with him. He was a lawyer, attentive, attractive, everything a girl wishes for when she's a little girl thinking about her Prince Charming."

Colton felt the tendrils of jealousy take hold and he was beginning to wish he'd never asked. This was a story that wasn't going to have a happy ending, he could already tell. He just wasn't sure who was going to be more devastated at the end of it, her or him.

Penelope continued. "Ever since that guy in college, I knew there wasn't a happily ever after in my future and I was okay with that until I met Maddox. With him, I dared to dream that maybe fate held more in store for me. We dated for about three months when it all came crashing down. I should have realized before. The signs were all there, but I chose to ignore them. But somehow I must have known. Just the fact I never told Cass and Julie about him showed I knew the truth even if I wasn't telling it to myself."

She'd gone quiet and her head was bowed behind a curtain of golden hair. He pushed it back off her face, before asking, "What happened?"

"He was *that* guy. The one I'd worked my whole adult life to avoid. A controller. An abuser. I didn't even know he was married until he killed his wife in a violent rage. I didn't know until I saw it on the news. I never told anyone about him. I never let anyone know just what an awful judge of character I am. That poor woman... and it could have so easily been me. I never saw that side of him. I chose not to see that side of him and now she's dead and he's rotting in prison. And I got my tattoo to remind me."

He spoke very quietly, "Remind you of what?"

Her voice was strident when she said, "I will never be that bird. I'm never going to be locked up in marriage. Marriage is a cage and I will never fall into that trap. I will never let a man have control of me that way. I will always be with the free birds, soaring as my own person."

She looked at him and he could see the desperate plea to understand in her eyes. "The birds come over my shoulder and I see them every day to remind me. I don't plan to ever let go of my freedom."

"Just because someone gets married doesn't mean you lose control of who you are or how you go about your life, Penelope."

"No, not for everyone, but I won't let myself be put in a position where it's a risk. I can't. I respect myself too much. I won't ever give up my freedom. Not to anyone."

And there it was, the reason she'd never open her heart entirely to him, no matter what he did or how many ways he showed her that he wasn't that guy. His heart plummeted. She'd told him from the very beginning she wasn't a long-term relationship girl. He just hadn't realized until this very moment exactly what that meant for the two of them. They didn't have a future. She was using him. He felt like she had feelings for him, but even if it was love, for Penelope that was a temporary love. She wouldn't allow it to become more.

While he planned picket fences and their two point five kids, she looked to a future that eventually would be without him. He felt like he'd been kicked in the gut, but it was his heart that was hemorrhaging inside his chest. He had to get out of here before he broke down and begged her.

***

Penelope's heart shattered. Cassie was right. If you say it with confidence, people will believe you. But she didn't mention how devastating it would feel to tell such a horrible, heart-breaking lie. The pain in his eyes had been like a physical blow to her chest.

Colton rushed out of the apartment with a mumbled excuse about an errand he forgot to do.

She knew she'd hurt him, but it would be okay if that kept Colton safe. She'd obviously learned something in all those acting classes in college, because he never saw that what she said was just as devastating to her as it was to him.

While everything from her story was true, her feelings on marriage had changed since falling in love with him. And yes, she could admit that to herself now. She loved him. She knew he wasn't that guy from her story. Colton would never do anything to hurt her. That's the problem though. He would do everything in his power to keep her safe, which included dying. Enough people had died from knowing her already.

He was her happily ever after, but she'd never get it if he ended up dead. Until they caught this guy, she wasn't willing to put Colton's life on the line. She'd never planned to hurt him like that. But when he asked about the tattoo, she saw an opportunity that she couldn't pass up. By hurting him, maybe he wouldn't hover so closely so that he was in the line of fire when it came. His life was worth the emotional trauma.

She knew he wouldn't stop playing bodyguard to her, but maybe he'd be standing a little bit further away when it finally happened. Maybe she could keep him out of the immediate danger zone of her body. She didn't know what else to do to keep him safe, even if it was only a few more inches away. Maybe that distance could make the difference. And if she was the one who died instead, maybe a little bit of hurt for him now would keep him from being devastated later.

It was only until this guy was caught. Then she'd come clean with Colton and let him know that she wanted what he did… a happily ever after together. Hopefully that wouldn't come too late for them. But it was just a risk she'd have to take.

Chapter 33

Saturday morning dawned hot and humid. For West Texas, hot was the norm even during spring, but humid was a rarity. The miserable weather fit Penelope's dark mood. She hadn't slept since Colton stopped sleeping by her side two nights before. He was still with her all the time, protecting her, but the chasm between them had become uncrossable. He stayed as far away as possible while still remaining in the same room to protect her. The separation hurt both mentally and physically, but she kept telling herself it was for the best.

But for today, they had the author signing at the bookstore to get through. It was going to be a busy day, which was a relief. Hopefully the frantic pace would keep her from thinking too much.

They drove to the bookstore together in the Bus. Penelope tried not to let Colton's stoic silence bother her. At this point, she almost wished she would have picked a fight with him rather than what she did. This pervasive air of hurt between them made it hard to breathe. Hard to function. Her arms ached with the need to hold him and to be held by him. She held the tears inside simply by sheer will.

They were the first to arrive at the store by a couple of hours. She went up to her office and he went silently to the reading nook. As she sat down at her desk, she let the tears fall. God, let this be over soon. She wasn't sure how much longer she could go on like this.

A knock at her office door sent her scrambling for a tissue to wipe up any sign of her tears. She couldn't let Colton see through her facade now. But when she opened the door, it wasn't Colton standing there.

Julie and Cassie crowded through the door. "What are you two doing here?" Penelope asked.

Cassie pulled Penelope into a hard hug, but thankfully didn't ask about her tears. Instead she answered, "When Colton chased off your last prospect for hired help, he recruited us to come in and work. We're your slave labor for today. Put us to work. Oh, and he also hired a couple of extra bodyguards to help keep an eye on things with the crowd."

Damn, could the guy get more perfect? She gave them each another hug. "Thank you guys so much. Today's going to be crazy so I hope you're ready to work. Wait a minute, did you say bodyguards?"

Cassie nodded. "Yep, he's not letting you take any risks today."

The Abilene Authors group showed up two hours later. There were four of them who came to do the signing.

Tony was just as she expected. He couldn't be more than twenty-one years old, tall with a lean, rangy build. He had shaggy blond hair that screamed surfer dude. He even wore a hemp necklace.

Accompanying him was Melinda, the group's graphic designer. She was rather quiet with a sweet smile and a studious look. Penelope would guess her to be in her mid-twenties.

There was another girl, introduced as Cheryl, who looked even younger than Tony and from the looks she gave the happy-go-lucky guy, she was along with the hope that he'd notice her. So far, Penelope wasn't seeing any sign of that.

The surprise of the group came with Tim. Easily in his fifties, he looked more like an aging NFL player than a writer. The guy was huge. He definitely rivaled Colton's size, but he had an intelligent and friendly look in his eyes that Penelope liked.

They were an eclectic group and it made Penelope even more curious as to how their cooperation worked. She was looking forward to hearing their talk this afternoon.

She led them into her office where she'd set up some refreshments for them while they prepared for the signing. "Make yourselves comfortable. I'm going to go downstairs and set up the table with the books you all brought with you. Thanks for that. I'll send someone up when we're ready for you. Do you all have any questions or concerns?"

Tony immediately dug into the food. "This is a sweet set-up. Thanks, Penelope. How long do we have until we need to be downstairs?"

She glanced down at the clock on her cell phone. "About twenty minutes." Melinda blanched, so Penelope rested a comforting hand on her shoulder. "It's going to be fine. Everyone here loves books and you all love to write them. It makes it easy for everyone."

Melinda nodded and gave a weak smile.

"I'll introduce you and get you started with a few questions about how your cooperative works. I think once you get going, it will flow for both you and the customers. Do you want one person to do most the talking? You know, act as the spokesperson for the group?"

A resounding, "Tony," came from the group.

Penelope chuckled. "Okay, Tony, you're unanimously nominated."

He grinned his cocky grin and said, "That's cool."

As she left her office, one of the buff bodyguards stood next to the door and nodded at her. She assumed the other one was downstairs somewhere watching over the growing crowd. As she started down to the main level, she was immediately overwhelmed with how many people were there. The bookstore was overflowing.

Standing taller than most, she spotted Colton as she descended the stairs. He was talking on his phone and scowling as he scanned the room, obviously looking for someone. When he saw Cassie he strode over to her, talked to her for a moment. She looked worried. Something was wrong. She rushed over to them. "What's wrong?"

"Chris has been in a car accident," answered Cassie.

"Is he okay?"

Lines of worry and fear covered Cassie's face. "I don't know. We need to get to the ER."

"Go. Of course, go. We'll be fine here. Both of you go and take care of care of Chris."

Colton's gaze swung suddenly to her. "I'm not leaving you. It's not safe for you here in this crowd."

"Don't be ridiculous, Colton. Your brother needs you. I'll be fine. Besides we have the extra bodyguards here." She waved her hand at the man who stood guard by the front door and watched their exchange in interest as he scanned the room.

Colton looked torn as he glanced from Cassie to the crowd in the store.

Penelope urged, "Colton, it'll be fine. Your priority right now is to make sure Chris is okay."

Cassie tugged Colton's hand. "We need to go."

He finally relented and quickly placed a kiss on her forehead. It was the closest he'd come to her in two days. Her heart stuttered.

"I'm going, but I trust you to be careful." He looked her in the eyes. "I need you to promise me to stay safe."

"I promise." She tried to ignore the shiver of dread that snaked down her spine.

After they left, she ignored the specter of danger in the air and set about starting the signing.

Penelope watched out over the crowd waiting in line. The customers were chaotic, but it was an organized chaos. Tony was witty and gracious and everyone seemed to be having a fabulous time. Even Melinda relaxed as Tony joked and worked the crowd. Jon did a fabulous job running the cash register while Alix and Julie kept the lines sorted and happy. Penelope was at Tony's elbow making sure his needs were met as she handled the crowds. Things were going smoothly until Tim, one of the Abilene Authors, came up to whisper discreetly in her ear, "There's an issue at the back door."

She looked at him and could see his concern. "What is it?"

"There's a little girl. She's lost her mother, but won't come with me. She's scared of me." He looked disgruntled at the thought, even though he had to realize he was a huge guy. She could see why a little girl would be intimidated by him. Hell, if she was lost and alone, she'd be intimidated by him, too.

She smiled at him. "Okay. Let me just tell Tony where I'm going and then I'll take care of it."

As Tim and Penelope headed toward the back of the store, one of the bodyguards fell in beside them. Penelope stopped and turned to him. "Look I know you're just doing your job, but it's just a lost little girl. She's already scared and having two huge guys with me isn't going to help the issue."

"Then he can stay here," he nodded his head at Tim, "and I'll go with you. Your protection is my job."

Penelope worked hard not to sigh. "Listen, I completely understand what you're saying, but she already knows him. I am not going to be responsible for traumatizing a little girl. Stay here. I'm going to stay in the store. I'm just going to find her mother for her."

He didn't look convinced, but he finally relented. "Okay."

Penelope spotted the blonde-haired, blue-eyed little angel with tears rolling down her cheeks by the back door. Her heart went out to her. She looked terrified. Penelope crouched down beside her. She couldn't be more than four or five years old. "Hello angel. My name is Penelope and this is my friend, Tim. Did you lose your mommy?"

She nodded quietly, still looking scared.

"What's your name?"

"Ka..Kat," she mumbled.

"It's okay. We'll find your mommy. Do you know what her name is?"

The little girl looked even more petrified as she shook her head. Suddenly she darted toward the back door and pushed it open. As soon as she hit the outside, she started running across the back parking lot. Penelope dashed after her, yelling her name. She was so little; any car could back up and never see she her until they hit her. Penelope saw her as she darted between a van and a Lexus and went running after her.

She was in between the van and the car when she realized something was wrong. The little girl ran into a strange man's arms, just as two men reached out of the van to grab her. She didn't have time to even take a breath and scream before she found herself on the floor of a van surrounded by four really tough-looking guys, all grinning from ear-to-ear.

Chapter 34

The hospital was only five minutes away from Penelope's bookstore, but Cassie was frantic by the time they arrived. Colton tried to reassure her while he drove since they had no idea what Chris's status was medically. "Cass, you and Chris have your twin connection and you've always known he was hurt before anyone else. Do you feel like he's in any danger?"

She was quiet for a moment as if trying to connect with Chris. Colton glanced at her and thought about their connection. The year before when Chris 'died,' Cassie always had that connection telling her he was alive even when all the facts said he wasn't. Unfortunately, none of them believed her then. Now they all trusted their connection implicitly.

She shook her head hesitantly. "No, I'm not getting a sense that anything is wrong."

"Then trust that feeling. It was probably just a fender bender. Try to relax until we know more." They pulled into a parking spot and ran into the ER, but it was mass chaos. A school bus carrying one of the area high school track teams had crashed and there were crying teens and harried adults everywhere. Trying to find someone who knew what was going on was next to impossible.

It was forty-five minutes later before they finally found someone to talk to. Unfortunately that person had no idea where Chris was at. The young nurse looked up at Colton from her computer. "Who did you say called you?"

"I don't remember her name. She just said that Chris had been brought in from a car accident and was in the ER." This was beyond frustrating. Colton gnashed his teeth with impatience. Worry for Chris and the stress of the week had taken its toll.

"Are you sure the caller identified the hospital as Texas Tech Health Sciences Center?"

"I thought so, but I was in a crowd when I got the call and there was a lot of noise. Maybe I misunderstood her."

The nurse picked up the phone. "Okay, let me call the other ER's in the area and see if I can locate your brother. Go have a seat and I'll let you know as soon as I find out something."

Colton gritted his teeth, but simply nodded and pulled Cassie down into a chair in the waiting room. He looked over at her as they sat. "Why don't you try his cell again?"

She nodded and looked up at him as she listened. "It's still going directly to voice mail and no one is answering the house phone."

"What was Jake doing today?"

"He went fishing with some friends from college. They wanted Chris to go with them, but crutches on a boat aren't a good idea. He left around 5:00 this morning. I'd call him, but I don't want to worry him until we know something."

Colton nodded as he looked around the waiting room, wondering what the hell happened to Chris.

Two hours later, they were no closer to the answer. The nurse who'd been helping them called all the area hospitals and then finally the Lubbock PD. There was no trace of a car accident with Chris Robertson in it. With no other choice, they headed out the door and back to Cassie's house to regroup.

As Colton turned onto Cassie's street, he exclaimed, "What the hell?"

Parked in her driveway was Chris's truck with no visible damage. He hadn't even gotten Cassie's jeep stopped before she flew out the door and up the walk, yelling Chris's name.

Colton rushed in after her and she was already coming back down the hall from the bedrooms. "He's not here. Where the hell is he?" She headed to the French doors leading to her patio and launched herself out them, calling Chris's name.

Colton got to the doors in time to see Cassie throw herself into a very sleepy, confused looking Chris lying on the lounge chair. He wrapped his arms around her as he sat up in distress. "Cassie what's wrong?"

She was crying and not capable of speech so it was up to Colton to explain. "We got a phone call you were in a car accident and in the ER. Where the hell have you been and why haven't you been answering your phone?" he growled at him.

"I've been out here enjoying the day. I've just been reading and napping. My cell is probably dead. The battery isn't keeping a charge for anything." He pulled Cassie off him so he could pull the phone out of his pocket. He flashed it to them. "Yep, dead."

Colton rubbed a hand over his face. "Dammit. I'm glad you're okay, but damn… We're gonna get that fixed first thing Monday morning." He nodded toward Chris's phone. "But why would someone call and tell us…" Realization dawned and the blood drained from his face. He reached back for his phone as he said a single word, "Penelope."

He dialed her phone first, but there wasn't an answer. Panic crawled up his gut. He left a message and tried not to sound as frantic as he felt, "Penelope, I need you to call me as soon as you get this." He hung up and dialed the store.

Alix answered, "Raider Readers."

"Alix, it's Colton. May I speak to Penelope?"

"I'm sorry, Colton. We were getting ready to call you." Her voice was full of sorrow. He knew what was coming next. He sank to the ground and both his siblings reached for him as she said, "Penelope's missing. We can't find her anywhere."

Chapter 35

Penelope knew she was in trouble when they didn't try to hide their faces. The four men surrounding her spoke Spanish. Unfortunately, they spoke much too quickly for her to pick up anything but a few random words here and there. From what she could gather, they were on their way to meet the Boss and then they would finally have access to the gift. She shuddered in revulsion and fear as she thought about Colton's theory and her erotica writing.

She couldn't see where they were going, but estimated they'd been traveling for around forty-five minutes. The floor of the utility van was hard on the rocky road they'd hit about ten minutes ago. With her hands tied behind her back, she had a difficult time maintaining her balance. Her shoulders were going to be covered with bruises from falling across the hard floor, but that was probably the least of her worries.

Right after they grabbed her, they had picked up the man and the little girl. They'd obviously been part of the set-up and were dropped off somewhere else about ten minutes later. The whole time they were in the van, Penelope watched the suddenly dried-eyed little girl in amazement. She was an incredible little actress. It never even occurred to her that danger lurked behind the tears of a scared, angelic-looking five year old girl.

She tried to engage her captors in conversation. They hadn't been open to the idea. A threat with a roll of duct tape meant she'd been quiet ever since. Instead, she listened to them and tried to gather information.

There were four men in the back with her, plus their driver. The driver looked nervous and young. He didn't even look old enough to have a driver's license yet. She looked around at the four men surrounding her. Three of them were also very young, barely in their twenties.

The one issuing the orders was older, mid to late thirties and both his arms were covered in sleeve tattoos. He had five teardrops tattooed below his left eye and a frightening looking ragged scar which travelled up his right cheek. His hard, cold eyes didn't miss a flicker of movement and she knew he wouldn't think twice about killing her. There wasn't a shred of humanity left in his eyes. He was the one she had to worry about.

She had no doubt they planned to kill her. Colton would feel responsible because he wasn't there when she'd gotten stupid. That alone almost made her lose her self-control and start sobbing, but she couldn't lose it yet. She had to figure out a way out of this. Mainly because Colton would never forgive himself if she died.

She couldn't dwell on him or she would panic. But that didn't keep her from wondering if Chris was okay. If things were serious with Chris, Colton may not even know she was missing yet.

The van suddenly lurched to a bone-jarring halt and she tumbled across the floor again. She didn't have time to right herself before the door slid open and hard hands yanked her up.

The heat of the day slapped her in the face, but the sight in front of her was even more of a shock. They dragged her up the steps of the old Martin homestead. She loved this house and this ranch. The last time she'd been here was with Colton. To know she'd probably die here seemed too cruel a fate. Were these men tied to the Martin family somehow? Surely the Martins didn't know about this.

Two men dragged her as she stumbled, trying to keep up with them. At the sound of galloping hoof beats, they immediately drew out guns. Penelope closed her eyes, praying one of the Martin family wouldn't die here today.

But it wasn't a Martin who rode up. It was Ethan, the Martin's ranch hand, and the men around her obviously knew him because they put away their guns and relaxed their stances. Ethan greeted Scarface, but never even looked in her direction. He couldn't be with these men could he? She didn't know Ethan as well as she knew the other men on the ranch, but he'd always been nice when she'd seen him around. He was always helpful and willing to lend a hand when she needed it.

In fact, he'd been the one who introduced her to Hannah. Oh my God! He'd been the one that introduced her to Hannah. Her stomach rolled and she tasted bile on the back of her tongue. These were the men who were responsible for Hannah's death. She had no idea how it all tied together, but there was no doubt in her mind that it was all related. She lunged for the railing, leaned over and lost her breakfast in the overgrown bushes.

The men surrounding her laughed at her discomfort. Finally, Ethan looked at her for a split-second. His gaze was filled with guilt and remorse before it slid away. Maybe she'd be able to use that guilt to get him to help her to escape. He spoke in rapid Spanish to Scarface, but she didn't have a chance to find out what they were discussing as they dragged her inside the house. They bypassed the main floor and headed directly to a staircase leading to the basement.

The basement was unfinished with a dirt floor and walls. It was dark and damp and had obviously been used as the root cellar. When they got to the bottom of the stairs, they shoved her to the ground and left her, not even bothering to untie her hands. The lock on the door clicked into place and Penelope was left in the pitch black. The panic she'd been holding at bay ever since she'd been grabbed came shuddering through her chest in great big sobs. What was she going to do?

***

Colton took great gulping breaths trying to get control of his panic. He would get her back. He had to believe that. To think anything else was unacceptable, but right now he had to get his head on straight so he could do that. He stood up and tried to remember the breathing techniques Penelope taught him when she was showing him her yoga breathing. Slowly, he shut his eyes and inhaled and exhaled to the count of five. He did that for five breaths, and then ten. Opening his eyes again, he splashed some cold water on his face, and felt more centered.

The worried faces of his siblings greeted him as he opened the bathroom door. He knew he was still pale from getting sick and they both looked at him with concern. "I'm headed to the bookstore. Are you going with me?"

They both nodded.

Colton grimly strode toward Chris's truck and started dialing his phone. Brian barely had time to answer before Colton began issuing orders. "Brian, Penelope disappeared from the bookstore. I'm pretty sure she's been kidnapped. I need you to meet me there as soon as you can."

"Damn, Colton. Okay, I'll be right there with a black and white."

"Thanks, Brian."

Next he dialed a number he had hoped he wouldn't need to call.

The crusty voice he knew too well answered the phone, "Bart Matthews, Homeland Security."

"Bart, this is Colton Robertson."

"Colt, how are you doing man? I'm hearing good things about Mad Rob's chances for the contract."

"That's fine Bart, but not why I'm calling. I need a favor and I'll owe you big time for this. My girlfriend's been kidnapped and I don't know the situation, but am hoping I can call on your resources if need be."

"Fuck! Penelope's been kidnapped? When? How?"

"I don't know all the details yet. I just need to know I can count on you if I need you."

"Sure…" he hesitated. "Colton, I don't know if this is related, but there's something big going down with the Mexican Mafia right now. There's lots of chatter and we don't know what it all means. Has your girl somehow gotten mixed up in something bad?"

"I'm afraid so, but at this point 'something bad' is all we know. We've been going in circles trying to figure out what's going on. A tie to the Mexican Mafia would be the first real lead in what's happening. Let me check out her disappearance and I'll call you as soon as I know something."

Bart's voice sounded grim, "I hope you find her soon, Colt."

"Me, too. Thanks, Bart."

When Colton hung up the phone, he closed his eyes and sank his head into his hands. His stomach churned at the thought of what she might be going through right now….if she was even still alive. God, he couldn't allow himself to think like that. She was going to be fine. He'd find her and she'd be fine. He had to hold onto that hope. He had to…

"Colton?" Chris asked from behind the wheel. No way in hell could Colton drive right now. "Are you okay?"

Colton shook his head while he looked out the front window. No, at this moment in time, he didn't feel like he'd ever be okay again. "No, and I won't be until we get her back safe and sound."

When they arrived at the bookstore, there were still plenty of people milling about from the book signing. As Colton stormed in the front door, Jon immediately directed, "They're all up in Penelope's office."

Colton bounded up the stairs with Chris and Cassie following in his wake. He was surprised when he stepped into Penelope's office to find the writing group still there.

Julie saw him at the door and rushed over to him. The circles under her eyes were even more pronounced than they'd been earlier in the day.

"Tell me what happened," he ordered.

She already had a notepad in her hand and looked down at it to check her notes. God bless Julie's organizing soul. She proceeded to tell him what they'd been able to piece together about the events that afternoon.

"What happened to the little girl?" Shit, Penelope wouldn't have ever expected duplicity from a little girl. She was too compassionate to even consider a tactic like that.

"She completely disappeared. We have no idea what happened to her, but assume she must have been part of a set-up."

"Why would Penelope leave the store? She knew it was dangerous."

Tim stepped forward. "First, I'm sorry. I should have been able to help better, but I never would have guessed that little girl was a decoy. Those were real tears and I truly thought she was just scared. This is my fault. I'm sorry."

It wasn't Tim's fault. It was his. It was his job to protect her. He told her that he'd keep her safe. Instead he left her alone to fend for herself and now there was no way to know if she was even still alive. He couldn't breathe. He turned back to Julie. "You've called the police, right?"

"Yes, they're on their way." He heard some extra noise downstairs and leaned out the door hoping it was Penelope, but it was the arrival of Brian and his police officers. Alix stood behind Julie, so Colton turned to her now. "I think it would be a good idea to close early today. Make sure none of the departing customers saw anything before they leave, but go ahead and go down to help Jon get the store closed up."

Alix nodded, seemingly relieved to have something to do. Worry lined her face and it seemed like she'd aged ten years since he'd seen her two hours ago.

He dragged Julie and her notes with him as he went downstairs to talk to Brian and figure out where to go from here.

Chapter 36

Penelope allowed her pity party to go on for ten minutes before she started talking to herself. The pitch black of the basement terrified her, so talking aloud helped to not feel so alone. She'd barely had time to see anything before they took the light. She had no idea what was down here.

"Come on. Buck up. Just think. What would Cassie do?" When kidnapped in December, Cassie almost single-handedly saved them all. "She sure wouldn't be lying on the floor crying about how bad it is." Using all her abdominal muscles, Penelope managed to get herself sitting upright. It was difficult with her hands tied behind her, but she crept around the room, doing a kind of backwards shuffle. She'd walk her legs backwards and then inch her arms further and further away, searching to see if she could find any kind of weapon or possibly even another entrance, although the total lack of light pretty much negated that possibility.

As she scooted across the floor, she'd move and then sit on the cold dirt floor. She'd then sweep her hands back and forth behind her, just, hovering above the ground to see if anything was there. "Okay creepy crawlies, I'm not here to hurt you or invade your home. You stay away from me and I'll stay away from you. Okay?" She continued to sweep her arms and legs. "But if you know where a baseball bat is, I'd love for you to share that information."

Finally she reached a wall and started to work her way around the circumference of the room. She calmed down from her initial panic and adrenaline which allowed her brain to work again. "Penelope, you dummy. You're a yoga instructor and damn flexible. As Cassie would say, use your strengths." She contorted her body until she managed to step inside her cuffed wrists and get them in front of her body. It required tweaking her still weak wrist, but that was minor in the grand scheme of things. She raised her shoulders to let the tension out of them from being pulled behind her for so long. "Ah, now see that's much better. You were born with a good brain. You just have to use it."

It was much easier to feel along the room now and she almost felt comfortable with it. She was singing "My Favorite Things" from *The Sound of Music* when she stumbled over the body and screamed. Fortunately, it was a live body because he groaned as she fell over him. She scrambled up to check him, locating first an arm, also handcuffed behind his back. She trailed her hands up his arm to the side of his head, where she encountered something warm and sticky. She was afraid it was probably blood and when she found the goose egg, he groaned again.

"Hey, are you awake? I'm sorry. I didn't mean to hurt you. I had no idea anyone else was in here. Do you speak English?" She continued to feel along his body trying to find any clue as to whom he might be, but all she found were more wet, sticky areas. His body was hot despite the chill of the basement so he was probably running a fever. Every once in a while a chill would rack his body so she snuggled up to him trying to share her warmth.

She felt along his arm again. "I wonder how long you've been down here. You're obviously hurt and all this dirt can't be clean. You have an infection, but I guess these guys aren't going to take you to the hospital, are they? I'm sorry you're in this mess, but I'm glad you're here. It's not so scary knowing I'm not alone. Just don't die, okay, because that would really freak me out. I need you to stay alive. Maybe Colton can get us both out of this mess."

Another chill took hold of his body and he shuddered.

"Just stay alive. It's good advice for both of us, don't you think?" She just had to stay alive and Colton would find her, right? And when she got the chance, she would take the opportunity to use her brain and find a way to get out of this. She rested her head against the ground as she thought.

She must have dozed off because the next thing she knew the man was moving and cursing. "Fuck." He nudged her with his face. "What the hell?" His voice was low and scratchy, but it seemed familiar.

She reached up to touch his face. "Hey it's okay. They threw me down here with you. I just wanted to keep you warm. You're running a fever."

"Penelope?" Disbelief tinted his voice.

Relief flooded her system. He was alive. She didn't realize until that moment how much she'd thought otherwise. "Damon? Thank God, you're alive. You've been missing for a week. Have you been here that whole time?"

"Fuck. A week? What day is it? Can you help me sit up?"

"It's Saturday." She grabbed his arm and he hissed in pain. "I don't want to hurt you. Tell me where you're hurt so I can avoid those areas"

He chuckled low and it was a sound full of bitterness. "It would be easier to tell you where it doesn't hurt. It's okay. Just help me sit up so I can get my bearings."

She gently tugged on his arm and used her leg as leverage behind his back, but finally they had him sitting up and leaning against the dirt wall. His breaths came out in gasps as he breathed through the pain. He was really not in good shape.

"Who are these guys, Damon? What do they want with us?"

"Fuck, Penelope, I really wish you weren't here." His voice was low and raspy like it hadn't been used in a while. "These guys are bad news. They're the Mexican Mafia and they don't play nice. You've got to get out of here."

"The Mexican Mafia? Why would the Mexican Mafia want me? I don't understand."

"I'm sorry. This has to be tied to me in some way. They've been trying to force me to use the dig and the shipments of artifacts for smuggling into the states. I refused and you can see how well that worked for me." Another shudder rolled through his body. She reached over to pull him so that he was leaning against her so she could share her heat with him.

"Are these the problems you've been having with the dig?"

"Yes, and why I haven't pulled the University into it yet. I didn't want to expose a bunch of college kids to the MM, but I haven't had much luck getting them off my back."

"Do you think that's why I'm here? To help coerce you?"

"Fuck, I hope not."

"Me, too. One of my employees was murdered last week and somehow I think she was mixed up in all this. I met her through one of the guys upstairs. I just don't understand how it all fits together."

"Which guy?"

"Ethan, he works at the ranch where we're being held."

"You know where we're at?"

"Yeah, we're about thirty-five miles east of Lubbock on the Martin family ranch. Ethan works here with them."

"The name doesn't sound familiar. I probably haven't seen him. I don't usually get to leave my lovely accommodations down here."

Just then they heard the lock jiggle on the door. "Whatever they do, just go along with it," Damon whispered urgently. "Don't fight them. These are not nice men, Penelope, and they won't think twice about hurting you or killing you. Cooperate with them."

Two men came down the stairs. One of them carried a lantern and she got her first look at Damon. She couldn't hold back the gasp. She knew he was in bad shape, but that knowledge didn't prepare her for how bad he looked. He was bruised, eyes swollen shut with both dried and wet blood everywhere. He'd easily lost fifteen pounds since the last time she saw him. She reached for him, but the men yanked her up by her armpits and dragged her to the stairs.

Damon yelled after them, "Don't hurt her!"

As they topped the stairs, the bright light of the sun burned her eyes after so many hours in the pure dark and she squinted her eyes against it. The men dragged her into what at one point in time had been the parlor, since it had a fireplace with faded, empty bookshelves surrounding it.

She gasped as she was pushed into the room and saw who stood there. "Thomas?"

He looked awful, disheveled as if he'd been in a fight recently, his face bruised and his arm held gingerly at his side. His eyes looked tormented.

He gestured to the men behind her. "You may leave us. Close the door on the way out."

Penelope shook her head, "I don't understand what's going on here. Thomas?"

Thomas sat down and sank his head into his hands. When he looked up at her, he had tears in his eyes. "Do you realize everything I've worked for in the past three years, you've completely destroyed?"

"What? How? I don't understand."

The desolation she saw in his eyes as he watched her terrified her. He stood up and walked over to a window that looked out over the ranch. He stood there for a moment before the muscles in his back flexed and he turned toward her with resolve. "I guess I can tell you. It's not like they're going to let you live after this. We're probably both dead at this point."

He glanced back toward the closed door. "We probably don't have much time. First, I need to know. Where's the book?"

She had no idea what he was talking about. "What book?"

"***The Gift***. The ARC Hannah was supposed to receive."

She shook her head for a moment before it hit her what book he was talking about. "You mean ***The Gift of Serendipity***? The Abilene Authors book?"

He turned and ran a hand through his hair in agitation. He muttered to himself as he turned and paced. "They renamed it." He suddenly kicked the chair and started yelling. "Goddamnit! All this because some artistic idiots decided to rename the goddamn book!"

Penelope shrank back. Thomas was on edge and she didn't want to be in his line of fire. He strode over to her and grabbed her by the shoulders. She could feel his fingers digging into the bones of her upper arms. "Where is it?"

Her mind scrambled trying to figure the best way out of this. She needed to tell him something that would keep her alive, but not endanger anyone else. "Colton knows where it is, but he won't give it to you if I'm dead. He's too smart for that."

His rage seeped out of him and he physically wilted before her eyes.

"Thomas," she said quietly, "what's going on?"

He sighed. "It was this huge, glorious plan." He laughed harshly. "I had it all set up. I had my contact from Dyess Air Force Base to feed us the routes. I had Dev who could encrypt them and write the codes. I had the writers to provide our cover. I had Hannah to put the information up on the blog and shuffle the book. It was all in place. We were all safe from discovery. It was brilliant, until you decided to take the book." He glared at her with a frightening mixture of rage and desperation. She didn't know what to do.

Penelope scrambled to keep up with his random ramblings. "I still don't understand. Yeah, I took an ARC but why didn't you just make another one?"

"Because the one you took had the microchip with all the codes for arming the devices in it. That book is the guide to all the nuclear devices being transported across the southwest for the next six months. The details in the book provide dates and times and shipment routes. The information is all in there via code, but without the microchip imbedded into the spine with the access codes, none of that information does us any good. That's the only copy of the book with a microchip."

He started pacing again. "This was my ticket to doing great things without the oversight of my lauded father. And the irony of it all was the huge joke on him. My glorious, patriotic father... and I used his land and resources to deceive the federal government for the Mexican Mafia."

"I don't understand. Why would you want to hurt him like that?"

"It's his fault my mother died. I was with her the day of the car wreck. She was upset, crying. He did something to upset her. She couldn't see the road clearly through her tears and never saw that the semi drifted into her lane. That's why she wrecked and died. It's all his fault and no one cares. All the neighbors love him. Even my brothers... none of them care. It was up to me to make him pay and this was the best way I knew how. To use the one thing he loves above everything else, this land, to aid the traitors against the government he loves."

His eyes turned hard and Penelope had a hard time believing that this was the same guy she'd dated and known and loved like a brother for so many years. How had she never seen this bitterness inside him?

"I had to make him pay. I owed it to her. He hurt her and I needed to hurt him, but now everything's falling apart and I'm not sure I can keep either one of us alive through this. These are not nice guys and I pulled you into this mess. I'm sorry for that Penny. You didn't deserve this. I'll do everything I can to get you out of this, but I don't have much leverage anymore. If you can, get out and don't look back."

The door suddenly opened and in walked a tall man in a business suit. He slowly clapped his hands together, each hit reverberating throughout the tense room like a gunshot. Two muscled men followed closely behind him. This had to be the guy in charge. "Oh, Thomas, you did always have such a flair for the dramatic. That's part of the reason why I've kept you around as long as I have. Well, that and you do come up with some rather inventive methods to aid the little business we have going here."

The man was younger than Penelope would expect a Mexican Mafia boss to be. He was probably in his early thirties. He wasn't a huge guy, but he had a presence about him that signaled his power. He was Mexican and spoke with a lilting accent which said that English wasn't his first language.

Thomas remained quiet as he watched the man walk into the room. She could see all his muscles tense up as he made an effort to hold himself in check and not respond to the man.

The man walked up to Penelope and looked her up and down. "You've caused poor Thomas a fair amount of trouble my dear." He waited for a response.

Since she was pretty sure 'Fuck You' wasn't going to go over well so she simply said, "I'm sorry. That was never my intention."

He nodded and sat down in a plush leather chair, the only piece of furniture in the room. He had his elbows propped on the armrests and his fingers were steepled so that she could read the 'PURE RULE' tattoos on his knuckles. He wore his suit with a relaxed elegance, although the tattoos peeking out around his open collar belied the professional look. He was attractive, but had cold, soulless eyes.

He watched her for several uncomfortable minutes before finally saying, "But now we're faced with a conundrum. You have my book. I have two prisoners and an operation going to hell faster than we can say 'Texas ranch'. Do you have any ideas as to what we can do about this situation we find ourselves in here?"

She didn't know how to respond to that so she just remained silent and watched him.

He turned his glare to Thomas and pulled a gun out of his pocket. Penelope couldn't stop the gasp that escaped her lips at the sight of the weapon. A cold shiver snaked down her spine.

Thomas said, "Now wait a minute. Let's not over-react. This is all fixable."

"You think I'm over-reacting? Maybe I should just shoot her now for all the trouble she's caused."

He pointed the gun at her, but Thomas stepped in front of her. "You don't want to do that. We can still get the book back and we can't recover it if she's dead."

"You make a good point, so I think I'll kill you instead." He turned the gun on Thomas and then shot him point-blank in the head.

Penelope flinched violently as she watched Thomas's body collapse. She was covered in his brain matter and gore. She stared down at his body in open-mouthed horror. Thomas was dead and somehow she'd been the cause of it. He had been a friend. And now he was dead at her feet. She dry-heaved, but having thrown up already, there was nothing left to come up.

The sobs shook her body. She was hysterical and knew that, but it was like watching herself through a television. She couldn't stop.

The boss stood and took the two steps to get close enough to her to backhand her across her face. Her head snapped to the side and her face was on fire, but the hit did its job. She was refocused.

He started laughing as he told the remaining two men something in Spanish. They took hold of her arms and dragged her back to the basement.

This time they left her at the top of the stairs before they took her light and locked the door behind. She slowly felt her way down the stairs. Movement from below told her Damon was searching for her in the dark. "Penelope, are you okay? I heard a gunshot."

Okay? Her stomach continued to roll and her legs were a quivering mass of jelly. She had parts of what used to be Thomas clinging to her. No, she was definitely not okay. But she didn't need Damon to know that. "I'm okay. Stay back from the bottom of the stairs so I don't fall over you." Her voice sounded hollow and weak to her own ears. She was sure she wasn't fooling Damon.

Finally she reached the bottom step, just as her legs gave out below her. She sunk to the ground and tried to gain control of her sporadic breathing. Damon inched up beside her and leaned into her trying to comfort her as best he could with his hands behind his back. "Shh, I'm so sorry, Penelope. You shouldn't be here. I'm sorry."

She reached up to him and gave a hysterical laugh as the ridiculousness of the situation hit her. "It's not your fault. I'm here because of a book."

"A book?" He sounded confused.

"I know." Her laughter morphed into hiccupping sobs. "I don't understand it either."

"What was the gunshot?"

"Oh, just the boss killing Thomas because of this whole mess. His brains are all over my shirt. Did you know I used to date him? And now his brain is all over my shirt." She shook and sobbed uncontrollably.

He curled his torso around her further. "Don't think about it. Maybe someone heard the shot and will come investigate."

She shook her head and slowly her brain began to function again. "I don't think so. We're at the far edge of the Martin ranch. They don't come over here this time of year and I'm pretty sure we're too far away from the main house for them to have heard it."

"Did you find out what's going on?"

"Yes." She gave a hysterical sounding giggle, "Oh my God. All of this. Thomas is dead. Hannah and Aaron, too. All because I took a book out of the bookstore. From what I understand it's a book that they're using to transport information to the various branches of the Mexican Mafia."

"Where's the book now?"

"It's in the saddlebag on Colt's motorcycle." She shivered at the thought of the unexpected danger she'd put him in. "I can't let them know that though. I won't endanger Colt's life."

"Penelope, trust Colton. He can take care of himself and maybe save you too. Just do what these guys say and let Colton figure out the rest. That may be the only way you survive this."

Trust Colton. That's what everything boiled down to, didn't it?

Chapter 37

Gone without a trace. How many people disappeared like that every year and their friends and family never found out what happened? To never know if they were dead or alive.

Never. Know.

The thought scared him to his very soul.

It had been three hours since he found out she was missing. Three hours that felt like three years. Every minute another section of his heart died.

He paced around the reading nook of the bookstore, trying to work through his aggression. They were all still at the bookstore, waiting for some word that never seemed to come. An hour ago, the group decided it was better to stay away from him and let him prowl the bookstore on his own. He didn't know what to do and it was driving him fucking nuts. So he paced and held his cell phone, waiting for it to ring. Someone needed to call. He needed to know. Something. Anything.

He stared down at it, willing it to ring. He'd been doing that for so long, it actually startled him when it did ring. He fumbled it trying to hit the 'answer' button. His heart went into hyper-drive, but he finally managed to hit the right fucking button. "Robertson here."

"Colton, this is Bart. Is your girl still missing?"

"Yes, why?"

"Where are you?"

"Raider Readers on 19th Street."

His voice was terse when he spoke. "I'll tell you when I get there. I'll be there in ten."

Colton hung up the phone and continued to stare at it until Chris interrupted his reverie. "Who was that?"

"Bart Matthews. It sounds like he may have some information about Pen's disappearance."

"Bart from Homeland Security?"

Colton nodded mutely.

"Damn, what the hell is going on here?"

"I sure wish I knew the answer to that."

Before either of them could contemplate it further, Colton's phone rang again. "Robertson."

"Mr. Robertson. You have something I want and I have something you want. I propose an exchange."

His gut clenched. This was it. Finally, something was happening. He scrambled over to the register where he'd stashed his notepad and pen. "I'm not discussing anything with you until I talk to Penelope." He heard some mumbling as the phone was passed.

"Colton?" Her trembling voice knocked the wind out of him and he just wanted to drop to the floor in thanks. Up until this moment, he really hadn't been sure that she was even still alive.

"Pen, are you okay?"

"I'm fine, but Colt, I need you to listen to me very carefully."

"Okay."

"They need a book. It's the book I use for my emergency reading, called ***The Gift of Serendipity***." He tried to focus on her words and not the shakiness of her voice. Just in case, he wrote everything she was saying down.

"Remember? I had it at your mom's house when I was reading on her porch with Bart. I left it there. It's on her bottom shelf. I'm pretty sure I shelved it by Celeste DeMarco's book, ***Acapulco Embrace*** and your Air Force manuals. I love…"

Her voice trailed off as the phone was taken away from her and the male voice was back. "You have three hours to locate the book. We'll meet you for the exchange at mile marker 341 on Hwy. 19 at 9:00. Don't be late and come alone, or else your girlfriend will be dead."

The line went dead and Colton's brain started scrambling. Pen was giving him a message. His girl was smart. She'd started the message by talking about his mom's house so he'd know it was all in code. There was no way for her kidnappers to know that his mother was dead. He just had to figure out what it all meant and quickly. Luckily, Bart walked in while he talked to her. Everyone gathered around and now they all looked at him with anticipation.

He looked first at Bart. "This definitely involves you or your office. She named you specifically. They're demanding an exchange. Her for a book. I'm supposed to meet them in three hours at mile marker 341 on Hwy 19. She told me how to find the book in code although I know exactly where it is. Let me repeat what she said so you all can help me figure out what she's saying."

After he repeated the message word for word, they all looked at him puzzled. To Alix, Colton directed, "Go get her book that she mentioned and we'll see what we can figure from that."

Then he turned to Jake. "The book they want is in my motorcycle. I need Cassie to take you to my apartment to pick up my motorcycle. The book is in the left saddlebag. Drive the motorcycle back here, but before you do, pull the gloves out of that saddlebag, doing your best to hide the book in between them just in case someone's watching. Slide it into your coat pocket and put on the gloves."

As they left, he returned his attention back to the message. "Okay, everything about reading on my mom's porch is a message since my mom's dead and Pen knows that." He looked at Bart. "We know Bart is you. That means she wants you involved and to know what's going on. Maybe you should tell us what brought you over here."

"Mainly it was just a gut feeling that this is all tied together. Our intel is telling us that one of the higher leaders in the Mexican Mafia is in the area. My office was called in on an investigation into a murder of one of Penelope's employees. Signs are that she was tied to the MM. Honestly, I'm hoping we can find your girl and that will lead me to this leader so we can shut him down."

"Question for you…"

"Shoot."

"What is your intel showing the MM is doing here?"

"The normal for them: drug-running, human trafficking, and there have been some rumblings of weapons smuggling."

Colton nodded. "That's what I thought. I think that's exactly what Pen is trying to tell us with the book. ***Acapulco's Embrace*** means Mexico or the MM. Obviously this book they're looking for means something. She also mentioned the Air Force. Could the MM be involved with something to do with the Air Force?" He turned his questioning glance toward Bart.

Bart frowned, obviously thinking it through. "Maybe something to do with Dyess Air Force Base in Abilene? Let me get some guys on it." Bart made a call on his cell phone and relayed a message to someone within his chain of command.

Chris chimed in, "What if somehow they're sending coordinates for their exchanges through the books? GPS coordinates, times, dates…things like that which could be hidden in the data on the front pages of a book or even a code somehow throughout the text."

"That would make sense." Colton tapped his pen on the paper. "That just leaves the porch and bottom shelf. What were you trying to tell me, Penelope?"

A thought occurred to him. He looked back toward Bart who had been on and off the phone with his people ever since he arrived. "Does your office have access to drones in the area?"

Bart cocked an eyebrow and looked around at the group, most without top-secret clearance, listening to their exchange before looking back at Colton. "I'm not really at liberty to say."

"Good enough. I think I may know where they are." He woke up the computer sitting at the register and with a few keystrokes found the online maps he wanted. "There's an abandoned farmhouse, here." He pointed at the coordinates on the screen. "I think she's being held here. There's no reason for anyone to be out there this time of the year. Pen told me they don't use that side of the ranch until fall and it's a long way away from the main part of the ranch. If you see people moving around out here, I'd lay odds those are the MM boys you're looking for."

"Okay, I'll get them to check it out." Bart got on the phone and called his men to relay the information.

By this time, Jake and Cassie arrived back at the store. Jake handed Colton the book out of his jacket. Colton barely glanced at it and immediately went to the bookshelves to find another book the same size. He brought them both back to Bart. "This is what they're after. There's information in here somewhere vital to the operations of the MM. Take it and get this cover onto this other book so that I have something to trade for Penelope. I hope it doesn't come to that, but it might and we need to be ready. Your people have one hour to get it done and back here to me."

Pen just needed to hang on a little bit longer. They were going to get her out of this safely. He had to believe that. The alternative wasn't acceptable.

***

An hour later and a plan began to come together. Surveillance showed someone was definitely holed up at the old farmhouse. The assumption was they were Mexican Mafia. The Department of Homeland Security with cooperation from the Texas Rangers planned to raid the house. Because the eldest of the Martin boys, Andrew, was a Texas Ranger, they were using the Martin ranch as their command post and were all congregating there now.

Unfortunately for Penelope's friends, they only allowed Colton to join them. None of them had been happy about that, particularly Chris and Jake, but he'd promised to call as soon as he had Penelope safely in his arms.

Colton now found himself in the midst of a team, not his own. Not knowing their individual strengths and weaknesses, but having to trust them with his life and more importantly, Penelope's. The thought terrified him.

As he looked around the room, he tried to take measure of each man, including Andrew Martin. He'd been the only Martin family member Colton didn't get to meet the day he and Penelope came out riding. Colton could see the anger simmering underneath the man's calm veneer. He was not happy that trouble like this had found its way onto his family's ranch. Colton could tell that he was worried about Penelope. Unfortunately, his brother, Thomas, had also mysteriously disappeared, but he remained cool and collected despite everything. In fact, all the Martin men were handling the pressure of the evening remarkably well.

Curiously, the only man from the Martin ranch who seemed negatively affected by the evening's events was their ranch-hand, Ethan. From across the room, Colton could see the man sweating profusely. He shifted from side to side as his gaze darted around watching the agents in the room. When he met Colton's gaze, he stopped fidgeting and looked away. The kid was obviously nervous. He probably should mention it to Bart. He was wound so tight, it would be way too easy for him to end up dead.

There were approximately twenty agents in the room from both the Texas Rangers and DHS. All of them were wearing body armor and various types of weaponry. Because of their intimate knowledge of the homestead and the surrounding terrain, Michael Martin and his boys were also included in the planning although they were given strict orders to stay in the back, away from the action.

A command post had been set up to monitor and control their communications. Each person wore an earpiece so they were all informed about what was going down with up to the second information coming to them from the crew monitoring the situation with a drone from above.

They were moving in to assault the old homestead with a mix of off-road vehicles, 4-wheelers and horses although the last half mile would be done entirely on foot so they didn't alert anyone they were coming.

Colton's special status in regards to this situation meant he'd be tied to Bart's side for the raid. He wasn't happy that he wasn't going to be the one to reach Penelope first. But he knew the importance of remaining detached during a mission, something he was just not capable of doing at this point, so he respected Bart's decision. He just didn't have to like it.

He glanced down at his watch again and tried to tamp down the surge of impatience. While these guys went over and over the details of the plan, they were getting closer and closer to the MM deadline. At this rate, Penelope wouldn't even be at the homestead by the time they got there. And knowing the brutal violence of the MM, if the raid went down after Penelope left, they would be signing her death warrant. No matter what information was in the book, they would see the raid as a sign of her betrayal. That would be a final act and she would die a torturous death.

Finally, he couldn't stand it any longer. He turned to Bart. "We need to go."

"Relax, Colton. We're almost ready."

Colton clenched his jaw in an effort to not argue. If he did, he'd increase his chances of not being there at all when Penelope needed him. He would do anything at this point to make sure she stayed safe. He was the only one on this team that he knew he could count on to make her life the priority.

After an interminable amount of time, they were finally on the move. They drove within a half mile of the homestead and then moved in on foot quickly through the rough terrain. The night concealed their approach as they moved swiftly toward the house.

Interspersed chatter of the forward teams crackled through his earpiece as they slowly picked off the ten men standing guard around the house. "One down. Two down. Three down." Until finally all ten were down without any apparent problems. Now they were just waiting for the final 'Go' command.

Sweat dripped down his spine under the heavy body armor while he looked at the house, glowing white against the darkened sky. He was crouched behind a tree with Bart standing next to him. Pen was in there somewhere. He was so close. It was taking every ounce of his self-control to hold his position.

Through his earpiece he heard, "Team One ready?"

"Check."

"Team Two ready?"

"Check."

They planned to storm the house as two different teams, one through the front and one through the back of the house. Both teams surrounded the perimeter and were waiting for the signal to go in.

"On my go. In three…two…"

Suddenly six men flew out the front door of the house brandishing automatic weapons. Something had gone wrong and tipped them off. In the middle of them were Penelope and another man he couldn't identify in the dark. Both had a gun pointed at their heads. The man didn't appear to be in the best of shape since two men were dragging him along. Penelope appeared pale and tense.

At the same time, Colton heard, "Hold your positions. Hold your positions," through his earpiece. Every muscle in his body clenched with the need to rush forward, but Bart held him back, whispering in his ear, "Settle, son. Don't get yourself and your pretty lady killed. We have snipers on them. Let them do their job."

That's right… the snipers. He tried to remember how many they had. Two… for six guys. Colton didn't like the odds of Penelope not getting hurt while the snipers took out six guys. He could see Penelope searching the dark. She knew they were there. He willed her to walk calmly along with the men so she didn't set them off. They were headed toward a black Suburban about twenty feet out from the house. What they didn't realize is that there were three men crouched behind that vehicle. From his position, Colton could see them clearly. In about ten feet, the shit was going to hit the fan.

Through his earpiece, he heard the command to the snipers, "Delta 1, Delta 2 take out the shooters. Now."

He started running as fast as he could when the call went out and gunfire erupted. Fear for Penelope made him push his body to the limit. The air moved as the bullets whizzed by him. He had to get to her to protect her. His movements felt like they were flowing through molasses as he pushed his body to move even faster. Finally, after what felt like hours, he reached her.

He tackled her and held her within the cage of his body, taking the brunt of their fall on his side. He rolled with her, cradling her head with his hands and wrapping his legs around hers, to shield her away from the shooting while protecting her body as much as possible.

Chaos and gunfire exploded everywhere. He could feel the rush of bodies and bullets around him, but his only focus was Penelope. They'd managed to put some space between them and the members of the MM. He could feel Penelope's tight muscles and frantic heartbeat underneath his hands on her back. He leaned down to talk quietly in her ear, "Sweetheart, we need to get under cover. When I lift you up, I need you to run as fast as possible over to those trees."

He felt her affirmative nod against his chest. He quickly stood, pulling her up in front of him so he could shield her body as they ran.

Once they reached the tree line, he ducked down tucking her in front of him with his back to the gunfire, so the bulk of his body protected hers from the continued danger. He immediately checked her body for damage. Up close, he could see the dried blood on her shirt and his heart stuttered in panic. "Are you okay? Tell me where you're hurt."

"Colt?" She reached up to touch his face, the handcuffs clanking as she moved.

He looked into her beautiful eyes and smiled. He hadn't known if he'd ever get this opportunity again. Relief flooded his body. "Yeah, it's me. Now answer me. Are you okay? Did they hurt you? God, did I hurt you with that tackle?" He continued feeling up and down her arms and torso.

She touched his lips with her fingertips to calm him. "Shh, I'm okay." She gave him a soft smile. "You saved me. That was a pretty impressive tackle back there. Are you okay?"

"As long as you're not hurt, I'm perfect."

"Yes, you are and I love you." She stroked the side of his face and tears fell off her lashes. "I'm so sorry I didn't tell you before. And then I didn't stay safe when I promised you I would."

All that mattered was she was safe and in his arms. Now. That's all that mattered. He reached down and threaded his fingers through her hair and promptly shut her up by kissing her. "It doesn't matter. You're safe now," he mumbled into her hair. Even after the events of the day, he could still smell the honeysuckle on her. He took a deep breath, taking in her scent and was surprised when he started feeling woozy. That wasn't right. He shook his head to clear it and the world tilted.

"Colton!" He heard her scream. His final thought was the gunfire had ended so she should be safe now. Then the world went black.

***

Relief was replaced by panic as she watched Colton collapse onto the ground. The shooting had stopped, so she started screaming. "Help! Someone please help!" She searched frantically over his body trying to find where he was hurt. It was when she reached up to brush the side of his head that she discovered the blood which seemed to pour out of the side of his head. She started sobbing. "Colton! Colton, can you hear me?"

Suddenly someone was there to help. "Do you know where he's hurt?"

She looked up to find Scott Martin taking Colton's pulse. Oh thank God. Scott was a paramedic with the volunteer fire department. He'd be able to help. "His head is bleeding. He was fine, kissing me and then he just collapsed."

Scott reached around to the side of Colton's head to find the wound. Someone tried to pull her away, and she brushed away the hands. "No, I'm not leaving him."

"Penny, let Scott work on him and we'll get someone to take these cuffs off you." She looked up, confused to find Michael Martin there. He looked at her with kindness. Oh no, he didn't know about Thomas. She felt her legs weaken. He reached up to steady her. "Come on. You'll be able to help him more once the cuffs are off and you need to get checked out, too."

She didn't want to leave Colton. There was so much blood coming from his head. What if he died? She shook her head. "I'm not leaving him. I don't care about the handcuffs. I'm not leaving his side."

Michael chuckled low. "Okay, okay, let me go find Andrew. He should have a key that will work on these."

"Michael," she grasped hold of his sleeve urgently and swallowed hard to hold back the emotion, "don't go into the house. Thomas..." She started crying as Michael looked back at the house. Grief filled his eyes as he looked from the house back to her. She could see the knowledge in his eyes. "I'm sorry," she whispered. "Just don't go in there."

He pulled himself up and nodded solemnly. "It's okay. We'll get it all sorted. Let me go find Andrew and we'll get those cuffs taken care of. Stay here and watch over your man." She continued to clutch at his sleeve and he slowly peeled her fingers. "Don't worry. I'm just going to go find Andrew."

As he walked off, Penelope turned back to Colton. Scott obviously heard their exchange because he met her eyes briefly and there were tears in his eyes that had nothing to do with Colton.

Another man joined Scott to help administer medical aid to Colton. Sometime in the last few minutes, the yard had been lit up by spotlights so Penelope could see exactly what they were doing. She could also see how deathly pale Colton appeared. She rushed back over so she was close to him. She was out of their way, but ran her hands up and down his leg so maybe he could feel her presence. They stripped off his shirt. She was surprised to see that he wore body armor underneath it. But it was even more shocking to see the purple bruising underneath that along with a plethora of bleeding scrapes and scratches.

Scott immediately started palpitating his abdomen and shot her a worried look.

"What is it? What's wrong with him?" She demanded to know.

He looked at the other man and nodded his head with some unspoken communication. The other man ran off and Scott turned to her. "Penny, right now his heartbeat is good, but he took a hard blow to the head. I'm worried about that just because he hasn't regained consciousness, although I really think it's just superficial. It's hard to tell out here. Regardless, he's lost a lot of blood from the head wound. He also took several hits to his body armor and I think that he may have some internal damage. We need to medevac him to the hospital as soon as possible."

"Internal damage? Medevac?" She lifted her head to the sky as she now heard a helicopter coming. "I need to stay with him. I have to, Scott."

He nodded. "I'll do everything I can to get you on the flight with him. It's going to be okay, Penny." He lightly touched the side of her face where the boss hit her earlier in the afternoon. "You probably need to be looked at, too."

Two men rushed over and placed Colton on a backboard. He was so still and pale. Someone tugged at the cuffs, but she never took her eyes off Colton. As soon as the hands let go of her, she rushed back over to his side, just in time to follow him onto the helicopter.

***

Colton cracked his eyes open, trying to figure out what bus hit him last night. Everything hurt, but he was surprised to realize he was in a hospital bed. He didn't remember coming to the hospital and had no idea what could have happened. The last thing he remembered was…Penelope! He sat up suddenly and gasped at the bolts of pain shooting through his body.

There was a whisper of movement along his right hand and he looked down at it, being careful to move slowly. Draped across his hand were the beautiful blonde locks that he knew and loved so well. Penelope was sound asleep with her head lying along the edge of his bed. He eyed her critically, checking for injuries. Her cheek was bruised and swollen and she had a couple of butterfly stitches above her brow. She had circles of exhaustion under her eyes, but otherwise, she looked to be whole and safe. He closed his eyes in relief.

He opened them again when he heard the whisper of the door opening. A nurse walked in and smiled at him when she saw that he was awake. She moved to the opposite side of his body from Penelope when he lightly whispered "shh," to her.

The nurse smiled indulgently to Penelope's sleeping form. "She's refused to leave your side, but she's exhausted after her ordeal."

"Is she okay?"

"She's fine. You're the one who got hurt. A bullet grazed your head and you lost a lot of blood. You also have several bruised internal organs and a cracked rib. You're one lucky man to be alive and now that you're awake, it looks like you'll probably stay that way."

He gave her a wry smile. "I certainly plan to."

Penelope stirred at his side.

"Good morning beautiful."

She gave him a blinding smile and that look alone told him that everything was going to be just fine.

Chapter 38

It took several days for everything to get sorted. After the raid, there were sixteen MM members in US custody. Three died and two mysteriously disappeared. Ethan was one of those who disappeared.

They were getting information from several of the MM members taken into custody who worked plea deals. Ethan went to work for the Martins three years prior. It was through his connections that Thomas became involved and he quickly rose to a position of power within the organization. From the little he'd told Penelope and through journals they found in his room, they were able to piece together his motivation. He felt like he needed the power and the retribution against his father, whom he blamed for his mother's death. A death that obviously affected him more as a child than anyone ever realized.

The MM used the Martin ranch as a regular dispersal point for both their drug and human trafficking. With so much land on the ranch and Ethan and Thomas working on the inside, it was easy for the organization to remain undetected while using the land. Thomas had the added advantage that he could closely watch Andrew's movements with the Texas Rangers and could warn the MM when things were getting dicey. Over the few years he'd been involved, Thomas managed to immerse himself into several fingers of the Mexican organization.

He'd succeeded in one aspect of his plan. Michael Martin was devastated. He'd appeared to have aged twenty years in just a few days.

It was through the ranch and Penelope's connection to it that the bookstore came onto the MM's radar. They were using the ARC's and Hannah's blog posts to transmit delivery times, dates and locations throughout the US. Through the archives of the blog, they were able to determine the organization had used the bookstore to disperse information for over a year and a half. Originally they'd worked by simply posting encoded messages on the blog, but then the scheme became more complex and the ARC's came into play.

The weapons smuggling and theft ring was a new venture within this branch of the organization. Abilene Authors were clueless as to how they'd played into it all or that they were even doing anything wrong, which in all actuality they weren't. They were as much a pawn as anyone else. It was their benefactor, Dev Masters, who was the connection. He was active duty in the Air Force from Dyess Air Force Base and had access to the Top Secret files about the weapons shipments. He encoded that information into the details of the books that he then directed the Abilene Authors to write.

When Penelope took ***The Gift of Serendipity*** home with her, it disrupted everything in the chain. That particular ARC detailed the drops coming up for the next six months for the entire West side of the United States. The Department of Homeland Security was still working to decode it all, but the book was already responsible for several huge busts in the Western US of MM cells.

Damon recovered fully from his captivity and his partnership with the Texas Tech Archaeology department was finally settled. The MM became interested in him and his dig while they were following Penelope. They saw his dig as another opportunity to help their drug flow into the US.

Colton's recovery was slower than he'd hoped, especially since Penelope kept her distance from him the entire time. She kept deflecting his advances, saying he needed more recovery time before he "taxed his poor, battered body." Two weeks of forced celibacy while sleeping with her and he was ready to show her how fully recovered he truly was.

Everything was on track with Mad Rob and just today, Colton had received word that they'd been awarded the Homeland Security contract. He'd called Penelope to let her know and told her to put on a party outfit because they were going out to celebrate.

He hoped to someday convince her to marry him, but he wasn't willing to risk their relationship by pushing it before she was ready. For now, he simply counted his lucky stars they both were alive and happy together. He parked his motorcycle in the parking garage and felt the zip of anticipation of a night out with Penelope. He needed to convince her tonight that he was fully recovered from his injuries.

As he entered the loft, he was surprised to find it dark, although some melodic jazz was playing lightly through the sound system. He could have sworn Penelope agreed to meet him here.

"Penelope!" he called, but there wasn't an answer. He started down the hall to the bedrooms, but his footsteps faltered when he noticed the fall of rose petals leading down the hall to his bedroom. A surge of arousal pounded through his body. Maybe he wouldn't have to work as hard to convince her as he thought.

When he reached the doorway of his bedroom, his breath caught and every drop of blood surged toward the length of his already engorged cock. Penelope knelt at the end of his bed in a position of submission. Her bra and thong were flame red scraps of barely there lace and her mile-long legs were finished off by incredibly sexy red heels.

But what took his breath away were her bindings. She had on a red leather collar with a metal ring on the front of it. A chain led down from the ring and attached to the cuffs connecting her wrists. There were several other chains draped around her shoulders as she was well and truly bound.

There was also a sign attached to the top of the chain. He walked forward until he could lift the note to read it. She kept her eyes lowered while he read the note.

```
My love,
    I am yours. My heart is bound to
you, now and forever. I love you and
want to stay yours for the rest of my
life. Please say you'll marry me.
Please.

Your humble servant,
Penelope
```

Shock and love reverberated through his system and he sank to his knees in front of her. He reached forward and lifted her chin so that she was looking at him. Her eyes were shimmering with love and tears.

"Are you sure this is what you want? Marriage?"

"I do. I love you, Colton. I've been an idiot. I had no idea what real love involved before I met you. Now I know. I know that with you, I wouldn't lose myself, but without you, I definitely would. You're the other half of my heart and I need you in my life. Every day from now on. You complete me. Please say yes."

"Not yet." He saw the flash of pain in her eyes before she lowered them back to the floor. He lifted her chin once again. "Where are the keys to this?" He waved his hand down her delectable body.

Her voice caught as she said, "On the nightstand."

He nodded and went to retrieve it. While he was there, he grabbed the small piece of jewelry which had been hidden in the back corner and slid it into his pocket. He unlocked her bindings and removed the collar and cuffs, then drew her up so that she was standing before him. She was so incredibly beautiful looking even with the tears teasing along the corners of her eyes. He kissed her lightly and then had to draw back before he got lost in her barely clothed temptation of a body.

He smiled softly at her. "If we're going to do this, we're going to do it right. As equals." A flicker of hope crossed her face. "Because that's what a marriage is…an equal partnership. That's what I want with you, Penelope. A partnership, between you and me, that lasts forever. I love you sweetheart, every stubborn, incredible inch of you, and I can't imagine spending my life with anyone else. Yes, I'll marry you, if you'll have me." He pulled the ring out of his pocket and held it out to her. "This was my mother's ring. I hope you'll wear it and agree to marry me."

"Oh, Colton, your mother's ring?" She looked up at him with tears shimmering in her eyes. "It's beautiful. I love you so much. Yes I'll marry you."

She flung her arms around his neck and he groaned long and deep as the press of her curves pushed up against his poor deprived body.

"Good." He whispered into her hair. "Now that that's settled, can we please get back to those handcuffs? I really, really liked where that was going."

THE END

Before the Mission Begins
(a novella prequel)
by Christi Snow

Coming Valentine's Day, 2013

Before his mission began, he went home. 24 hours to say goodbye to his twin sister.

Instead he found her. A girl that was nothing like the one he thought he knew.

They have 24 hours. 24 hours before he deploys on an extremely dangerous mission. 24 hours together in a freak West Texas snowstorm. 24 hours that will have to get them both through the awful next year.

When the resident good-girl decides to take on the visiting bad-boy, 24 hours is all it takes to change their lives forever.

This is the story of the 24 hours that no one knew ever occurred…until now.

The timeline of this novella is set before the When the Mission Ends trilogy occurs, but this book is actually meant to be read between *Book #2,* **Operation: Endeavor**, *and Book #3,* **Operation: Endurance**.

Operation: Endeavor

Author's Note:

Texas Tech is a real university and Lubbock, TX is a real town. In fact, that's where I graduated from college and have amazing memories from there. As a result, when I sat down to write my first series of books, I wanted to pay homage to that school and town I love so much.

I probably wasn't thinking that through when I decided to create all the murder and mayhem of this trilogy in that locale. Don't let the events in these books influence your perception of either the school or the town. While the places are real, the events absolutely are NOT.

I also took great liberties in the layout of the campus, the kinds of activities the University would allow, Lubbock PD, Texas Tech Health Sciences Center, and some of the surrounding businesses. Please don't hold it against them or me!

This is a work of fiction and should be looked at in that light.

DON'T FORGET!

Book #3 in the When the Mission Ends Trilogy
Operation: Endurance
Releases April, 2013

And if you want to learn more about Chris & Julie's mysterious history, watch for:
Before The Mission Begins (novella #.5)
Releases Valentine's, 2013

ABOUT THE AUTHOR

As an avid reader my entire life, I've always dreamed of writing books that brought to others the kind of joy I feel when I read.

But…I never did anything about it besides jot down a few ideas and sparse scenes.

When I turned 41, I decided it was time to go after my dream and started writing. Within four months, I'd written over 150,000 words and haven't stopped since. I've found my passion by writing about sexy, alpha heroes and smart, tough heroines falling in love and finding their passion. I'm truly living the dream and loving every minute of it.

My tagline is…

Passion and adventure on the road to Happily Ever After. I have to admit, I am loving this adventure!

You can find me at:
www.Christi-Snow.com

CPSIA information can be obtained at www.ICGtesting.com
Printed in the USA
LVOW051937020613

336548LV00001B/7/P

9 781481 035613